WHILE
YOU'RE
AWAY

WHILE YOU'RE AWAY

Jessa Holbrook

razor
bill

An Imprint of Penguin Group (USA) LLC

A division of Penguin Young Readers Group
Published by the Penguin Group
Penguin Group (USA) LLC
345 Hudson Street
New York, New York 10014

USA / Canada / UK / Ireland / Australia / New Zealand / India / South Africa / China
Penguin.com
A Penguin Random House Company

Library of Congress Cataloging-in-Publication Data

Holbrook, Jessa.
While You're Away / Jessa Holbrook.
    pages cm
Summary: "Once a cheater, always a cheater?"—Provided by publisher.
ISBN 978-1-59514-732-5 (paperback)
1. Women college students—Fiction. 2. Man-woman relationships—Fiction. 3. Triangles (Interpersonal relations)—Fiction. 4. Commitment (Psychology)—Fiction. I. Title. II. Title: While you are away.
PS3608.O48288W55 2014
813'.6—dc23

2013030120

Printed in the United States of America

1 3 5 7 9 10 8 6 4 2

KENNEDY

ONE

To make it sound classier, Tricia Patten called it a Gods and Goddesses party.

Everybody was supposed to show up in togas. A lot of skin and a lot of beer to celebrate the crazy weather, almost eighty degrees in April. Unfortunately, *The Avengers* was a thing. That's why half the Aphrodites at Tricia's lake house that night were getting flirty with a palette of Thors.

"I don't think this is what Tricia had in mind," I told my boyfriend, Dave Echols, grabbing his hand and nodding at the mixed-deity crowd as we set up our stage gear.

With a grin, Dave said, "She wanted a party, she got a party," and leaned over to kiss me.

Dave and I were the intermission entertainment—a local band that would already be at the party when the deejay had to go pick up his mom at work. Usually, we played our own songs. But tonight it would be an hour of funny indie covers of frat rock songs.

As I tested the pickup on my acoustic guitar, I cut a quick look at the crowd. A spotlight seemed to follow me, and not in a good way. Everyone hesitated and ran their eyes down my costume. The best expression was bafflement, but the worst was amusement. I forced a smile and kept setting up.

I hadn't gotten the memo that a sheet over a regular little black dress was enough of a costume. Geek that I was, I'd raided my sister Ellie's closet. She danced for the Columbus Repertory Ballet Theater, so she had plenty of bits and pieces that added up to a goddess. A gauze wraparound skirt over a silver-shot leotard. Silver slippers with matching ribbons crisscrossing my legs.

Producing extra ribbon, Ellie threaded it through my thick, dark hair. Alternating white with gold, she plaited and twisted, taming my wild halo. Then, because it was a permanent part of her ballet DNA, she knotted it in a perfect chignon on the top of my head. Pulling tendrils out around my face, she considered the look. After taking a picture with her phone, she declared me ready to rock and sent me on my way.

When I'd left home, I felt good—pretty, even. A little bare, because I never wore my hair up. But good.

That confidence burned away as soon as I stepped onto the temporary stage in front of Tricia's French doors. The party was packed. A wood dance floor stretched over the pool. Snacks and drinks circulated under a white light-strung arbor. And there I was, the trying-too-hard girl on stage, crazy obvious in front of a sea of sheets and plastic plate mail.

Power-mingling, Tricia buzzed the stage. "You guys are so great. Thank you so much for doing this."

"Anytime," Dave said, zeroing in on her.

As soon as he did, Tricia turned her attention to him and him alone. Why shouldn't she? With his fresh, all-American face, Dave got all kinds of attention. He was the blue-eyed, blond-haired boy next door, wrapped in a flag and carrying Mom's apple pie. Seriously, at Fourth of July parades, people practically worshipped him. And after our gigs, girls did. By the bucketful, even if they had boyfriends.

It always bothered me when Dave flirted. Even if it meant nothing, I couldn't help but feel a twinge of jealousy whenever he turned his attention elsewhere.

Tricia had her own boyfriend—none other than Will Spencer, our high school's biggest player. Exactly nobody understood how she'd caught him and kept him. Tricia was well-off, gorgeous, and genuinely likable, definitely a catch. She stood apart from other girls, with a mane of copper hair and green eyes clear as glass. But Will had never seemed like the type to settle for one girl. Or ten. Or a hundred. Not when he could have his pick *and* have them all. Will and Tricia were the senior class's enduring mystery.

I couldn't help but wish the enduring mystery would step away from my boyfriend.

"I'm so glad you do private parties," Tricia purred, clutching Dave's mic stand.

Dave powered up his amp and smiled. "For you? Anything."

My heart sank, but I said nothing. Dave flirted with everyone. Every*thing*. Once, I'd seen him wink at a baby, and then a dog. People fawned over him, and he couldn't help reflecting some of that glow back.

To be fair, he flirted with me, too. When we played, sometimes he'd lean over to murmur in my ear. Between the mics, just loud enough for me to hear: *You killed that verse, love the way the lights catch your eyelashes.* Things no one else could, or would, ever say to me.

Which meant I had to get over myself and get back to work. Giving my guitar a quick tune, I strummed a few chords—the universal notes for "stop flirting and let's get this gig started."

"Later," Tricia said, and when the crowd surged, she was gone.

Dave stepped back. Nudging me, he turned on the smile for me and me alone. In the uneven light of the party, his eyes looked more stormy than blue. There was a quiet place in that gaze, one that helped me find my center. I felt too bare in this costume, and now I was asking everybody to look at me.

But when Dave kicked off the first number, I started to feel better. A hum wavered across my bare skin. It shielded me from the chill trying to roll off the river. My gaze lingered on Dave's, and he broke the night with his honeyed tenor. On the chorus, our voices tangled in harmony. For a moment, it was just the two of us. Just him, and me, and the music.

Then, the power kicked on. It was electricity, holding his gaze and holding on to the audience at the same time.

They laughed because we wanted them to. There's something inherently hilarious about two people with acoustic guitars playing LFMAO and Kanye; that's part of the act. But half a song later, everybody started to sing along. They put their cups up and they danced. Gods and goddesses moved in time—in our time.

Soaring on the rush of making music with Dave, I felt like I could touch the heavens. My fingertips burned, and sweat rose on my skin. I poured my whole body into the music, and I shimmered. So did Dave, golden and handsome.

His flush warmed his skin; his sweat gathered in the fascinating dip of his collarbone. When he threw his head back to laugh, everyone looked. Everyone had to. They all wanted to touch him, and I understood completely.

I never minded sharing him when we performed. On stage, we were like one, and the adoration was for both of us. We were so stratospheric together, how could I mind? It was when the music stopped that I had a problem. When we descended the stage, it was like Dave never touched the ground. He mingled and flirted and was adored, while I grew shy without music to hide behind and was relegated to watching from the sidelines. I crashed. And it hurt every single time.

After the set, the adulation started. Dave didn't bother to take off his guitar once the deejay reclaimed her stage. Instead, he waded through the party, arm curled around his black Epiphone Jane, her strings gleaming beneath the café lights. Idly, Dave stroked the guitar's curves as people plied him with drinks and compliments and bites to eat.

My guitar in its case, I walked off, completely unnoticed. I pulled out my phone, checking Instagram to see if anybody had posted shots of our set. It was a good way to look like I was busy instead of simply alone.

Dave getting all the attention didn't surprise me anymore, but I didn't think I'd ever get used to it. Our songs really were *ours*, collaborations. Even when we sang other people's songs, it was half-and-half, and full harmony whenever possible. But once we broke the set, I didn't exist, and Dave was the star.

Across the party, a script unfolded, and I watched it play out. Again. Heatherly Watkins, whose parents plainly didn't understand the way adverbs worked, plastered a hand in the middle of Dave's chest. I couldn't hear them over the din, but I saw her laugh, *Ha-ha-ha-oh-Dave-you're-so-funny.*

There was a particular shape to that. Her head tipped to one side, and she looked at him through her lashes—careful to laugh, but not so hard that something horrifying like a snort escaped. I would have felt sorry for her, but the burning in my chest distracted me. I hated watching Dave's post-show game, for lots of reasons. Tonight it especially bothered me.

I ducked beneath an arbor, putting my back to Dave and Heatherly. My best friend, Jane, was around there somewhere. She could be counted on for a ride home, for sure.

As I searched for Jane, the one and only Will Spencer drifted toward me. Tricia's boyfriend. Notorious player. All confidence, in Hollister shorts and a vintage T, he trailed a finger across my shoulders.

Though his touch skimmed like a feather, it felt like a kiss. A whispered secret that carried an unexpected shot of heat. Caught short, I held a breath as I burned from the inside out. That urgent, animal reaction held me in place.

He circled and stood in my way. "And you are?"

My brain kicked in right before I told him my name. Of course he knew my name. Not twenty minutes ago, I'd leaned into a mic and said, "I'm Sarah Westlake, this is Dave Echols, and we are Dasa." Even if Will and I hadn't gone to the same schools since pre-K, my identity wasn't a mystery.

I think it was the costume that interested him. It made me feel like I had bigger breasts and curvier hips than my usual clothes. Like I was just out there, every inch of me exposed. I crossed my arms over my chest before I answered. "Athena."

"Goddess of wisdom, keeper of owls."

Surprised, I said, "Exactly."

"Good choice." Then, he nodded toward the makeshift stage. "Good set, too."

All at once, everything was *fine*. All because Will was *that* guy. Above it all but incredibly there. Even when I was a freshman and he was a sophomore, he was at the top. High school royalty, full of noblesse oblige.

He had black hair that curled in the heat. Black brows and black lashes set off beach-blue eyes. Going into senior year, he'd grown into his height. Broad shoulders, narrow waist—half the people at that party would have paid good money to be a Thor hammer hanging from Will's belt loops.

Instead of walking on among his people, Will lingered. With *me*. Leaning against the arbor rail, he studied my face. Just my face. His gaze never drifted lower, but it didn't have to. The way he stared at my lips made them sting.

Summoning up some bluster, I replied, "Thanks. Now explain yourself."

"What do you mean?"

"What's this?" I asked, gesturing at his non-costume. "The host is your girlfriend. I know you got the Evite. 'Gods and Goddesses' sound familiar?"

"Atlas is a god." Will tugged his T-shirt, flattening the silhouette of a man holding up a globe.

"No, he was a Titan. There's a difference."

Waving a hand dismissively, Will caught my eye in a sideward glance. "If Thor can stay, so can Atlas. You don't think it counts?"

The spark in his smile made me contrary. I raked my gaze down to his sneakers and back up to his gym clothes. For the first time ever, I was doing some flirting of my own. And it felt amazing. With a careless shrug, I informed him teasingly, "Sorry, no."

"No?"

I shook my head. "Nope. And like you said, Athena is wise, so I must be right."

"Obviously," he said.

He thrust the stack of empty cups into my hands. Then, he grabbed the hem of his shirt and peeled it off. His skin was pale from winter. It made the dark dusting of hair on his chest stand out. It trailed down to his navel, disappearing into shorts that hung too low. Way too low—and I was staring.

"Now I'm Hercules," he said, taking all but one of the cups back. "Get a beer, Athena. Dance a little."

With a wink, he tossed his shirt over his shoulder and walked away. As cut as his chest, his back rippled as he walked. Two dimples at the base of his spine taunted as he moved through the crowd.

Clutching my cup, I shook my head and called after him. "Hercules doesn't count. He's a demigod!"

Will looked back. It felt nice, having all of a demigod's attention. Even in the middle of a party packed with guys dressed to flirt, he stood out. It was like something had outlined him, tracing him in silver. Every edge, every detail—when I blinked, I still saw his shape in the dark.

With a brash smile, Will saluted me. Then he pointed to the table with the keg, shooing me along without a word. I felt a wash of heat, nothing to do with the weather. In fact, as the sun slipped down, it grew colder. In my skimpy costume, I shivered. I probably should have gone home, but this is why I stayed:

The wicked, infamous Will Spencer looked back at *me*.

TWO

Half a beer and four mini gyros later, Dave had shucked off Heatherly, but that was only to talk to Olivia.

What I needed was some quiet to recharge. Some dark sounded good, too, where I didn't have to watch Dave work the crowd. If I happened to run into Will, well, that wouldn't be the worst thing in the world.

Breaking away from the party, I started down the lawn toward the shore. Haze drifted over the river, creeping onto land. It swirled along the banks and against the Victorian strangeness of the Pattens' boathouse.

I'd never explored the grounds at Tricia's house. First of all, being at a house that had "grounds" made me itchy. My family wasn't poor. We had a tri-level with a cute backyard, next to another one just like it.

The electronics plant in town had jumped the Internet gap. No one needed to move closer to a city to get by. That meant that everybody lived in the suburbs, and my house sat in the quaintest, most tree-lined part of it. It was middle class. The definition of nice.

Unlike Tricia's family, who owned the aforementioned plant. The most historical piece of land in the county was their home. The house was a renovated saltbox, artful gray wood and pristine white shutters. It cast an austere shadow over the pool and the guesthouse.

With its long, symmetrical windows and identical shutters, it seemed to gaze ruefully at the party. As if it accepted that most of the senior class needed to do keg stands, but it didn't really approve.

Tricia's was a serious business kind of house. But down the sloping lawn, resting on the shores of the river, was the boathouse. And it was amazing. The Pattens had their pictures taken there every year for the company Christmas card. The ugly-charming sweaters changed, but the fairy-tale boathouse never did.

A bit of 1920s whimsy that practically screamed for shimmy skirts and flasks of hooch, the boathouse had pillars made of whole trees. Twisted branches framed the dock, all whitened and weathered. And to match the mist coming off the water, a thin trail of smoke swirled from the boathouse's stone chimney.

I followed the sharp, alluring scent. It meant somebody was down there, and I suspected it was just the person I wanted to see.

Caught by the water's chill, I hurried into the boathouse. Stacked rowboats filled the middle of the floor. They tilted, threatening to topple. It was too early in the season for them to rest in their berths. But a few bobbers and buoys did. They thumped lazily against the wood dock. The sound echoed, pulsing like a heartbeat.

I called out as I oriented myself. "Hello?"

"Hey, Athena," Will called back.

At first, I hesitated. I'd hoped to hear his voice, but now that I had, I was unprepared. I felt the ghostly trace of his finger across my shoulders again. Trying to shrug it off, I ducked beneath a string of floats.

Damp clung to the air. A high-tinged scent surrounded me, old wood cut with smoke. When I rose on the other side, heat swept over me. Orange flames danced in the stone fireplace, and a silhouette stood in front of it.

Still shirtless, Will raised a bottle to me. "You get lost?"

I didn't think he'd understand needing a breather. I was angry at Dave, not to mention exhausted from the press of so many bodies near mine.

Will, on the other hand, wore crowds like a cloak. People orbited him; he had presence and space in the middle of them. It seemed to me like Will got his energy *from* them.

I shook my head. "Just being nosy."

"You ever been out here before?"

"First time," I said, turning to take it in. Branches curved above, casting odd shadows when the light moved.

"Welcome. Make yourself at home."

Will had made himself at home. A rowboat sat on the ground beside the fire, thick blankets heaped inside it. Two amber bottles gleamed by the hearth. I smiled when I realized the labels proclaimed them root beer.

Turning my attention to him again, I said, "Not your first time out here, huh?"

"Occasionally," Will said, "you have to listen to the silence to appreciate the noise."

A quizzical smile touched my lips. "Is that your secret philosophy?"

"Nothing secret about it."

He shrugged, his bare shoulders catching the firelight just so. Orange and gold traced him, marking every elegant curve of his body.

Tugging his shorts up, he gestured at the rowboat. "Take a load off. Stay a while."

My conscience whispered a warning. Dave wouldn't like it. And I didn't know if it was safe. Not because I thought Will would hurt me. Completely the opposite, in fact: Will had a reputation for making girls very, very happy. A *lot* of girls. But I didn't back away, and slowly, I shook my head.

"I shouldn't."

"Neither should I," Will replied. "But here I am."

This pensive, thoughtful version of Will piqued my curiosity. I'd never thought of him as somebody who . . . well, thought.

It was more like, he wasn't a Moleskine-notebook kind of guy. He'd never penned an editorial for the school newspaper, and he wasn't the inspirational speaker on the mic at pep rallies.

Will was the guy running up and down the court, waving his hands. He demanded a frenzy and he got it. People cheered louder and louder, until the roar filled the gym and echoed on our skin.

Until that moment, Thoughtful Will didn't even exist in my imagination. Will Spencer was the blue-eyed bad boy, the one who walked with swagger because he *had* it, not because he was trying to cultivate it.

And because I couldn't see what he'd see in me, I lowered myself into the boat. After all, the thoughtful part had come as a surprise. Maybe he really did want someone to talk to. Conversation wasn't what most people had in mind when they thought of Will.

Most of the blankets were wool, but the comforter on top was smooth enough. I slid against it. The boat's keel wobbled on wood instead of water. Blushing, I wanted to sit down like a normal human being, but it was a boat. On land. It was awkward just to spite me.

Graceless, I twisted in place, trying to get comfortable. Draping my legs over the side, I leaned on one elbow, then the other. Finally I gave up and propped my arms on my knees. Watching Will move in front of the fire, I wondered what the turn of his shoulders meant. If the tip of his head signified something.

Finally, I said, "You're holding out on me."

"Is that so?"

"Oh yeah. I see you, hiding out here with the good stuff."

Glancing toward the bottles on the hearth, I waited for him to catch my smile. The tease in my voice. I don't know why I did it, except Will Spencer, thoughtful, had distracted me completely. I forgot to be quiet and serious. I forgot that I was the forgotten half of my own band, an introvert in a world of extroverts. He made me forget, and I liked that. To prompt him, I said, "Well?"

With a laugh, Will raised the bottle in his hand. "Last one."

"Now I'm sad."

His feet whispered against the smooth, wooden floor. Sinking beside me, the boat shifted under his weight. Somehow, he knew exactly how to sit in a dry-docked rowboat stuffed with old bedding. His whole body was easy. Liquid, limber. Shadows spilled across his jaw and down his throat.

Splaying back and trailing one arm against the gunwale, he broke the smoky quiet with a smooth gesture. The bottle dangled from his fingertips. Casually, he touched the cool glass to my bare skin. "I can share."

"I haven't heard that about you," I said. He touched the bottle to my skin again, and with a shiver, I leaned back. The boat's curve angled us closer. My gaze fell on his bare chest and the really, completely perfect turn of his collarbone.

Taking a lazy swallow of his root beer, Will didn't move. He didn't have to. When I raised my head, I met his eyes directly. They were so dark, they seemed almost black. It was unnerving to sit so close to him. To get swallowed up in eyes that hid everything going on behind them.

His lips parted, and he said, low, "That's very provocative."

Of course he wouldn't ask what I'd heard. He probably didn't care. Or he was aware. Girlfriend or not, Will Spencer was supposed to be the bad boy that was good for you.

My freshman year, he made out with Stephanie Kim on the catwalk, during the second act of *Our Town*. Running the follow spot, Stephanie was used to people scurrying behind her, rushing to get from one side of the theater to the other.

So when she saw Will heading her way, she didn't think anything of it. Plenty of people ended up in the wings and above them. Now, she was a little surprised when he stopped beside her. But it was a good view. Why not?

Suddenly, he was closer. He smiled and raised a finger to his lips to shush her. To this day, Stephanie swears she doesn't know how it happened. One minute, she was waiting for her next cue. The next, she had her arms wrapped around Will's neck and his tongue in her mouth.

The green flash of the cue light interrupted them. When it went off, he slipped away. She swore she thought he said something to her, but she never remembered what. She did remember that she couldn't let the stars go without their follow spot, so she turned back to her post. Will left her there, smiling like a loon.

That was literally the first and last encounter they had. He didn't avoid her; she wasn't embarrassed. Afterward, if they passed in the hall, they smiled. But that was it. That kiss on the catwalk was a perfect moment, exactly enough.

It was one of the cornerstones of Will's semi-epic reputation. Sometimes, it seemed like he'd had a moment with the entire senior class and half the junior class, too. But Will wore it well, and it felt right when he trailed his fingers across my shoulders again. It shocked me how different those little touches felt from Dave's big gestures. When Dave slung an arm around my shoulder, I was content. When Will touched me, I was on fire.

"You're quiet," he said.

I didn't know why, but I replied, "You're smart."

It made him laugh. A scoffing, almost baffled sound escaped him. Shifting toward me, his eyes narrowed. Newly keen, they studied my face in the firelight. There was something in them I'd never seen before.

He was human.

Will Spencer, senior royalty, rich and popular and perfect, was *human*. That realization popped and sparked like a match, devouring the air between us. So when his touch drifted—when his knuckles grazed my cheek—I wasn't afraid. I leaned in for the kiss, and I didn't feel wrong for doing it.

Nobody else had kissed *this* Will, I was sure of it. A soft, surprised sound caught in his throat. Another hint of human, a little touch that was wonderfully real. I heard him set the bottle on the floor. The boat rocked beneath us, beating a gentle rhythm against the floor. His lips, so thin and teasing a moment ago, were lush beneath mine.

When I leaned into him, my hand fell on his still-bare chest. So much skin, his body so sculpted. It would have been a lie to call him Adonis. He wasn't a blond, frosted, pretty thing. He was dark and tempting.

Music from the party drifted on the wind, distant and enchanted. We were surrounded by the soft call of waves, the lazy beat of the keel as we filled the space between us with sighs and murmurs.

I parted my lips, and he slipped into me. This was a deeper kiss, one sweetened with root beer and the spicy bite of cinnamon gum. My mouth stung, and all I wanted was a better place.

One where we could spread out together. One where my hair was loose so he could thread his fingers into it. His fingers seemed to long for that, too, twining and curling around the tendrils at my cheeks.

Subtly, he took control. Even as I grazed my blunt nails against his skin, he pressed me into the blankets. His fingers bloomed on my cheek. When they slid down my throat, I didn't stop them. Why would I stop them? The thought floated away; my body spoke for me. I melted beneath him, forming to his shape.

He had so much bare skin to explore. His shoulders shifted beneath my hands. His breath fell on my lips. Humid heat collected between our bodies, different from the dry, lazy waves that still rolled from the fire. Stroking the small of Will's back, I rose up for another kiss, hungry and shameless.

I didn't care that we were basically strangers. That I'd never been like this with anybody. That this was probably wrong. In fact, that seemed to be a reason to keep going. I'd seen a Will no one else had seen. The secret in his pale eyes, the real him that he shrouded in big smiles and lazy flirtation.

More than anything, I had the dizzying sense that it wouldn't be a *moment*. Other girls had been with the shiny, flashy, veneered Will. Of course *they* slid apart. It was once and then done for them. This was different. This Will belonged to me and just me. I knew it was ridiculous to think so, but it was the way I felt.

With a rough murmur, he pushed up on his elbows. Dark hair, slightly damp with sweat, clung to his forehead. Tilted at angles, his dark brows questioned. Shadows swirled in his pale blue eyes, more questions, and pure amazement. His teasing lips had gone flush, and he stared at me, stunned. That's when he realized that I should belong to him, too.

THREE

This was another new Will for me—uncertain Will, full of realization and trembling over what to do about it. Dipping lower, he brushed his lips against mine. The caress was sweet, almost distracted. Then he opened his eyes, peering into me. Lips parted again, this time to speak.

Before he could say a word, loud, echoing laughter silenced him. We broke apart in a shock. Panic left me fluttery and frightened. What if that was Dave? Even if it wasn't, the interruption reminded me that I wasn't supposed to be here—not with Will. Swallowing hard, I twisted around, just in time to see Emmalee Dekker and Simon Garza straggle into the boathouse.

It was an unexpected combination. Simon was a social justice warrior and the editor of our school video-magazine. He had a hate-on for the sports programs that sucked up all the air and funding at East River High, and he wasn't shy about sharing it. Especially not with Emmalee, the captain of our girls baseball—not softball, baseball—team. The day he was supposed to interview her for a friendly feature about her successful Title IX protest to *get* that team, he ambushed her instead.

So it was weird to see Simon and Emmalee together at all. Will said exactly what I was thinking, his voice low and just for me.

"How drunk do they have to be to be making out?"

"That's a Level Epic," I said. "They're four hundred and twenty-three miles from Just Drankin'."

We were going to have to say something. They didn't know we were there, watching. And then not watching, because we weren't creepers. Just people caught in the wrong place at a very, very wrong time. A nagging sense of worry slipped through me. These were people who tolerated each other on the best day. What if they regretted this later? What if they weren't even sober enough to realize what they were doing? Despite my unease, I hesitated.

Maybe they'd been secretly crazy about each other the whole time. Jane called this the hate-to-hot conversion when it turned up in movies. The whole *Let's argue for three-fourths of the movie before we realize we're soul mates* thing. I loved it. It was romantic when two people knew there was something there and refused to let go. It was a triumph of romance: fight to get that happily ever after. And fight afterward a little, just to keep it spicy.

Sadly, H2H is why Jane refused to go to rom-coms with me anymore. Though she was a total filmaholic, that's where she drew the line. She said all they did was teach guys to be douche bags and teach girls to put up with it. She had this special barfing noise she saved exclusively for scenes where the unhappy duo realized they were in love. It was literally the most disgusting thing I'd ever heard.

Standing, Will caught my hand and pulled me to my feet. He must have felt my same unease, because he was suddenly his public self again. Smooth and composed, he walked right toward Simon and Emmalee like they weren't grinding against one of the pillars. Somehow, Will made it seem friendly and not even a little embarrassing when he said, "Hey, guys, didn't realize you were in here."

The two of them broke apart. When they did, it was obvious they were only barely holding each other up. In fact, if it hadn't been for the pillar, they might have already been on the ground. Rubbing a hand over his wild ginger hair, Simon summoned a smile.

"Hey, Will. Hey."

"This place gets a lot of traffic," Will said. Then he offered Emmalee a smile. "You okay?"

"I am so good," Emmalee breathed. She caught, and missed, the front of her toga. It gaped open and looked like what it was: rumpled bed sheets, starting to fall off. Fortunately, she was part of the little black dress brigade. No danger of actually exposing herself, but she looked uncomfortably close to disheveled.

Stumbling on nothing, Simon lost his balance. That set off a reaction down the line: Will steadied him, and then Emmalee pitched forward. I caught her and miraculously didn't fall over myself.

Emmalee's skin smelled sugary sweet, but her breath was all beer. Sour, tangy, too-much beer, and her skin was fever hot. Her weight shifted against me, like she wasn't sure both feet were on the floor.

I'd been drunk like that once. Once. That night ended with me throwing up in Jane's azaleas and passing out facedown on her bedroom floor. I barely remembered anything else, and remembering *that* made me feel protective of Emmalee. And ashamed that I hadn't been the one to step up first.

"Maybe we should get you home," I said.

Will nodded, looking from Simon to Emmalee. "What do you think? Get you home?"

"Um," Emmalee said, knitting her brows. "Trish said I could stay in the guesthouse. She did. She did say that, in fact."

I nodded reassuringly. "She did, I believe you."

Simon didn't answer right away. Not because he seemed to be hesitating, but because he seemed to be drifting off a little. They really were at Level Epic on the drunk scale. Suddenly, he patted Will on the chest and nodded, "Can you drive me, man?"

"I can't. I had a couple of beers," Will said. "But Dave'll usually play tipsy taxi if we need him to. Right, Sarah?"

And with that one question, everything contracted. My heart squeezed so hard, it felt like it stopped. My throat tightened, and my back tensed. Suddenly, I was a wire, coiled tighter by the moment. Like a guitar string, tuned carelessly to the point of snapping.

The last time I saw Dave, he was basking in the warm glow of Olivia Bernowski's attention. Still wearing his guitar, still caught in the high from our gig. It was true that he didn't drink. And because of that, he would drive people home if they needed a ride. Drunk people, mostly. High people, people who got into fights and lost their ride home. People left behind when their friends ditched them for another party elsewhere.

Guilt churned in my stomach. Dave Echols was my partner. My friend. And he was my boyfriend. My boyfriend who restored guitars, and played them like a demon, and looked extremely fine in a pair of 7 For All Mankind jeans. Yes, he was flawed. And yes, I was angry at him. But in that moment, it provided little comfort that he was currently just up the hill, completely clueless that his girlfriend was in the boathouse, adding yet another point to Will Spencer's high score.

I knew that nothing would happen between him and Heatherly.

Or Olivia. Or anybody. It never did, not with them, not with the people who crowded around him after our other gigs. It was true that he was addicted to the attention he got. Despite my repeated requests that he stop, he couldn't. He had driven me to become a sick, jealous monster. No matter how many times he told me that it was just after-show glow, it gnawed at my confidence. Now the first time somebody showed me a little bit of attention, I threw myself at him.

I felt angry and guilty at the same time. One question kept spinning and multiplying and echoing in my head: *What have I done?*

"Sarah? Where is Dave?" Will prompted.

Question. Dave. Ride home for Simon. I had to concentrate. Forcing myself to answer, I couldn't make myself look at Will. "He should be back at the party. Let me walk Emmalee to the guesthouse. If I see him, I'll send him this way."

Will produced his cell phone. With a few swipes across the surface, he held it out. "Text me if you don't."

Fumbling, I swayed under Emmalee's weight but managed to dig my phone out, too. Shame crawled on my skin, a blush so deep it had to be visible in the dark. I *was* just a moment for Will. One of a hundred. A thousand. I had known better. I wanted to blame it all on him—but I couldn't.

It was my fault. I'd looked into his eyes and seen what I wanted to see. A guy who looked at me and got excited. A guy who wanted to get closer and didn't care if it complicated things. So much for all the things I made myself believe. He was just Will Spencer, same as he ever was. Everything else was my own pathetic fantasy.

Touching the back of my phone to Will's, I downloaded his contact info and made myself speak. "Okay, cool. That's what I'll do. You ready to go, Em?"

Emmalee nodded and let me sling her arm over my neck. She was dense muscle, and I was wispy musician, so I staggered a little. But I managed to get her walking in the right direction.

As we ducked through the front doors, I swore to myself I'd never mention this night to Dave. It was a one-time, completely hideous total lapse of sanity. That's all it was. And for sure, I didn't need to tell him. It would only hurt him, and what good would it do?

My head, my *heart*, wouldn't let me. For just a few moments, I had reached out for something special. I had been someone different. The girl who made Will Spencer stop and catch his breath. I was the center of the glow for once. I was the special one.

Except now I realized I wasn't. I was every other girl that Will had seduced. Except this time, the girl had thrown herself right in his lap. I wasn't special. I was desperate. My stomach rolled; I felt so small.

Nope. No need to tell Dave at all. I was going to punish myself for a long, long time.

After safely depositing Emmalee at the guesthouse, I plunged back into the party. Deserving every bump and jostle, I waded through a sweaty sea in search of Dave. Turning at the edge of the shuttered pool, I rose on my toes to scan the crowd.

Everyone seemed to merge together. It was like a cloud of party, one body blending into the next and everyone swaying in time. Straining and searching, I felt ridiculous. With a torch, I could have been the Statue of Liberty in a sea of random deities. When someone dropped a hand on my shoulder, I almost yelped.

It was Tricia. Raising her voice over the party, she said, "Have you seen Will? He disappeared a while ago and I have no idea where he went."

My heart sank. I really was a monster. I'd cheated on Dave so easily, and I'd forgotten all about Tricia's existence. Drugged by some insane fantasy of a special connection with Will, I'd plundered ahead, hoping to erase my anger over Dave. But now I felt worse than ever. I was still angry, but now I was also a shitty girlfriend and friend.

As casually as I could, I said, "He's down at the boathouse with Simon. That's why I'm looking for Dave, actually. Simon needs a ride home, and Dave usually—"

"I know!" Tricia interjected. Sincerely. Sweetly. God, she was so sweet. "He's so nice. And now that you mention it, I think I saw him loading up his Element with a couple of boozers a while back. He's probably on the return trip now."

"Great," I said.

And then I stood there, like an idiot. I couldn't text Will right in front of his girlfriend. Or could I? Was it suspicious for me to have his number? Lots of people probably had it. Thinking twice about everything was exhausting, and it made me look slightly crazed. Tricia patted my shoulder, misreading my expression completely.

"I'm sure he's okay. He'll be back anytime now."

Choking on my reply, I nodded. "You're right. I'm . . . I think I'm going to walk up to the driveway and keep an eye out for him, though."

Before I could break away from her, she stopped me. Tossing back her coppery hair, she said, "Wait, Will's at the boathouse with Simon?"

Even more lies slipped from my mouth. They came so easily, I was ashamed. With numb lips and a pounding heart, I rolled my shoulders and said, "Yeah. Since the house is locked, Simon went down there to throw up in private. Will was holding him up. As soon as I realized what was going on, I came right back up here to find Dave. I can't deal with puke, you know?"

With sympathy I didn't deserve, Tricia nodded. "Absolutely, totally."

Finally escaping, I did exactly what I said I was going to do. I headed up to the driveway. Texting Will as I walked, I felt the blush return. Not a delicious sting of anticipation. This was more like the deep, aching slap of humiliation. Fingers flying, I hit send, then slumped to lean against the garage.

Dave already on his first shuttle. Will be back soon.

Instantly, Will responded. Thx. S passed out. U think he'll help me carry?

Y, he's helpful like that.

K. Sorry to see you go.

Fear and uncertainty swirled in my head. I slid down the garage door a little. I felt heavy, and exposed. My phone lay in my hand.

I reminded myself: this meant nothing to Will. Less than nothing. One more notch in a collection that would have whittled the biggest bedpost into toothpicks.

In the dark, I considered my options. Then I texted Will again, as subtly as I could. Let's keep the root beer to ourselves, ok?

All right. You ok? came his reply.

No. I wasn't. I wasn't okay about one single thing, and it was my own stupid fault. Tears welled in my eyes, and I swiped them away. The whole time, I berated myself. *Stop it. This is your fault. You knew better, and you did it anyway. You're not allowed to feel sorry for yourself.*

I tried to imagine Jane saying it. She could be really unforgiving when she wanted to be. With her asymmetrical bobbed hair and hard-angled clothes—mostly black, with a nice mix of bloody red sometimes—she could be terrifying. I wanted her to terrify me. But instead, thinking about Jane's reaction only made me want to cry more.

My phone bleated again, the screen lighting up. It was a spotlight. It refused to let me hide, even in the dark. Dragging a knuckle beneath my damp eyes, I made myself look. A blank avatar stared back—blank because I didn't know Will. He wasn't my friend. We were strangers to each other. But something sharp pulled in me, a sudden, piercing tug, when I read his text.

U there? Won't say anything if u don't want me to. Then, another text pushed it up. This one read, Can we meet up later?

Silken calm slipped over me. I was already replying when Will sent another.

Was it just me?

It was a plaintive, perfect question. Headlights skimmed down the long drive. They stole the luxury of a long, thought-out reply. Though a chill pressed around me, I barely noticed it. I still felt guilty, but I wasn't ashamed anymore.

Instead, I typed out my response as quickly as I could. I hit send, then put away my phone. It was out there in the ether, floating in the night.

It wasn't just you.

FOUR

I texted my sister Ellie, and she saved me from the rest of the party. I couldn't go back in there, not with those texts from Will taunting me. Not knowing that I'd walk in and see Tricia hostessing away, completely unaware she'd been betrayed. Especially not knowing that I'd have to face Dave, even if he was oblivious.

Sliding my guitar into the backseat, I tried to sound light when I climbed into the front. "Homeward, Jeeves."

"It's early," Ellie pointed out, ignoring my put-on expression. "Bad gig?"

Really, I should have known she'd ask. She and I were both pathologically addicted to our arts. That's probably why we didn't fight like most sisters. Sure, there was the standard-issue stuff. Closet raiding, special cereal eating, little battles. But never any wars, because we connected on a completely different level.

We saved the hardcore rivalry for our older sister, Grace. She was off at Loyola. Acing her GREs, getting a degree in financial mathematics that would make her crazy rich. Grace liked to complain that she was the one who'd have to take care of Mom and Dad in their old age.

Obviously, dancer Ellie and musician Sarah wouldn't be any help. Grace didn't believe that success could exist if it wasn't quantifiable by equations and tables and charts. She was the alien in the family. She just didn't know it.

But because Ellie and I shared that wavelength, it also meant that Ellie was hyperaware when my artistic schedule changed. Much like I would be shocked if Ellie were home on a Saturday morning—prime matinee time—she knew that I shouldn't be heading out this early. A gig usually meant that Dave drove me home, sometimes just before my midnight curfew. A round of homework, one last tour of e-mail, Facebook, and Twitter, and then bed—an early morning for me on the weekends was noon.

Clicking the seat belt into place, I shook my head. "It was good. Short, though, and really crowded."

"Oh, good," she said.

The other nice thing about Ellie was that she took me at my word. With surgical precision, Grace would dissect every single bit of that sentence to see if there was something more beneath it. Not Ellie. Whether she believed me or not, she didn't push. She also didn't pry, and I was glad.

I still didn't understand what had happened with Will. Or more importantly, why it had happened. Was I only trying to get even with Dave? Was I just another one of Will's endless conquests? Or was it possible that I hadn't imagined anything, and Will and I shared some inexplicable pull? I felt split in pieces, and none of them matched. It turned out that it was possible to feel guilty and elated at the same time. To be ashamed and emboldened at once. Though it had been wrong to even try it, I wanted another taste of Will.

The quiet in the car gave me too much time to think. I wanted to get home, because there I could burrow in my own bed and welcome sleep. In the morning, things would be clearer. Emotion would give way to reason. That's what I needed, a good night's sleep. A return to normalcy.

Reaching over, I grabbed Ellie's hand and squeezed it. "Thanks for picking me up."

"Anytime," she said and drove on home.

I was wrong. In the morning, everything felt more scattered than ever. I wasn't ashamed to admit I couldn't figure it out on my own. That's why I grabbed my keys and headed straight for my best friend's house.

"Morning, Westlake," Jane said. "Somebody beat you with the hangover stick?"

With a groan, I replied, "You suck, I hate you."

Because Jane was my best friend, I muscled past her and right inside. We had fridge privileges at each other's houses, so I never felt bad about busting into Chez Dubinsky. But instead of taking my usual route to the kitchen, I headed to Jane's bedroom and flopped facedown in her bed.

A moment later, Jane tossed a pillow onto my head. I heard her drop into her desk chair. It squeaked in F minor, and she refused to fix it. I felt her sling her feet on the edge of the bed. Every move she made added another squeak; it was maddening.

"Are you seriously hungover?" she asked.

"No. Not even. I had, like, half a beer last night." Sighing, I rolled onto my back. My head felt stuffed full of cotton. My heart kept beating weird, random patterns. Was it possible to die of guilt? Maybe the deathblow would be unconfessed guilt. With that possibility in mind, I looked to Jane. "And maybe also a taste of Will Spencer."

The chair squealed when Jane all but threw herself out of it. "What?!"

"Yeah . . . I know . . ." I moaned. The judgment was coming. I was waiting for it. Practically anticipating it.

Instead, Jane knocked me even more off-balance when she said, "Whoa. Okay, lay it on me. How was he, with one being *I'm permanently traumatized* and ten being *I think I saw the face of God?*"

Pushing up on my elbows, I stared at her. "Jane! I cheated on Dave!"

"Oh, I'll get to that," she assured me. "But, well? I'm intrigued! I want to know if the rumors are accurate. Or if they're the most carefully orchestrated PR campaign since Gwyneth Paltrow morphed into macrobiotic Martha Stewart."

I shrugged, unsure of where to start. "I don't know."

"Sarah!"

"Eight? Point five?"

Jane clapped her hands together, rubbing them like some cartoon villain. "So he's not perfect! I knew it!"

"It probably would have been more like nine, nine and a half if we hadn't been in a rowboat. And if we hadn't been interrupted. And, you know, if I hadn't been *cheating on my boyfriend with someone who has a girlfriend.*"

Bouncing from her chair, Jane sprung onto the bed. The headboard thumped the wall, but Jane didn't care. Her house was chaotic on the best day. Her dad was a life coach, and her mom specialized in DIY carpentry.

If Jane didn't have a cause to shout about, her dad had top-of-the-lungs advice or was yelling because her mom was ripping apart an armoire to distress it. Frankly, a little headboard thumping was the quietest it got around there.

Jane looked down at my face. She blotted out the entire ceiling; she was nothing but brown eyes and orange juice breath. "Explain yourself, Jezebel."

With a roll of my eyes, I plastered my whole hand across her face. "I feel bad, okay?"

"I said explain, not defend."

Ugh. I sat the rest of the way up, then slumped against Jane's shoulder. She was going to give me a hard time because that was just her way. But I knew she had my back, no matter what. And the truth was, I didn't know if I could explain. Not completely. Dave had flirted with the entire world for as long as I'd known him. Never before had I ever considered going behind his back. But Will had happened so naturally.

Flapping my hands uselessly, I finally dropped them in my lap. "I don't know. Heatherly was all over Dave after the set we played . . ."

"Loved the T.I. cover, bee tee dubs," Jane interrupted.

"Thanks, I arranged that," I said and slipped right back to the topic. "But it was Heatherly, and then it was Olivia . . . and look, I know I'm not the main draw when it comes to Dasa, but come on. They both know Dave's my boyfriend. Also? I was up there, too. He wasn't harmonizing all by himself, you know?"

Sagely, Jane nodded. "Double jealousy whammy, okay. Now please explain. How does this end with you sampling Will Spencer's unlucky charms?"

I played it back in my head. Was the talk about my costume relevant? Would anything in the boathouse have happened without it? I thought of him trailing his finger along my back. The way he looked at me and seemed to really see me. I didn't know what to put in and what to leave out. It was easier to purge everything and let Jane sort it out.

Well, almost everything. The texts afterward, those I kept to myself. They were mine, and they were secret. I wasn't ready to let them out of my grasp.

After I told Jane the almost-entire story, I sat back and watched her curiously. What would she say?

Jane seemed to struggle with her own reaction. Her face contorted, three different times. Like she started to say something, then changed her mind. Finally she landed somewhere between amused and concerned. "I mean, it's not cool, right? You know that."

"Oh yeah, trust me. I know."

"And that magical connection was probably just party and hormones," she continued.

I wasn't ready to concede that. It had felt like more. It still felt like more, even the morning after. Even feeling as badly as I did for what I had done, I had this spark, the faintest glow deep inside that insisted there had been something more there. The secret texts, the ones I wasn't ready to reveal—they proved that Will had felt it, too.

But Jane needed a narrative, so I nodded. "Okay."

"So don't do it again," Jane said resolutely. "And don't beat yourself up over it. Everybody makes mistakes. What's important is how you recover from it."

Eyeing her curiously, I wondered what she would have said if I hadn't been her best friend. If I'd brought the situation to her as gossip about somebody else. Somehow, I had a feeling Jane would have been a lot less understanding. Was she secretly judging me? Nudging her, I said, "But I was so wrong. And Dave doesn't deserve that."

"Okay, look, I don't want you to think I'm all down on Dave or anything—he's fine. He's a nice guy. But I'm not, and I never have been, a real big fan of the whole rock star thing he does after shows. I don't care if it means anything, it makes you feel bad. And he knows it makes you feel bad ..."

Suddenly defensive of Dave, I said, "I never told him to stop."

Jane crystallized, hard and unyielding. "Yes, you have. And you know what? You shouldn't have to tell your boyfriend to stop paying attention to everybody in the room but you. So yes, you did a bad, bad thing with a bad, bad boy. Bad Sarah. No gelato. But it's not that easy. You would be absolutely furious if Dave did this to you. You'd never speak to him again. You've never thought about cheating on him before. Why last night? Why Will?"

If Dave had hopped off stage and danced with me, I never would have talked to Will in the first place. If he hadn't been working the party without so much as a look toward me, I never would have gone to the boathouse. Or if I had, it would have been with him.

I had done a terrible thing, and I felt more confused than ever. Because while it was true I wouldn't have ended up in that boat with Will if Dave had been at my side . . . I was secretly the smallest bit glad that he hadn't been.

FIVE

Sunday mornings in Dave's garage studio were a tradition. Or a long-standing date. Or a commitment. I don't know; they were something permanent, anyway. Each time I looked at him, I shrank a little. Could he see it on me? Didn't he realize what I had done?

Sinking into the threadbare plaid couch, I tried to keep my guitar level in my lap. Fingers trailing the fret board, I mapped out a C7 chord, then played it. A faint, flat buzz emanated from the strings.

"Is that off?" I asked Dave.

"No, it's fine." Distracted, he turned around twice, then picked up a bag of brushed chrome bushings. "Traded Nicky for these. Did I tell you he's putting green tuning heads on that Rogue of his?"

Shaking my head, I played the C7 again. It sounded sweeter this time. Like music instead of practice, and that was the goal. "He'd be better off buying a new guitar."

"Exactly what I said."

Dave didn't look up from his workbench. Instead of taking cars apart, Dave restored old guitars. Sometimes, we spent whole afternoons scouring thrift shops and flea markets for them.

A guitar with possibilities put a light in his eyes. Always so tender, his hands would skim the body, studying the instrument's curves. In the end, he always said, "I guess I have to take her home." Then he did, over and over.

Each time, he swore he'd refurbish the guitar and sell it—his contribution toward the recording studio time we needed to cut our demo. But Dave's collection of guitars never shrank. It just kept growing.

Running scales, I watched Dave thoughtfully. He'd gotten his hair cut a little too short. It didn't spike out, but it wasn't as smooth as it usually was. Morning sunlight sparkled in the field of blond, making him look a little like a Japanese manga character. His red plaid shirt brought his color out—and made his mouth look like candy.

From my corner on the couch, I measured him with looks and memories. In the beginning, we were music, first and foremost. Even though that had turned into my hot hands under his white T-shirts, and his lips on mine, music was still our center.

Because we were good at lyrics but not titles, we called ourselves Dasa. Our first names, smashed together. His first, because Sada looked either depressing or cruel, depending on your frame of mind. Fortunately, Dasa looked good on a chalkboard marquee.

We hadn't had any big professional gigs yet, but we played a lot of local shows and coffee shops. Parties like Tricia's and a couple bat and bar mitzvahs. The community college radio station loved us. We made decent money selling our mini-CDs online. And none of it would have happened if it weren't for coincidence.

We met freshman year, two gangly, goofy dorks who both brought guitars to school on the first day. For me, it was a security blanket.

Carrying a guitar always gave me something to talk about with strangers. Pulling it out and playing whatever was popular was a good way to start making friends.

I sat on the top step of the atrium, where all the underclassmen congregated. I wore brand-new shoes and even newer jeans—and back then, really unfortunate braces.

Thirty minutes before first bell, I'd already played through most of the Billboard Top 40. I'd met three girls who would share classes with me, a couple of guys who wanted to ask questions about the guitar, and then there was Dave. Just as I finished off some Taylor Swift by request, a voice behind me asked, "Know any Iron and Wine?"

Tipping my head back, I smiled. My whole heart jumped up, because there was this guy, a really rather cute guy, hefting his guitar case up for me to see. He stood there, waiting for an invitation, so I slid over a little. Shaking my fingers out, I slid into the first chords of "Flightless Bird, American Mouth" and waited for him to join in.

And he did, singing along in a sweet tenor. Everyone near us stopped, turning to listen. It was a delicate song, with notes that drifted into the air like dandelion silk. Harmonizing with him, I sang along when we hit the second chorus.

Eyes meeting, we didn't shy away. It was like we'd been singing together forever, not for a few minutes. There was a special current there, something instinctive. Our voices darted and tumbled, swirling together effortlessly.

Parts of that morning were preserved in my memory, kept pristine no matter how much time passed. I remember that the sky was unmarked blue, but it smelled like rain coming. That the stone steps in the atrium were rough and cold and never warmed up. And that when we finally stopped playing there was applause, but I didn't really hear it.

"Do you write?" Dave asked. He curled his arms around his guitar. A silver ring on his thumb hummed against the strings. It was a low, whispering sound that I felt on my skin.

I answered with a lazy chord and a nod. "A little. Do you?"

"Yeah."

For a moment, we ran out of words. The music was so good, so easy. Talking wasn't like that. We were just a couple of fourteen-year-olds on the first day of school. Strangers, and potential losers, suddenly weirdly aware of each other.

To patch up the gap, I checked my position and picked out a few notes that I hoped he recognized. "Creep," by Radiohead. It was ancient, but it was the ultimate *I feel awkward* anthem.

His expression transformed with a smile. All at once, his too-soft face resolved into richer angles. High cheekbones and blue-gray eyes that crinkled when he smiled. His bangs fell casually across his brow, and he smiled the smile of somebody who'd already gotten his braces off. I barely had time to wonder what it would be like to feel his lips on mine when he leaned over and graced me with one perfect kiss.

When he pulled back, he looked dazed. I felt it. With shaking hands, I found my chord and looked to him shyly. Falling into the music with me, Dave extended the opening long enough to say, "I have a studio in my garage, sort of. If you ever want to come play."

Later, he told me he'd never carried a guitar with him. He'd just woken up that day, the first day of high school, and decided he should. At the time, it felt like destiny. Then it felt like love, and it still did. Dave was spun sugar, the sweetest kiss—I loved the way he laughed in my ear and whispered my name.

With a brand-new kiss, Dave drew me back to the present. His breath was warm, lingering on my lips. When he drew back, there was a smile in his eyes. Leaning forward, he bumped my nose and said, "So . . . ?"

Usually that was a sign that it was time to put music aside for a while. Making out with Dave was fun, ice cream on a hot day.

The phantom of Will's kiss stung my lips. It burned, a brand that sent heat through me. It rushed with each heartbeat, not sweet at all. I felt the shock all over again, the pull when he opened his eyes and looked in mine. Was it just lust? Was I just jealous of the attention Dave got—and gave?

There was only one way to find out.

SIX

"Dave," I said, setting my guitar between my feet. For once, music could wait. Even though I'd melted back in this couch with Dave too many times to count, suddenly I felt shy. My palms went sweaty, and my heart started to waver. Twisting in the couch, I got to my knees and leaned over the back of it. Reaching out, I managed to rasp my fingertips against his back. "Hey, you."

"Hey," he replied with a smile. Flecks of sawdust drifted from his workbench. Bright stars in a streak of sunlight, they fell gracefully to earth. Teasing, he let his caressing hands slip off the half-finished guitar. "You want something?"

Wanting something was an understatement.

I wasn't about to say, *Yes, come over here and make me forget the boathouse.* So instead, I tugged the hem of his shirt and half met his eyes. Then I shocked myself by skating way too close to danger by asking, "Have you heard from Simon since you drove him home?"

"No, why?"

I beckoned him with a crooked finger, pulling my guitar into my lap. "Oh, because you were too busy playing taxi, I didn't get a chance to tell you the whole story. Our friend Simon was *this* close to hooking up with Emmalee Dekker."

Abandoning the workbench, Dave wandered closer. He didn't have a roll in his hips, but there was something definitely slow and sure in his step. "No way."

"I have the texts to prove it. While you were driving Simon home, I was directing *her* back to Tricia's guesthouse. She was so grateful when she texted earlier. Said she'd gotten coyote drunk . . ."

"And you saved her from having to gnaw her arm off in the morning."

"Exactly," I said and curled up a little when Dave kissed my neck. Walking his fingers against my arm, he nudged at the guitar. "I thought you wanted me to come over here."

Still attempting to flirt with my own boyfriend, I teased, "I did. I've been working on something. You want to hear it?"

"Okay," Dave said. His stormy blue eyes lit with the challenge. "Go for it."

I started playing through a song I'd started last week. I had most of the chorus down, but the verses weren't coming together. Half of the lyrics were dumb stuff like "and then he gave me scrambled eggs," just as placeholders. Like he always did, Dave jumped in, singing notes to fill empty spaces in the melody.

As I slid through the chorus, I leaned over the guitar. Dave was there to meet me. At first, he teased with the faintest touch, a feather-light caress. Then he brushed my hair back over my ear and claimed his kiss. It was sweet and playful. A flush rose to my cheeks, and I felt airy and light.

Dave knew me. He knew me really well, and his kiss lingered when he slowly drew back. Stroking the tender skin behind my ear, he pressed one more kiss to my lips before drawing back. He looked like a fairy-tale prince all over again.

When I cycled through the few lyrics I had, I let the last notes trail away. Dave still nodded his head in time. His eyes were half-closed, and his golden lashes fanned against his cheeks.

Reaching out, I drew my fingers across them gently. The party really had been a momentary lapse of reason, I decided.

"Kind of rocker girl, not like your usual stuff. It's definitely going somewhere," Dave said, pulling away and nodding toward my guitar. "Needs some work on the second verse, though. Scrambled eggs, really?"

He was only teasing. We always used placeholder lyrics. Sometimes they were so silly, they became inside jokes.

"Those are the secret lyrics. The real ones would blow. Your. Mind."

Dave stroked his hand along the curve of my guitar. Lightly, he leaned in and teased suggestively, "I know another way you can blow my mind."

We hadn't gone there yet. Maybe somewhere medium close to there. On this couch, even. Clothes off, but only from the waist up. It wasn't a sore point or anything, Dave was fine with waiting—which was good, because I wasn't ready for more. But that didn't mean that he wouldn't occasionally hint toward something more.

With a kind smile that told him it wasn't going to happen, I pointed out, "Rehearsal. We have a show at the Eden coming up."

Like he was indulging me, Dave smeared a quick kiss on my lips and rolled to his feet. He never pushed too much, which I appreciated. But sometimes I couldn't help but want him to want me enough to push for it. The view when he walked back to his workbench was nice. Dave had a lot of things going for him, including his tight, cute butt.

I loved Dave. I loved so many things about him. For example, every rehearsal, that morning included, he greeted me with a tall zebra mocha, one extra pump white chocolate. I'd ordered one on our first movie date; I used to love them. They were too sweet now, though I'd never told Dave that. If I had, I'm sure he'd produce a regular half-caf with cream instead, because that's what I bought for myself now.

The trill of an incoming text startled me. Fishing my phone from my purse, I blinked in surprise. The blank avatar flashed on the screen. It was Will. I felt my pulse flutter. Instant heat engulfed me. All my edges sharpened, my teeth and my eyes, even the curve of my hips. Suddenly, I was a wild thing, just barely contained in my skin. I hadn't gotten a hint of that while I was making out with Dave. It was like Will had traced that finger across my shoulders again. The phantom tingle of a cinnamon kiss rose to my lips, all before I'd even read his message.

In need of some wisdom. U have any?

I glanced up. Dave was oblivious, trimming off strings and lavishing his full attention on tuning the new-to-him guitar. We were supposed to be rehearsing, but he just couldn't leave a half-finished guitar alone. Somewhat irrationally, I felt like he should realize that my attention had shifted elsewhere, that another guy was texting me. That somebody else wanted to be with me in a way he didn't. He didn't notice. He hadn't even looked over. And before I knew it, I fired off a reply to Will.

Depends, I said. U have any root beer?

His reply came back almost instantly. Come see for urself.

Four words, and they realigned every nerve in my body. I felt fresh and limber, like I could run a race in record time. There was no reason to wait. The starting line was in front of me. At the end waited Will, with his dark looks and his sure hands and his pale eyes that looked right into me. That *saw* me.

Before I knew it, I'd tossed my phone in my purse and thrown the strap over my shoulder. "That's Jane. She's got a flat, I'm gonna go pick her up."

Wire snips still in hand, Dave looked over. He never could resist the chance to play the hero. "Does she need help changing it?"

"No, we can change it. I just need to take her to get a spare. She thought she had a donut, but . . ."

I let the lie trail off. It gave him a chance to figure it out. To look at me and see the electricity racing along my skin. One final chance to get that I was walking out the door to see somebody else. This was his opportunity to ask me to stay.

After all, I was walking out in the middle of our Sunday studio time. Three straight years of Sundays, and we had missed exactly one.

He gave me a little wave. "All right, if you're sure. Tell Jane I say hi."

"I will," I promised.

The school was dark, the grounds entirely abandoned.

All the spots were empty in the school parking lot. I parked next to the custodian's dock, then hesitated. Will had told me to come to the side door on the loading dock. Until this morning, I didn't know this part of the building existed. It was an adventure. A treasure hunt, with Will at the end of it.

Buzzed on forbidden adrenaline, I drove straight to school, and it wasn't until I stopped to check out the surroundings that I began to feel anxious.

The back of the school was off-limits, the kind of spot where illicit and dangerous things might take place. They kept the Dumpsters back here. The incinerator, too, the stink of strange burning things hanging in the air. It was grubby and industrial. If I hadn't been meeting Will, I would have thrown it in reverse and peeled out of there.

After I locked my car, I hurried to the side door. This felt like no-man's-land. It was only the promise of seeing Will that kept me going. Knowing that he was waiting somewhere nearby set my senses alight.

The sensation grew as I knocked on the thick steel door to the side. Inside me, everything tilted on a seesaw. First, exhilaration. Then worry and guilt. But exhilaration won out, that night in the boathouse etched into me.

I shivered, feeling that first kiss again. Feeling everything again.

I was practically breathless when the door swung open. Will looked amazing. His distressed jeans clung to his legs jealously. In a nod to the season, he wore a cream-colored sweater that made his hair seem even darker. His eyes even bluer. He could have walked off a New England pier, all wind-tossed and casually sexy.

Reaching for me, he cast a furtive look into the parking lot. Instantly, I knew. He didn't want to get caught here, either. It was a secret, forbidden place for him, too. Though there were heavy, industrial sounds behind him, I was thrilled when he pulled me inside. My body fell against his chest, with his possessive hands sweeping up my back.

"I'm not going to kiss you here," he said.

My hands spanned his hips. I steadied myself against him, thumbs slipping into his belt loops. Tipping my head back to look up at him, I reminded, "You picked the place."

"I didn't pick the boiler room," he said. "It's just the fastest way to get where we're going."

Feeling bold and wild, I smiled. "Then let's go."

Still, he didn't move. It was like he couldn't help himself. He actually seemed to fight against an instinct that drew him closer to my lips. He leaned in, in spite of himself. The warm outline of his mouth nearly traced mine. There was nothing but a breath between us. Tugging his belt loops, I flattened myself against him.

Summoning more strength than I had, Will pulled himself away. "This isn't actually the place."

Lacing his fingers in mine, he backed down clanging metal steps. Machines two stories high pounded away, making so much noise it seemed to echo in my head.

Leading me through a tangle of pipes and steam, he reassured me with a squeeze of my hand. There was no point in saying anything, and no need to.

Then suddenly, we turned down a darkened hall. Will led me through two more steel doors, and the noise was trapped behind us. This new hall felt claustrophobically small after the giant machine room. It was dark, too. Light in the distance illuminated the white-plastered walls, but we stood mostly in shadow.

Will's gaze dropped to my lips, and when he spoke again, his voice was lower, a smokier tone, one that snaked over me lazily. "Any guesses?"

"About where we are?"

I laughed nervously. We weren't in the boiler room anymore. There weren't any machines here. There was just a long, narrow hallway. At the end of it, a bluish light flickered. It danced along the walls . . . like waves. I stopped, holding a finger up to shush him completely. I perked up my ears, really listening. But instead of picking up sound, I noticed a scent: chlorine.

I looked up at him. "Are we under the pool?"

Will traced a finger against my lower lip. "You really are wise. Come on. I want to show you something."

Leading me toward the light, Will smiled when we turned the corner. There, instead of another long plastered wall, was a window. It had to be twenty feet long, maybe more. And from our vantage, we looked up, into the deep end of the pool.

Our school had a full-size, Olympic-quality natatorium—a gift from the Pattens, of course. Everybody at East River High School had to take swimming and pass a swim test—it was the bane of freshman year. I had never seen the place like this before.

My hand tightened in Will's, because it was so unexpectedly beautiful. Now the strange, inside-out sounds made sense. It was the groan and call of waves above us. Lights from inside the pool illuminated the water. Bright wave prints danced over us as we stood there together.

This was something magical, a hint of romance to cut the ravenous want that I felt when we got too close together. Players played, sure, but Will already knew he had me. This was something more—proof that there was something more between us.

Softly, I said, "Will, it's wonderful."

"I love this place," he murmured.

Suddenly, silver foam and a dark streak filled the viewing window. A deep, plunging echo seemed to waver through it, the sound of a splash from the inside. Pressing closer to the thick glass, I watched in amazement. Legs kicked, a body twisted. It took me a moment to realize what it was. When the second streak whipped past us, I finally understood. We were watching dive practice.

Eager to see the next dive, I said, "I didn't even know it was here."

"Me either. I found out when the custodians needed some help bringing the chlorine in. Jake and I happened to be standing around after a pep rally, and they snagged us to help."

Touching the glass, I left foggy fingerprints behind. "It's amazing."

I stepped back. Right into Will's arms. "Can they see us in here?" I asked.

Shaking his head, Will trailed his hands down my waist, down to rest on my hips. "It's a one-way mirror. I checked it out. It's about eight feet down. If you dive to it, all you see is yourself."

I turned in his arms, the same time he took a step forward. Pressed between his warm body and the cool glass behind me, I took a soft, shallow breath. Mingled now with the chlorine was Will's warm, spicy scent. He smelled so good, I wanted to press my face against his neck and just breathe him into me.

Then I thought, why shouldn't I? I didn't feel tentative with Will. There was no barrier, none of that shy anxiety about doing or saying the right thing. I wanted to, and so I did.

Brushing my nose against his throat, I shivered with a deeper breath. Nosing along the fine, strong line of his jaw, I filled myself with him, letting him overtake my senses. The fleeting quiver of his pulse against his cheek made my own race.

He answered with hands that tightened on my waist. His thumbs trailed restlessly, hitching beneath my shirt by increments. It was a touch of fire when he found bare skin. His caress stirred heat through me everywhere. He touched nothing more intimate than my ribs, but I was dizzy with it, anyway.

It was easy to kiss Will Spencer. We moved in tandem, both turning at the same time. It was like we were machined to fit together, the right key in the right lock. Rising on my toes to meet his mouth, I looped my arms around his neck. Stretched against him, I felt long and tall, and strangely lovely. I wasn't transformed by his touch. I was *revealed*.

Will pressed into me. Every inch of him felt strong and hard, wound so tight he might snap. His grip on my waist tightened. Lifting me, he sat me on the window's narrow ledge. It was barely wide enough to perch on, but when my legs tangled around his waist, I realized I wasn't supposed to.

He held me up. Stealing the breath from my lips, he returned it on another kiss. His tongue was velvet on mine, seeking and teasing. I'd never been kissed like that before. Not with Dave, not with anyone. This wasn't innocent, a kiss for its own sake. It wasn't naïve and curious, not at all.

This felt like the beginning of something. A seduction that dared me to imagine what might come next. I felt like I'd been waiting for this. Needing it, even without knowing it. My fingers twisted in his hair, and he surged against me. It wasn't a thrust, but it promised one. It whispered darkly, *This is what it would feel like if . . .*

Another splash echoed overhead. From the corner of my eye, I caught a glimpse of a halo of bubbles, swirling and racing for the surface. I was happy to sink beneath it. Down, into the dark, into Will's arms. Into an uncertain, inevitable future.

SEVEN

Sitting back to back with Will, I leaned my head against his. This was the only way we could talk without crashing into each other.

Even still, we held hands. Our fingers twisted and teased. Slipping together, then apart again, they whispered with caresses. It was like our hands continued doing all the things we couldn't. Because no matter what we wanted, we really did have to talk.

If I said too much, if I said it the wrong way, would he leave? My heart said no, but how could I be sure? A different kind of tension threaded beneath my skin. It pulled tight, shortening my breath as my pulse raced.

Pretending things weren't complicated didn't actually simplify them. Nerves frazzled, I shaped my lips to say it.

"You have a girlfriend," I said. I kept my voice down. Since diving practice ended, the dark hallway took on an eerie quiet. I didn't want all my secret thoughts and feelings to carry. No one could know what I was feeling—no one but Will. I glanced around, but we were alone. I was glad for that, because his response caught me off guard.

"Yeah. Tricia's great."

Jealousy filled me, not that I was entitled. But I didn't want Will to think she was great. I wanted him to think I was better. I wanted him to admit he was mine, so I could admit that I was his. How else could we ever be together?

Casting a look over my shoulder, I said, "That night—you asked me if it was just you."

"It sounds wrong," Will said. His shoulders rubbed against mine. Fingers darting, he caught my hand in a new grip. His fingers trailed along the underside of my wrist. The skin there was tender, and his fingertips rough. "Or maybe it sounds like bullshit, I don't know. But it's different with you."

A shiver skated through me. "How? Is it just, you know . . . physical?"

"No."

"Are you sure?"

When he laughed, I felt it vibrate through him. "If it were, the boathouse would have been enough."

"Okay, crazy confession time," I said. I squeezed his hand, rolling against his shoulder. All I wanted was a peek at his face. I caught a glimpse of it in the shadows, half-masked by dark. The light caught his eyes so that they seemed unnaturally blue. Bright as the pool above us, and just as variable.

"Yeah?" he said, prompting me.

"Before anything happened, I felt like I knew you."

"I thought you were on to me," he said. With a wry little smile, he rested his weight against my back. "That Athena, she's just too smart. She cut right through the douche-bag party-boy and saw my true nature."

I wanted to gather him in my arms. I wanted to protect him from the rest of the world, who looked at him and couldn't see past the surface. I was sad that he hadn't had a chance to just be until now. His whole life, stuffed into a shape that didn't fit him . . . it was like I was the only one who realized that Pinocchio was a real boy.

Twining our forearms together, I raised our joined hands. Fingers skimming our shoulders, I turned and brushed a kiss against his fingertips. "There you are, Will."

Roughly, he said, "Here I am."

Reality pressed in. Closing my eyes, I was forced to admit things were crazy complicated. We couldn't just pack up a convertible and ride into the west together. He'd been dating Tricia for a while. They were homecoming king and queen, and on track to sweep the prom, too. And Dave? Dave wasn't just my boyfriend. He was my partner. We had years of history behind us, and I cared about him.

"I'm waiting for the 'but,'" Will said.

What a way to prove he did know me, in some basic, primal way. Already, he keyed into my silences.

"Dave isn't just my boyfriend," I said. "We're partners."

"The band," Will said.

"Even that makes it sound easier than it is. We actually have something, music-wise. I don't believe in muses or anything. But when we sit down and write a song together . . . it really is like there's some force out there, pouring music and lyrics into us."

"I've seen your website," Will said.

It touched me that he'd looked at it. That made the rest of what I had to say even harder. I wanted him to understand that Dasa wasn't so much about me and Dave as a couple. It was about us as artists.

With a frown, Will looked back at me. "You know, I've heard you play without him. You're really good."

"I'm better with him." I sighed. This was a mess; I was making it worse.

Will turned. I guess he thought I needed to see him when he said it. Catching my chin gently, he searched my face. Then he met my eyes, unwavering. "I don't want to take that from you."

Nervous, I nodded. I appreciated the gesture, but part of me wanted him to protest, to want to be the only guy in my life. Covering his hand with mine, I wondered if this was the part where we agreed to meet back up in five years and see if we could make it work then. A knot formed in my throat. It twisted tight, because the thought of giving him up made me want to cry.

His expression melted dramatically. All at once, his eyes were seeking. His brows tilted, reflecting my pain. Soothing, he stroked my cheek, knuckles grazing my jaw. "Hey. Hey, shhhh. There's nothing wrong here. We can figure this out."

"Can we?"

Framing my face with his hands, he kissed me. Then he pressed his brow against mine. Opening his eyes, he gazed into me, and I gazed back. Wrapping my fingers around his wrists, I felt for his pulse. I wanted it to keep the same beat as mine. When I breathed, I wanted him to breathe, too.

With a whisper, he said, "See me when you can see me. You don't have to stop hanging out with Dave. I'm still good with Trish. For now. Until you can figure things out. We'll keep talking. It'll be fine. We'll be fine."

I believed him. When he said it like that, it made perfect sense. I didn't have to scrabble to hold on to my dream or to Will. I had time to figure it out. As reasonable as that sounded, it plucked at my nerves. Everything between us felt like it was in the future tense; I didn't want to be the one holding back. But I didn't dare to be the one who jumped first. There was just so much at stake.

Desperate to hold on to something, I rushed to close the space between us with a kiss.

Will was already there.

The next morning, I pulled up outside Jane's house and hit the horn once. Her quiet neighborhood was funkier than mine. Older bungalows and crazy yard people who couldn't stop at one garden gnome when five hundred would fit beneath their old oak trees. Jane's house had a cute old-fashioned porch on it, and a paint job that I liked to call Early Modern Bordello.

Compared with the boringly boxy houses on my street, Jane's neighborhood was practically garish. And since there was no lack of backyard chickens and roosters, I didn't feel bad hitting my horn, once. Jane was the one *desperate* for coffee before homeroom, but I always ended up waiting for her to emerge.

When she finally did, she was still scrambling to put herself together. Her purse twisted awkwardly from one wrist while she tried to shove a textbook into her bag. As soon as she got it together, she jogged up to the passenger side of my car.

Knocking on the glass, she leaned over to look at me. She mouthed, "I'm on to you," before flinging the door open and jumping inside. Her stacked bracelets jingled, and her faux-leather jacket squeaked against my definitely straight-up plastic seats.

"I have no idea what you're talking about," I said. But tension laced me tight. Did my second meetup with Will show on my face? Was he talking about it?

With a laugh, Jane broke the tension. "I'm just messing with you, jeez."

I waited for her to buckle up, then took off. I headed in the opposite direction of the school. We needed coffee, and Jane insisted on the fair trade shop out by the highway. Our town, East River, wasn't big enough for a true rush hour. Easing into traffic, I waited until I was in the express-ish lane to tell her what was happening.

"Okay, so maybe something *is* up," I said uneasily. "But I don't want you to be mad at me."

With an arched brow, Jane told me that I should explain. Hooking a finger at me in the air, she wriggled it until I started talking. It was her way of demanding without being demanding.

Usually, that move made me laugh. She had so many great, weird quirks. I was just feeling guilty, so I reached over and closed her chattery finger in my fist.

"I don't want you telling anybody this . . ."

"Since when do I spill on you?" Jane asked. "Speak, mouth."

I really did want to tell her about me and Will. It's just that when I went to say it out loud, I realized I didn't know how to explain it. There were so many lingering questions I hadn't yet answered. There were so many details that needed to be unpacked carefully.

In our last conversation, Jane and I had come to what seemed like a conclusion: Will was the bad candy, and I shouldn't have any more. And at the time, I'd agreed.

So I had to find a way to make sure Jane understood there was something more with Will. Yes, there was cheating involved. And yes, it was complicated. But there was so much at stake.

Anyway, the really short version was, I didn't want to be judged before seven in the morning. So I offered up the next best thing.

"Did I tell you that Emmalee and Simon almost hooked up?"

"What! No!"

"Yeah. In a big way. They made it to the boathouse before Will and I broke it up."

Whistling low, Jane shook her head. She wore shock well. When people caught Jane by surprise, they felt the massive quake as it rolled through her. "People used to call that place the V Stop. 'Cause that's where you stopped—"

"Being a virgin," I said. "I know."

"Holy crap, how did that even happen?"

Cracking my window a little, I sighed in relief. Cool air flooded into the car. It scrubbed at my flushed skin. I was suddenly so hot, I wanted to peel my clothes off and jump into a deep, dark pool. That stray thought brought memories of the pool back in vivid color. And thoughts of being wrapped around Will in the cool, shadowy blue made the flush worse.

Managing to steady my voice, I said, "The usual way. Too much party, not enough sober."

"But they didn't actually . . ."

I shook my head. "No. No. Nothing like that, just kissing. They were so slogged, I practically carried Emmalee back to the guest-house. She texted me yesterday, said she was vee vee vee grateful that I saved her from the Balrog. Any idea what a Balrog is?"

"They're fire demons with scourges," Jane said. She whipped out her phone and started Googling, presumably trying to find a picture of a Balrog somewhere that she could show me. There was nothing Jane liked better than visual aids. Her Instagram was a wonder to behold.

I kept talking. "Yeah, so that was a visit from weird town. Oh, and by the way, I made out with Will again."

Jane's Googling came to an abrupt halt. And there went the quake. Jane's eyes shifted from wide and curious to narrowed with incredulity. In fact, there seemed to be a little bit of betrayal in there as well. After all, she had helped me decide it would never happen again, and there I was, telling her she was wrong. "Excuse?"

Rolling my shoulders, I tried not to squirm. "He texted me, he wanted to talk."

"You don't talk to a guy like Will Spencer! You ride him like a pony, and you go, whee, I always wanted to have a pony, and then five minutes later you say, I'm over it now, thanks, bye!"

Defensive, I said, "He's smarter than he looks."

"So is a Slushy Magic, but you don't hook up with it!"

Leave it to Jane to get real without hesitation. All my life, I'd told her basically everything, and she forgot *none* of it. Every kiss I'd ever had, every weird bump I'd ever grown, every nauseating, embarrassing phobia . . . Somewhere in that crazy genius head of hers, there was a running log: every dumb thing Sarah ever did. And now, there was a new event in the number-one slot.

Struggling against her seat belt, Jane seemed like she wanted to burst out of her seat and shake me. "One time is an accident, Sarah. Twice is . . ."

"I know."

"If you know, why did you do it?" Then, randomly, she held up her phone. Sure enough, she'd found a horned demon brandishing a fire whip. I'm pretty sure if Jane had a whip, she'd have cracked it at me. "He has a girlfriend. You have a boyfriend. People's feelings are at stake here."

Frustrated, I flipped on my turn signal. "Yes, I am aware of that. I'm not proud of it. I'm just trying to figure things out."

"I'll help you," Jane said, frowning. "Gird your ovaries and dump your boyfriend before you attempt to get a new one."

I said nothing. Because Jane, if nothing else, was fair. And sensible.

And allowed to tell me the truth, even if I didn't want to hear it. Since I was silent, Jane felt the need to fill the quiet. "Look, you know I love you. But right now, I'm like . . . This cheating is not you. And I don't understand how you got here."

"It's hard to explain."

We passed the billboard for the coffee shop, and Jane shrugged. "Well, then I guess you're just going to have to sit down and try."

EIGHT

We were going to be late for homeroom, but I didn't care. Neither did Jane. We sat in the back booth at the Daily Grind, Jane nursing her coffee and boggling at me.

I told her everything. The very first thing Will said to me, and the very last. I admitted the secret texts, the ones that I hadn't told her about before. And I admitted that our attraction was so intense we couldn't even talk to each other face to face.

I tried to ignore the really exaggerated reactions. That was just Jane's way of processing a massive load of information in really short order.

Though Jane snorted when I explained that the temptation was just too much, I thought it was important to include, because it was important to me. The physical was a really, really big deal. I'd always felt like Dave was a step or two ahead of me. He never pushed or pressured, but I knew he was ready for sex and I just wasn't.

Now, though, I wondered if I just wasn't ready for it with *him*.

When Will touched me, I wanted more. When Dave and I made out, I felt happy, but I only wanted exactly as much as I had. It was delicious, but ephemeral. Like cotton candy that immediately melted on my tongue.

At the same time, I had no idea if Will was the kind of guy who'd remember my favorite coffee order or hold my hand at the movies. If he'd write me e-mails in the middle of the night and remember my every detail. Maybe I wasn't ready for sex with Dave because I was afraid it would change that?

"I'm just confused," I insisted. "And trying to figure it out. Will gets that things with Dave are incredibly complicated."

Finally allowed to weigh in, Jane practically lunged over the table. "O-kay, does he understand your special snowflake circumstances? Or is he just excited that he gets to nail two girls at the same time? Maybe he 'gets' that things are so complicated because as long as you're confused, he doesn't have to offer you any commitment. He's taking advantage of you, boo!"

I'm not sure what shade of red I turned. I couldn't see myself. But from the wildfire way it spread across my face, I was betting it was something in the scarlet family. Even the tips of my ears burned. Offended, I said, "It's not like that."

Jane groaned, clapping a hand over her face. It wasn't even necessary. She just did it for effect. "Literally every single person in the history of infidelity says two things: It's not like that, and she just doesn't understand me like you do, baby."

"That's really gross. And overly specific."

Fortified with another slug of ethical caffeine, Jane sighed at me. "Sare-bear, seriously."

Crossing my arms over my chest, I waited. There was no point in arguing with her. She was going to say whatever hideous thing she had to say. The love affirmations almost always came before the Angry Hammer of Jane fell on the unsuspecting villagers.

"You're smarter than this, Sarah. You deserve better! If you want to get a little something-something on the side . . ." she started.

I cringed.

"Then go for it."

I froze. Where was the Angry Hammer? Where was the part where she told me that I was a reprehensible human being who deserved to be shunned? I demanded shunning, damn it. Okay, I didn't. But I did feel a little disappointed. Obviously, kissing Will had caused a teensy bit of brain damage.

"So," I said. "I'm super confused now."

Scooting along the booth bench, she slung an arm around my shoulders. "Don't get me wrong, you're a jerk for screwing around behind Dave's back."

There was the Jane I knew and loved. Having my actions described that way actually made me feel a little better. Somebody had to say what I knew in my heart. Cutting her a long, sideward glance, I prompted her. "But?"

"But you're going to do it anyway. I can talk logic, but you don't care."

"I do," I insisted.

"Nope," Jane countered. "You want my opinion?"

Carefully, I said, "I actually do."

Jane shrugged. "It doesn't matter what I think because you're dickmatized."

Horrified, I leaned away from her. "Jane!"

"You've been with Dave how long? Almost three years, right?" She didn't wait for me to confirm it; she already knew. "The crazy phase is over. You're together, it's good, it's fine. Maybe it's a little boring, but it's safe and comfortable. Then Will Spencer comes out of nowhere, and he gets you hot. He's not safe. He's not familiar. And he's not good for you. You're all enchanted and dazzled."

"I don't know where you get this stuff."

"From observation, yo. So, my opinion is, I have no opinion." Draining the last of her coffee, she offered me a gentle smile. "You know I'm here for you, but I already told you what I think. Beyond that, you'll have to figure this one out on your own."

I couldn't believe she was surrendering. Maybe I hadn't explained it well enough. "It's just complicated with Dave. I do love him, and you know, Dasa's really important to both of us!"

"Sweetie. You're the engine in that machine. I know you think you have to have Dave there to make it run. But believe me, you don't. So . . . go debase yourself with Will. Or don't. I'm officially Switzerland."

As confused and conflicted as I was, I realized that Jane's position of no-position was the best thing she could do for *us*, as friends. Her head was clear enough to see that we weren't going to agree on this and it would be too easy to let it come between us.

My phone bleated, and I glanced at it. The blank avatar: Will. What was he doing texting me so early? It wasn't like we could hook up at school. But I wasn't at school yet, was I? There was a whole town full of places to meet up, if only for a few stolen minutes. Thoughts racing, I pulled up the message hungrily.

Where r u? Need to see you.

"Is that him?" Jane demanded.

I shielded my phone as I replied. Since she was Switzerland, she could sit on her side of the table and just wonder. Keeping my desperation to myself, I tried to play it cool. Biting my lower lip, I considered my words, then sent back, Sorry u'll just have to keep needing me, not even @ school yet.

Watching me with keen eyes, Jane waited until I put my phone away. Then, suddenly, she flailed. "Seriously, though, Sarah, really? Of all the people with a reputation for the sexing, you picked Will?"

Now I *was* offended. "He's not the guy you think he is."

Jane raised her hands. "I'm going to get a warm up. And ponder you getting your freak on in a dinghy. And under a pool. What's with all the water, little mermaid?"

I called after her. "Stop making it sound weird!"

As she walked away, she hummed "Row, Row, Row Your Boat" beneath her breath.

My own best friend, the moral center of my universe, had stepped back. I was on my own, and I had to figure it out. Everything felt funhouse crazy, a hall of mirrors where I could see a future with Will down one corridor, and one with Dave down the other.

They both existed as possibilities, but I couldn't make out the end. There wasn't a bright neon sign pointing me in the right direction. All I knew was that I had to pick one and hope that I had chosen wisely.

I drained the rest of my coffee and wondered.

My morning classes kept my mind off things, at least until our pass-through period: a twenty-minute break between third and fourth period. Some people hit the library to finish up homework at the last minute. A couple of clubs held micro-meetings. For most of us, though, it was just a chance to socialize and chill.

For me, it was a chance to catch up with Will. Already tight with anticipation, I walked the main hall, scanning for him. When I didn't spot him immediately, I shot off a message. Still needful?

Y but w trish.

A rock sank in my stomach. It was cool. It was fine. Jealousy gnawed at me all the same. "Not gonna do this," I said under my breath. I had other things to occupy my time. My newest song, for one.

East River had a pretty great music department, including a couple of soundproof rehearsal booths. I went that way, head down and determined. When I closed the booth door, I shut out the world. I heard my own heartbeat in my ears, my own breath rushing through my chest.

Just when I had lost myself to the music, the booth door opened. The soundproof seal cracked like an egg. A rush of noise flooded in, then died when the seal caught once more. It was Dave, shamelessly cutting in on my session. And the weird thing was, I wasn't disappointed to see him.

He checked the latch, then turned to me. His crimson hoodie and tan shorts looked tailored to him. Though Dave wasn't a jock, he took care of himself. He was lean and sculpted, and his clothes hung on him like he was walking the runway for Abercrombie & Fitch. With that dazzling, boyish smile of his, he said, "I thought I'd find you here."

Though it wasn't cold, I shivered. Jane was wrong. This wasn't as simple as she made it sound. Dave and I had been together for a long time, but he was still crush-worthy on a daily basis. He smelled good, like molasses and spice. When he approached, everything stilled—I felt warm and safe, not a hint of drama, even in the distance.

"I didn't expect to see you until after lunch," I said.

"I figured," he said, sliding right into my arms, "since you were working on a new song Sunday that I'd probably find you here."

"You know me really, really well."

"And I said to myself, self . . ."

With a laugh, I interrupted. He smelled so good, and I traced swirls up his back, ropey and familiar. This is what I needed. What I wanted. "Did you really say that?"

Touching a finger to my lips, Dave said, "Shhh."

We still had a whole year of school left together, and all the milestones that came along with it. Ditch Day and senior prom, graduation—we'd do those things together. There were gigs on our calendar; we were going to rule homecoming from the stage.

On the other hand, Will was going to graduate in a month; he'd be long gone before my senior year even began.

Tightening his arms around me, Dave leaned in to kiss my neck. Melting into his embrace, I hid myself against him. He felt good, certain and safe—and sweetness wasn't a bad thing. I liked his kisses, and I liked the fact that I didn't feel even a little guilty. I was allowed to have this; he was *my* boyfriend. I ignored the whisper in my head that added, *for now.*

Between touches, he went on. "And I said to myself, Sarah works too hard. She's way too intense. She probably needs some help relaxing."

Curling my toes, I leaned into him. The funny thing about the booths was that it was absolutely forbidden to touch the acoustic tile walls. That made it a delicious challenge, to hold each other up and let go at the same time.

Unless we were both going to perch on the booth's tiny wooden stool, this wasn't going to go much further than a few tingling kisses. But the right lips could make a few kisses go a long, long way. Already, my blood warmed, pulsing slowly through my veins, a happy, lazy beat. Pressing into Dave, I traced my name on his back, and stars and swirls.

My eyes drifted closed, and my thoughts trailed toward the future—I couldn't deny that a future with Dave felt more certain.

Dave's lips rasped sweetly on my throat. His hands were so sure on my back—they anchored me against him. I insinuated myself against Dave's chest.

Drifting to my lips unerringly, Dave murmured a few notes from one of our ballads before blending the buzz away with a caress. The sound booth was a cocoon for us, our place in the world and no one else's. We both knew the song he'd hummed to me, and we moved with it subtly. Not dancing, but something like it. We swayed together in time—perfectly in time.

He nosed against my ear, his breath tickling when he asked, "Better?"

"Getting there," I replied. I nestled against him lazily, drifting on a sweet, pleasant cloud.

We couldn't hear the bell, but we both had a good sense of the minutes passing. With one last nuzzle, Dave leaned back. One hand still pressed to my back, he smoothed my hair with the other.

This was love—safety and security and certainty. Having things in common and having a plan. My Instagram account was full of our good times, and so many firsts. Playing the fair together, sneaking out of town for a concert together. And there were the things that couldn't be captured in a selfie. Knowing each other, being comfortable. So many people wished for that, and I had it. All wrapped up in a boy with a summer smile and golden hair. This was too special to throw away. He was too special.

"What are you smiling about?" Dave asked, his nose crinkling in curiosity.

"Just you," I said. "Just us."

I rose up to kiss him again and sighed happily. I didn't need Jane's help after all. She could be Switzerland till the end of time, for all I cared. Maybe she'd been right about the dazzling, but right there, surrounded by a hushed and gentle world, I knew what the right choice was. Maybe it had taken all of this to finally realize what I had right in front of me. It was Dave. It had to be Dave.

Didn't it?

NINE

After a concentrated couple of weeks, everything was back on track, and I felt so much better.

I threw myself back into Dave's arms, and it was great. Will faded into the crowd at school, sort of. He and Tricia were everywhere, on the prom ballots, at the pep rallies. It ached to see him moving on without me, even if it was with his actual girlfriend.

Still, he hit me up with occasional texts like, wish i could get u alone.

Stupidly, I answered in kind. tag, ur it.

Our flirtation continued, but didn't feel as urgent as it once had. Dave flirted all the time. There wasn't anything wrong with soaking up a little extra, harmless attention. Will would text-tag me at lunch, even though we didn't share the same lunch schedule. I'd tag him back in the pass-through period. Sometimes, I'd roll over in the middle of the night, and my phone would be glowing.

Ur it. Come out come out wherever u are.

Finally, one night my conscience got the better of me and I replied, u still have a girlfriend.

Will's reply? Only bcuz u still have a boyfriend.

I did have a boyfriend. Dave was real. And present. And to be honest, I'd started to get the impression that Will was just messing with me. The blank avatar that kept popping up in my phone was a tease. It wasn't personal, like when we really talked. It made me ponder new and naughty ways to steal a kiss, but there was no depth to it.

Jane had obviously been right: the more days passed, the more convinced I became that the thing with Will had just been novelty and spark. I had a great boyfriend, who actually wanted to spend time with me, and we had a lot going for us. We were gearing up for a show at the Eden, a three-story club in the next big town over.

We'd talked our way onto the stage there for the first time last year. We showed up with raw hunger, a couple of YouTube videos, and a willingness to fight for even five minutes.

Honestly, I think the owner gave in just to shut us up. He offered us thirty minutes on a Thursday night, the deadest night of the week. Despite that, we killed it. Jane filmed the whole thing, and sometimes I still liked to watch clips from that show.

After that set, we didn't have to beg to get in the door anymore. Instead, the owner booked us every couple months. We got a split of the receipts and that much more experience in front of a crowd. I was looking forward to another show. And trying to ignore the nagging daydream of Will standing just off stage, waiting for me to walk off into his arms.

Dazzle, I reminded myself. And lust. That's it.

But it didn't prevent the lust from rising to the surface. Especially when I parked in the driveway and my phone lit up again. This time, it said, what about tonight? With a groan, I replied, sorry, playing the eden tonight.

Did he have a sixth sense? Had he waited until it was absolutely impossible to meet up to finally get specific? I was so frustrated, but it was probably for the best. My heart and my hormones weren't as ready to give up on Will as my brain was.

I found my sister Ellie on the front porch as I came up the walk.

"Hey, you," she said, genuinely glad to see me. Late afternoon sunlight spilled over her silky chestnut hair. Her golden skin gleamed in it. She was compact and graceful and beautiful. And she was in the process of savaging a new pair of pointe shoes.

They were too unforgiving to break in like regular shoes, which is why Ellie was shaving the soles with a Stanley knife. She'd already pried the heel tacks free and torn out the insoles. Still to come was the ritual door-smashing and cutting of the satin. She spent more time defacing shoes than she did going to the movies. Or on dates. Or really, anything.

When I had to pull an all-nighter to wrench the last, perfect lyric out of my head, Ellie understood. And I understood Ellie's hours at the barre practicing a single position, again and again. The goal was perfection. Transcendence. Capturing that one, elusive moment when the whole universe vibrated on the same note.

That's why I felt comfortable dropping myself at Ellie's feet to lean against her knees. We got each other. And I knew she'd never use all the twisted up, messed up drama in my head against me like our responsible oldest sister Grace would. Grace had been dating the same guy since freshman year in college. For the last year and a half, they'd been seeing each other long distance.

"Very effectively," she informed us at Christmas, while said boyfriend chatted up our dad.

Ellie and I spent a month repeating that to each other. It got to the point where we just had to make the face, and we'd bust up laughing. *Very effectively dating, thank you very much, and good day to you, sir. Ta-ta, farewell.* All that laughter seemed so far away now.

"I had a weird blip," I said at last. "No, I'm still having it."

With her shoe, Ellie bopped me gently on the top of the head. "That's so descriptive. No wonder you're a songwriter. Are you going to put that to music later?"

"Ha. Ha."

Chuckling, Ellie reached for her jar of homemade shellac. It smelled like the devil's aftershave. It was her secret formula: no one knew what was in it except for Ellie.

"Do you think it's normal to get crushes on people, even if you're really happy?"

With a knowing laugh, Ellie went back to her shoes. "Completely normal."

Though she sounded certain, I wasn't reassured. "Things are so good with Dave, you know? But I just keep having these weird . . . fantasies, I guess, about another guy."

"It's not against the law to think," she pointed out. Then, sensing that I needed all her attention, she put her shoes aside. Wrapping her arms around me, she squeezed me tight. Her delicate perfume engulfed me.

"No matter how happy you are with somebody, it doesn't make you blind. You see how Mom gets over Robert Downey Jr., and she's been married to Dad for thirty years."

Fair point, but the details bothered me. "Yeah, but there's no chance she's going to hook up with him."

"Yes, but there's a difference between what you want to do and what you choose to do."

My mouth actually dropped open. I didn't know how I'd missed that in all my ruminations, but it was so obvious now. Invisible forces weren't at work. The universe wasn't conspiring. Will had made me feel sexy; who wouldn't fantasize about that? But the feeling should be enough; I didn't have to act on it.

Dave was love; Will was lust. It felt so obvious now. I felt confident that a switch would flip for me and Dave if only I let it. Maybe prom night, maybe just some wonderful, random Tuesday night— everything would go from sweet to sultry, and I'd have everything I wanted.

Ellie gave me another squeeze. Then she poked at me, leaning around to grin. "Did I just blow your mind?"

Exhaling my relief in a laugh, I nodded. "You did, actually. Thank you."

The Eden's main stage felt like home.

The boards were uneven, their soundboard fought with our amps, and the lights were blinding. It was paradise. I loved the sting of a hot halogen on the back of my neck, and the way the music seemed to pound into me in waves. Tonight, Dave and I were Dasa, and we owned the club.

Fingers stung on the guitar strings, I smelled someone else's beer on my mic, and I didn't care. The crowd surged close to the stage. Most of the time, it was impossible to make out individual faces.

Except tonight, as Dave and I launched into the last song before our encore, I noticed a bright, redheaded gleam, right next to the footlights. It was familiar, but I couldn't place it. The impression nagged at me for a verse and a half, until I realized who it was: Tricia Patten.

At first, I felt a pang of irrational fear. She'd found out about me and Will, and she was there to beat me down. Never mind that Tricia was five feet tall and made out of cotton candy.

Then all at once, the whole front row came into focus. It was the whole senior court, Tricia and her best friend, Nedda Coleman. Jake Thompson, center of the varsity baseball team; his girlfriend, Latonya Waite. Arjun Patel, Mason Sedgwick—it was like the entire A-list from Tricia's party had transferred directly to the live room at the Eden.

Dave realized it the same time I did. With a crooked smile and a nudge, he nodded toward them. The popularity of the crowd wasn't the impressive part. It was the connectedness. Tricia had paid us a hundred bucks for an hour of music. All these people had seen us there, and now they'd paid to see us again. On purpose. They were alive and bright and excited—they were there for a show.

By the time the final note rang out, my throat was raw and the crowd was roaring. Grabbing my mic, I leaned into it, introducing ourselves the way I always did. Then, I added, "And if you give me two minutes to grab a drink, we'll be back to take your requests."

They applauded, and I shrugged broadly at Dave. We didn't usually take requests at the club, but we didn't usually have an audience this enthusiastic. From his broad smile, I could tell he obviously didn't mind.

Peeling off my guitar, I placed it in its stand and bounded down the back steps. They didn't serve us at the bar, but there was plenty of bottled water in the office fridge. Sweaty and elated, music rang in my ears. I was probably making too much of it, but there was no high like coming off a great show.

Or so I thought.

As I checked my Instagram, someone reached from the shadows and hauled me into an alcove. It was a cool recess where the club

stored extra cases of soda and old music equipment. Before I realized it, I was pressed against a concrete wall, and strong, broad hands
enveloped mine.

"Tag," Will murmured, then branded me with a searing kiss.
"You're it."

Pinning my hands to the wall beside my head, he parted my lips
with a teasing tongue. Slick and sensual, he covered me completely
with his body. That's all it took to burn away everything I'd just shared
with Dave. One touch. One kiss.

I tightened my fingers in his and surged back. It was just the way
I imagined it, like he'd read my mind. The connection was there, I
realized, half-savage and hungry for more of him. It wasn't something
I'd created to explain the attraction. It *was* the attraction, a fierce and
undeniable pull that left me aching for more of him than I could possibly have.

Shifting, Will pressed his knee between my thighs. It was a subtle
movement, but it made me ache. Shameless, I pushed back; if I was
going to have to spend the rest of the night throbbing with want, so
was he. Will murmured low in surprise, and I swept in for another
kiss.

It didn't matter that we were dangerously in the open. That our
significant others were both nearby. That we had nothing else in common. That I didn't even really know him. Will wasn't comfortable or
predictable or safe, and I liked that. I needed it.

Short of breath, Will broke away and pierced me with his pale
blue eyes. "I've been trying to get you alone for two weeks. I thought
we had an agreement."

"You're the one who disappeared," I said. Jealousy pricked at me.
"With your girlfriend."

Will swayed into me, deliberately. His thigh rasped against mine. "Says the girl eye-fucking her boyfriend out there on stage."

With that, I kissed him yet again. I wanted to taste how dark he could be, how wrong we could be together. I was glad I wasn't wearing a skirt, because I'm not sure I would have pushed his hands away if they'd slipped beneath it. My face was hot, but for once it wasn't with an embarrassed blush. It was with flash heat, and need.

All but panting, I freed my fingers from his. My mouth stung, and so did the rest of my body. I was glad I had to get back to the stage, and fast. One, because the crowd was intoxicating, and two, because I was afraid of what I might do if I were alone with Will much longer. I was reckless under his touch.

Both hands on the concrete wall, he pushed away from me. It was like all the light and heat had suddenly gone out of me. My fingers curled wantonly. I wanted him back; I wanted to grab him back, but he let the cold fill the space between us.

Pink tongue darting at the part of his lips, he looked away. "You better get back before somebody catches us."

Twisting a bottle of water off one of the cases, I nodded. I didn't want to leave. I didn't trust myself to speak. My body still trembled, my knees coltish and weak. It was afraid it would be obvious to anybody who looked at me, that I was slick with heat that had nothing to do with the show.

But I had to. I had to get back to Dave. He *would* come looking if I was away too long. Just like Tricia would eventually come looking for Will. Swallowing down the bitterness of that, I took a deep drink of the water and made myself walk.

Breath hot in my throat, I stepped into the hall, but I couldn't help myself. I had to look back. It was wrong, but it was so good to realize that he was out of breath, too. He looked torn and ravenous, and his eyes burned just for me.

By sheer determination, I managed to ask him, "What do you want from me, Will?"

His voice broke, and his eyes flashed. And he said the one thing I had no defense for. It rang in my head, and haunted me, even as I took the stage again.

Even as I returned to stand beside Dave, Will had said the one thing that guaranteed I would come back to him. When I asked Will Spencer what he wanted from me, he said:

"Everything."

I wasn't prepared for just how much that meant.

TEN

Somehow, after our set, we ended up at a private party with the senior A-Team. When Arjun asked if we wanted to roll with them, Dave accepted enthusiastically. Jane was invited, and I was glad for that.

She was my touchstone, the lucid center of an insane situation. I was also relieved when the party took us to a park on the far end of town instead of Tricia's house. That would have been too much.

But after Jake broke out the beer and Dave decided to play solo from the edge of the picnic table, I started to wish I was somewhere else. Anywhere else, especially when Tricia shimmied up to me with a Coors Light and a smile.

"I didn't get a chance to talk to you at the club!"

My throat constricted. It felt like a trap. Like, any minute, she was going to rip the friendly look off her own face and call me out. Trying to fight the dizzy sense of terror, I plastered on a smile of my own and struggled to sound sincere. "I know, I'm so glad we're here now. Way quieter."

Slinging an arm around my shoulder, Tricia nodded. "You know,

I was telling Dave, you guys are really good. If I turned on the radio tomorrow and you were on the top-twenty countdown, I wouldn't be surprised at all."

"Thanks, that's really nice of you."

If Tricia knew the truth, she wouldn't be playing besties with me. A low weight settled in my stomach. I wasn't sure what felt worse: realizing that I was the trashiest person in the world, or the fact that Tricia didn't. When she leaned her head close to mine, I stiffened. What if she smelled Will's cologne on me? What if she suddenly came to her senses and saw the filthy evidence all over me—

"I have time for polite," Tricia said, airily unaware. "I'm only *nice* when I mean it. Which reminds me. I had a thought . . ."

"What's that?" I said. I sucked down half my beer, looking around plaintively.

Laying her head on my shoulder, Tricia held up a finger. She stopped to listen to Dave, who was charming a crowd by covering Ryan Adams's arrangement of "Wonderwall." I had to admit, it was beautiful. It was no wonder everybody gathered close to him. I didn't find it any less bothersome than before. When Tricia broke free of his spell, she sighed.

"We have a deejay for prom, but he kind of sucks," she said. Fixing me in her bright, determined gaze, she said, "So you guys should play instead."

I didn't know what to say. Prom was crazy soon, and a really big deal. We had played the Eden, and plenty of parties, but senior prom was a couple of hours with a huge and captive audience. And because the most popular students in school were the prom committee, it was like a seal of approval. Go forth, it told the masses. Buy Dave and Sarah's digital EP.

Tricia took my silence for hesitation. Steamrolling right ahead, she said, "I know it's next week, but you've played stuff on short notice before, right? My party, for one."

"Right, we have," I agreed uneasily.

"We have a grand to throw around. And it would make everybody really, really happy if you'd play."

A thousand dollars? I hadn't even expected payment. I wanted to faint. I couldn't think of a single reason to say no. At least, not a single reason that didn't have to do with poaching her boyfriend and taking advantage of her good nature at the same time. That was a pretty big reason, but not one that I was willing to admit out loud.

Lowering her voice, Tricia said, "We can get you into the after-parties, too."

"To play?" I asked.

Before Tricia could answer, Dave called out. He was flush with swagger, rolling his shoulders and nodding at me like I was just some peon waiting for his beck and call. "Hey, Sare, come play 'Scrambled Eggs' for us."

Nedda giggled, a sound that bored right into my brain. What was he thinking? He knew that song wasn't finished. And he knew those weren't permanent lyrics. With all the fawning attention around him, it really felt like he was trying to embarrass me intentionally.

Tricia sat up, giving me an encouraging push. "Think about it, okay?"

"We'll do it," I said. To Dave, I called out, "Let me go get my guitar from the car."

Waving off any company, I stalked toward the road where we'd parked the cars. The river whispered, and the trees seemed to close around me. It felt private here in the dark, secluded enough that I could risk something. With a few quick strokes on my phone's screen, I sent a message into the dark.

Then I stood beneath a white ash tree and waited—for Tricia's boyfriend to come help me forget about mine.

When Dave arrived at my door on prom night, he wasn't wearing a tux. That was fine, because I wasn't wearing a gown, either.

We were dressed for a show, but my clothes had a secret twist. The waterfall skirt mimicked the shape of my costume at Tricia's party. Ellie recreated the chignon from that night, too. Will had to be there with Tricia, but he had to see me, too. I wanted him to watch. To miss me, and want me.

"Next year, when you guys are seniors, I'm going to take so many pictures," Ellie said.

"I brought a wrist thingy," Dave said, offering me a plastic clamshell full of stargazer lily. "If you want to take pictures this year."

Shaking my head, I murmured to Dave, "Dad doesn't realize it's prom night—let's keep it quiet."

Secretly, I had admitted to myself that I had no choice but to make a break with Dave. As good as I sometimes felt when I was with him, there were times when I felt equally bad. Everything felt sweet and safe and secure with him, until it didn't. He still walked into the crowd to soak up the attention. And he still wasn't taking my songwriting seriously.

None of that erased our history together. I wondered if I wanted too much. But then I got angry with myself. Was it really too much to expect my boyfriend to respect me?

Maybe it was insane to look to a playboy to make me feel like the only girl in the world, but I had to face it. That's what it was like when I was with Will.

In my heart, I felt selfish because I wanted to keep Dave, too. I wanted him to be there in case I was wrong about Will—if it turned out that Dave was the right one after all. We had the band and our history and had shared so many firsts together. Maybe the broken things could be fixed . . .

Though Jane remained neutral, I kept coming back to the first conversation we'd had. Especially because it had become the running theme of my texts with Will. Pick somebody. Decide. They made it sound so easy, but it wasn't. I had more to lose with Dave than just a first love.

"Nervous?" Dave asked as we headed for the venue.

I guess I had been quiet, but I shook my head. "It's just prom."

With a nod, he reached for my hand. "Next year, we'll go together. If they don't want us to play again."

He said it so simply, so confidently. Like it had never occurred to him that one day we might not be together. The realization nearly broke my heart.

Rooting around in his glove box, I pulled out Dave's bottle of vocal spray. It tasted like juniper and glue, and it felt like a thin wash of slime. But doing the throat-coat routine meant he wouldn't try to talk to me until we got on stage. I hated that I wanted that, but I needed the quiet to put myself together.

The hotel ballroom was much more than I expected. I guess I had my brain trained for movie prom. I'd seen enough of them: school gym, paper streamers, butcher paper, and tempera paint backdrops announcing the theme. This was a glittering wonderland, café lights like stars draped everywhere, swaths of organza draping the walls. Hundreds of tiny glittered balls dangled from the ceiling. They cast flashes of rainbows everywhere. Since we were there early to set up, we weren't even seeing it at peak perfection.

Unpacking my amp and a new pack of strings, I took to the stage to set up. Even with my head down, I saw glimpses of what could have been in the shadows. Will in a fitted tux, and me in something vintage and ethereal from ModCloth. My red lipstick and his blue eyes, the only splashes of color as we danced.

That's exactly what I saw when Will walked in with Tricia, just as I segued into our third song. Fashionably late, they moved through the sea of seniors like the royalty they were.

Tricia floated in a champagne lace mini, layered with matching silk that fell in a creamy train behind her. In a garish sea of bright cummerbunds, Will stood out in his black-on-black tux. It cut perfectly across his shoulders and his hips, setting off his equally black hair and brows. When he looked across the floor, his eyes pierced, bluer than ever. He would have been at home on a red carpet or on the cover of *GQ.*

When I missed my cue in the chorus, Dave frowned. He looked concerned, not angry, but there was no way to explain why I was suddenly distracted.

Seeing Will smile at Tricia was torture; somehow it was worse to realize that he planned to dance with all the girls. His friends, virtual strangers—I knew for a fact he didn't know at least two of the girls he swept across the floor. They walked away from their encounter with Will Spencer like new foals, long-legged and clumsy.

Song after song, dance after dance. None of those smiles were for me. None of those touches. This was all my fault, a whole night spent watching Will adore everyone in the room but me. I let the guitar strings dig into my fingers. If they cut through my skin, down to the bone, it didn't matter. I couldn't possibly hurt more.

It was prom night; he was beautiful and he was out of my reach. It wasn't my hand he held up; I wasn't the one with a fairy-tale gown swirling around me as I turned in his arms. My numb lips wouldn't be kissed. They just grazed the cold curve of the microphone as I played on.

I don't know how I managed to sing. I don't even know how I managed to stand there without crying. Inwardly, I reminded myself that he wasn't my boyfriend. He didn't belong to me.

But it didn't matter. As the night wore on, I felt like I was playing the soundtrack to my own nightmare. I was so glad for our break in the middle that I abandoned my favorite guitar on the stage and literally ran for the girls' bathroom. To avoid company, I locked myself in a stall and leaned against the wall. My breath came in short, hard pants.

I wanted to cry, but I couldn't let myself. I had to be back on stage in ten minutes. So instead, I pressed my head against the door and stared hard at the ceiling. I didn't know who I was anymore. A bad person. A bad girlfriend. Just a girl realizing she had no idea what she really had or what she really wanted.

But that wasn't true. Seeing Will glide across the dance floor with everyone but me clarified the one question that had been hanging over me since the boathouse. I wanted the same thing Will did, or at least what he claimed he wanted. *Everything*. All of him—all to myself.

The question was, when would I make that happen?

ELEVEN

Some people might call what happened next fate. Or proof of a higher power. In all likelihood, it was probably just proof that we lived in a small town.

When prom ended, I begged off the after-parties and left Dave to his usual swarm of adoring fans. When I got home, I turned off my phone, closed up my windows, and disappeared into a long, hard sleep.

Morning came, and I didn't feel better. But because I knew everyone was still passed out at various hotel rooms and parties, I decided to make a run to Florek's.

The old music store was my safe place. I loved the musty scent of it. The mixture of oils and resins, old paper and new reeds. No matter how messed up my head, an hour or two browsing new sheet music and old instruments made me feel better. Free, instant therapy.

Winter was over, and spring nearly was, too. That meant that the roads were especially pothole-y. They always waited until the rainy season stopped to start fixing them. That meant three or four months of dodging chunked-up asphalt on every single errand.

Turning down Epler Avenue, I bumped over one pothole. This was the older side of town, where the old Main Street met up with the new one. Cute joined-up storefronts competed with strip malls for attention. For some reason, the roads were the worst here.

I jounced in my seat, no big deal. Except, in the bounce, I missed the very next gaping crevasse in the pavement. It was a grave of a pothole, big enough to bury the jerk who was responsible for patching them in. I hit it so hard, I heard concrete bang against metal.

And then I had a flat, instantly. Pulling off to the side, I put on my hazard lights and climbed out to see the damage. I already knew it was bad. Just the sound and the jolt told me that the tire was seriously messed up.

When I saw the damage, I groaned. The rim was bent. Not a small, unfortunate dent that a garage might be able to bang out with a mallet. It looked like a cartoon tire, practically flat on one side. The whole thing was shot. Karma had a hardcore sense of humor. In the very beginning, I'd lied to Dave about Jane getting a flat. Now the flat had caught up with me.

I made a mental note to never lie about something that could actually happen again. It was metaphysically safer that way. Not to mention physically.

Traffic shot around me as I trudged to my trunk to grab the donut. Wind yanked at my hair and clothes. The cars passed so closely, I swear, I felt the doors nearly brush me. Nervous, I fumbled opening the trunk.

Finally, I got the keys into the lock and flung open the trunk door. The unpleasant scent of old motor oil and rubber greeted me as I peeled back the rug. Cursing under my breath, I unscrewed the jack and freed my spare. When I turned to put them on the ground, I yelped.

Standing there in front of me, his hair tossed by the wind and his pale blue eyes serious, was Will.

"Where did you come from?" I said, stunned.

It wasn't even noon, the day after prom. He should have been dozing in a suite somewhere.

He nodded vaguely, toward nothing in particular. His black Miata sat parked at an angle in front of the strip mall. "Coffee run. Then I saw you."

I don't know how he made it sound so forlorn. There was an emptiness in his voice that was hard to hear.

It implied so many things, things I'd just started to realize. It was thrilling to kiss him. To have a secret, shared with just him, had been exhilarating. But last night wounded me. There might have been a time when it was enough to just want him. When it could have been a harmless crush, and I could have enjoyed that without wanting more. It was too late for that now.

When we were together, I was finally free. Finally myself, exactly the way I wanted to be. That meant that a little bit wasn't enough anymore. Knowing I couldn't have him, not all of him, left me raw and broken.

Hearing his voice made me realize he must have been miserable, too. When we shared a look, it was like we recognized each other. That's the only way I could explain it. Something innate was built into us, lonely and waiting to connect. Beneath all the hunger and longing was something else—something real.

Reaching for my tire iron, I tried to sound neutral. Casual, though

I felt anything but. The middle of the street seemed like a bad place to talk with Will. Something would inevitably happen—something that we couldn't risk anyone else seeing. Though my heart felt like it was trembling, I managed to smooth out my voice. "Some luck, huh?"

Suddenly, Will caught my face in his hands and set fire to me. Lips smearing against mine, he buried his hands in my hair. The waves twined around his wrists. I shivered at the rough skate of his fingers against my scalp.

There was no sweetness in this kiss. Tender and feral at the same time, Will claimed me. As if he was afraid I might escape, he gathered me closer, kissed me again.

He kissed me in the middle of the street, where anyone could see. And people saw; car horns blared around us. They tore by, drafting dangerously close. But now I didn't care. My flailing hands failed. The tire iron hit the ground, the metal ringing out like a church bell.

Head swimming, I lost my connection to the ground. It felt like floating—absolute weightlessness. Gravity no longer applied. The world around us became a dreamy, hazy place. Like the background in a painting, or a radio playing just to fill up the quiet. Nothing else mattered. I only needed Will to anchor me. His hands on me, his lips on mine, his taste on my tongue. Folded in his arms, I had come home.

Finally breaking away, Will stared into my eyes. His shoulders actually shook with short, panting breaths. For all I knew, mine did, too. I'd never felt so intoxicated in my life. So bleary and blissful and *right*.

"I've been waiting for you, Sarah." As if he had finally just broken, Will trailed his fingers down my face and murmured, "I couldn't wait anymore."

After we changed my tire, Will followed me home. At the time, he said it was just to make sure I got there. I think it was a lie we both needed to hear.

Inching along the back roads to my house, I couldn't stop glancing in the rearview mirror.

When he pulled in behind me, I stilled. For a fleeting moment, my instincts said *run*. But not from him. Just so he would chase me. So he could catch me.

Climbing out of my car, I didn't want just a kiss. I wanted more. I wanted to merge with him, to be inside his skin and to have him inside mine. Those late night fantasies we all had and blushed about and never dared to say out loud—with Will, they were possible. Agonizingly possible.

Up on the porch, I pulled out my keys. And in a breath, Will stood too close behind me. His hands grazed the curve of my hips. A low, appreciative sound rumbled from him as he touched my hair. His breath sounded so thin, and mine felt it.

I couldn't get enough air. Blood rushed in my ears, sweeping away the familiar music of my empty house. My *empty* house. Closing the door behind Will, I realized I didn't know what happened next. The foyer felt strangely disapproving, like the walls were infused with parental concern.

"I want to show you something," I said. Then I blushed, because there were so many ways to take that. Slipping my hand into Will's, I led him not to my bedroom, but to the music room at the far end of the house.

When the three of us girls were little, it was a nursery, stuffed with toys and books. French doors separated it from the rest of the house, and the other three walls were nothing but windows. The walls, painted bright yellow, rose high around the windows. Even in the grayest part of winter, it was a warm, inviting place.

Taking the longest path to my destination, I looked back at Will. He filled the hallways in my house in an exhilarating, terrifying way. Lights and shadows I took for granted painted him in unfamiliar angles. His spicy scent lingered in the air. He didn't touch anything but me, but he left his fingerprints everywhere.

Bringing Will into my music room was a test. I had to see how he would react to something that was as necessary to me as breathing. Lips dry and palms hot, I let go as I crossed the threshold. Spreading my arms wide, I realized how small the room had become. When I was little, the windows and ceilings soared. The space seemed endless.

Now it was packed with music and too many guitars. Recording equipment, a half-assed sound board. The really good tech stuff sat in Dave's garage studio. These were my bits and pieces, the ones I used when I experimented.

When Will stepped inside, it was like he was stepping into a part of me. Relief flickered through me when he didn't just grab an instrument and start goofing on it. That's what people often did, when they didn't understand how personal a guitar could be.

Instead, Will was respectful. He held his hand over the smallest guitar—my very first. And he smiled. "You got this when you were . . . six years old."

"Good guess," I said, sinking to sit on the little love seat in the middle of it all. "Five."

"That's incredible."

Reaching for my favorite piece, I made room for him to sit with me. If he wanted to. Edging my nail against the strings, they pealed softly. It sounded almost like laughter. High pitched, far away.

Gossip shared in the back room at a party. Fingering a simple chord, I strummed it.

"My grandpa played," I explained. "He let me sit in his lap. I felt the music vibrating on the back of the guitar. And his arms felt so strong around me . . ."

Will sat. Draping his arms over his knees, he watched me intently. "He must have had pretty long arms."

Laughter bubbled right out of me. "He was six six, you're good at this."

"I do what I can."

"Have you ever thought about running away to join the carnival? I hear you can make good money guessing people's age and weight."

Comfortable anywhere, Will settled into the corner of my couch. "Are you trying not to kiss me right now?"

Playing a sweeter chord, I looked up from the strings. Sunlight streamed through the windows behind him. It lit his hair and cast shadows beneath his brows. He was the devil and the angel on my shoulder. Studying the play of emotion across his teasing mouth, I played another chord.

Finally, I answered, "I'm trying not to talk to you."

A painful smile touched the corners of his mouth. It didn't take a genius to realize he was hurting. More accurately, that I was hurting him. An echo of that pain flickered through me. That connection again. Sometimes it felt like we were a single piece, split in two.

He handled it with more grace than I would have. Clearing his throat and looking away, he said, "We don't have to talk. We don't have to do anything. Be anything. This could all be a dream we once had."

The same moment he said that, I struck a bittersweet chord.

Slowly, I set my guitar aside. It was time to stop hiding. Though it was terrifying to say things most people only thought, it was necessary. It felt important.

"It's so strange," I told him. "You were almost imaginary to me before that party. I think, before, if I'd moved toward you, you would have moved away. That it would have been impossible for you to see me."

He nodded. We both knew it was true. As he slid closer, he struggled to keep his hands in his lap. I was glad to see that, because I was struggling, too. There were things I needed to say. Things I had to clarify, things that weren't even clear to me yet. But my body didn't care. My skin tightened when our knees touched.

Licking the part of my lips, I steadied myself before I went on. "I don't know why our magnets flipped. I don't know why I see you and I want to do unspeakable things . . ."

"You could speak those things," he teased gently.

"I sort of am," I pointed out.

"You're right. Sorry. Go ahead."

"But I'm not going to lie to you." I gestured at the music room, at all the things in it. "This is what I love. This is who I am. And Dave is a big part of that."

"So figure it out," Will said. His restraint faded, and he stroked a hand up my knee. Leaning into my space, he let his gaze wander. It trailed over me. Over my lips. It lingered there, and he slipped imperceptibly closer. "Stop making everything so hard, Sarah."

My voice fell faint. "What about Tricia?"

"I'll handle that," he said, buzzing ever closer.

Maybe he was right. Maybe things were simpler than I was allowing them to be.

Tired of denying myself, I pushed up, trying to capture the teasing kiss he promised. Instead, he darted away. His blue eyes sparked. Dark, flashing, they dared me. I tried again; once more, he pulled away.

Electricity crackled through me. It snapped and burned, running rays of heat to the tips of my fingers and the soles of my feet. He couldn't just kiss me on the street and then expect me to wait for his permission. Without waiting or begging or hoping, I took what I wanted. Catching the back of his neck, I pulled him to my lips.

Then it was fire. First light after winter's dark. Our tongues played in a slick, silken tangle. We skipped past shy exploration. We didn't need to pretend to be civilized together.

Tugging Will's hair, I arched beneath him. His sculpted chest, his flat belly—I laughed drunkenly in his mouth, because hip to hip, I felt how much he wanted me. Before I could return the favor, he pulled away. Completely. Everything inside me protested. He took all the heat with him, leaving me to shiver because he moved too quickly for me to catch him back.

Overheated, Will put deliberate space between us. He stood there panting, face streaked with red, mouth bruised and still slick.

"Let me know what happens," he said.

I couldn't tell if it was an order or a plea. And I didn't have the chance to ask. He left, and left me there to figure it out on my own.

TWELVE

It didn't take much to get Dave's full attention. When I walked into the garage studio and said, "We need to talk," he froze.

There was a new guitar undergoing surgery on his workbench. It looked like a lost cause. Leave it to Dave to throw himself at the impossible.

Leaning back against the workbench, Dave crossed his arms over his chest. Already defensive, he studied me with his stormy blue eyes, an unexpected touch of darkness in an otherwise sunny face. "What's going on with you lately?"

"Can we please . . . ?" I asked, gesturing at the couch.

"Is it about 'Scrambled Eggs,' Sarah?" he asked. "I'm sorry. I thought you'd want to show it off, it's a good song."

Wrong guess, and it made me feel even worse that he was so ready with an apology. And not a good one; it rankled me that he kept calling it that when he obviously knew I didn't like it. All this time, I thought he'd been clueless about certain things. That he was a good person who just didn't realize how I felt when he flirted, or how little

I liked being the lesser partner in the band. But I was starting to realize that maybe that wasn't the case.

"It's not the song. Could you . . . can we just sit down together? Please?"

Pushing off the bench, Dave approached me warily. "I don't think I like where this is going."

I wanted to yell at him to quit being psychic and just sit down and take it. Instead, I bit my tongue and waited for him to make it to my side. Three years was a long time to be with someone. We had more history than most couples our age, and I didn't want to just blurt it out. At the very least, we deserved a real conversation.

Reaching for his hand, a felt a bittersweet pang. His rough fingertips rasped against mine. Neither of our hands were silky. We'd calloused them with hundreds of hours on our guitars. Those scars were badges; we'd earned them together.

"I don't know how to say this," I began.

Dave stiffened. "Now I'm *sure* I don't like where this is going."

Forcing myself to look at him, I faltered. He was good at hiding his hurt behind bravado. When we got a lousy review, or when we auditioned and got cut, he was all bluster. He could rage for hours about how ignorant a particular judge was. Creatively, in ways that were almost inspired. But in the end, his impenetrable façade always boiled down to hurt.

But I had to do it. I had to. "You really won't like it, and I'm so sorry. I'm just . . ."

"You're breaking up the band."

"No," I said abruptly.

Now confused, Dave squinted at me. "Pardon?"

"Not the band."

Though I hadn't had a plan when I arrived, one formed almost immediately. I was going to hope that Dave could handle separating the us that was theoretically romantic from the us that was creatively amazing. Music mattered to him as much as it did me; he wouldn't want to abandon that.

Squeezing Dave's hands in mine, I pressed on. "We're so good together. As partners. As musicians, and I don't want to give that up."

Drawing back, Dave pressed his lips together. "Wait. It's *us*?"

The sheer shock on his face set me back. I guess all along, I had felt like he might know something was going on. Obviously, he knew I was upset at the after-party. But he was clueless as to any larger problem. Everything about him read stunned.

Sick to my stomach, I pressed on. "Look, you . . . I've told you before that it makes me crazy the way you flirt with *everybody*."

"I don't flirt," he insisted, furious. "I talk to people. What's wrong with talking to people?"

"You talk to girls," I replied. "Constantly. They cluster around you and hang all over you. And you know, I get it. I mean, we got together freshman year. You never had a chance to see anybody else, and . . ."

"What the hell?" Dave said shortly. "When did I ever say I wanted to?"

"You don't say it. You show it."

Slowly, Dave's eyes narrowed. "Is there somebody else *you* want to see?"

It was impossible to hide the surprise and the guilt. This conversation was already off the rails and it hadn't even started. There was no point bringing Will into it. But I took too long to reply, and Dave hopped to his feet.

"Who is it?" he demanded.

Pushing a hand into my hair, I looked up at him in dismay. "I don't want to do this like this, Dave."

He paced away from me. Every step was sharp, precise. When he cut his hands through the air, when he turned on his heel, it was frighteningly angular. This wasn't bluster, though hurt probably fueled it. This was anger, straight up. "I talk to people. That's it. If you're messing around with somebody else, that's not on me." He narrowed his eyes. "You should see your face right now."

I refused to just sit there and let him berate me. Hopping up, I stood my ground. I'd made some mistakes, yes. But that didn't mean he had a right to bulldoze me. "Everybody thinks you're perfect, Dave, and you're not. I don't care if you think it's just talking, it's a lot more than that. It's disrespectful, and it's humiliating."

"Then why didn't you say something before?"

Throwing up my hands, I exclaimed, "I have! A million times, and you think it's fine! Well, I don't. And you know what else? You have no business making fun of my music *while* you're flirting. That's not something a supportive boyfriend does."

Dave rolled his eyes broadly. "Now you're being ridiculous."

My voice rose with my anger. "Do you have any idea how small you made me feel?"

"It was just a joke, Sarah!"

"Well, it wasn't funny," I snapped.

Stalking over to the wall, Dave punched the button to close the garage door.

"If you're so worried about other girls, why do you keep pushing me away?" he finally asked.

I stared at him incredulously. "What?"

"*Not yet*," Dave repeated—mocked, in my voice. "*I'm not ready yet. Can we slow down?* I'm not going to pressure you to do something you don't want to do, but you know what? Maybe I do like the attention. Maybe I like knowing that somebody *would* sleep with me, even if it's not my girlfriend."

What a low blow. It felt totally unwarranted. The longer he stood there with his calm anger, the more I wanted to explode. He was infuriating. I wanted to scream, and jump up and down, and that was insane. How could he make me so angry, so quickly?

This definitely wasn't the right way to break up with somebody. It was messy and horrible. If I could just catch it and hold it with both hands . . .

Deliberately calming myself, I tried to salvage it. "Maybe I'm not ready for a reason. I'm not going to apologize for that. I mean, maybe we're not like most couples."

"Define 'most.' "

"Most regular couples," I said flatly, "are into each other and can't stop touching each other and stay up all night thinking about each other. You know, the kind of people we aren't, but we write songs about!"

"Whose fault is that?"

"Mine," I shouted. "Yours! Creatively, we're perfect, but as a couple . . . we're not working."

Coldly, Dave asked, "Who is it?"

"Do *not* change the subject!"

Repeating himself furiously, Dave raised his voice with each word. "I said, who is it, Sarah?"

Furious, I spat, "Does it matter?"

Shaking his head, Dave shot me an ugly smile. There was no joy in it, no pleasure at all. It was all teeth and hurt. A particularly rav-aged kind of vindication. He sounded almost snakelike when he said, "It obviously does to you. You're trying so hard to protect him."

The accusation struck like a whip. Was I trying to protect Will? Or was I trying to protect myself? In that moment, I felt so ugly and so ashamed. When I first kissed Will, I was sure I'd seen something there that no one else had seen.

But now, this far away from him, faced with someone I knew, and loved, and needed to hurt, I had my doubts. I doubted everything. My heart and my feelings. What I thought I wanted, what I believed I needed.

Standing on the edge of a precipice with Dave, it suddenly seemed too far to fall. But the look on his face, twisted and cold and angry, told me it was much too late to step back.

I fought away the tears, turning away to press the heels of my hands against my eyes. I didn't want Dave to think I was trying to manipulate him by crying. It just happened. They just poured out, when I realized how much I had destroyed. Three years came crash-ing to an end in three minutes. It didn't seem fair.

Though I needed to collect myself, Dave didn't intend to give me the chance.

"Don't think sobbing's going to fix this," he said.

That's right, the perfect boyfriend, the one who really knew me. Zeroing right in, stabbing all the right places.

"Look," I said, forcing the tremble out of my voice. "We need a break. Romantically. I don't think we need a break musically—"

Barking a laugh, Dave sneered but waved me along. His hands said, *No, go on, keep talking*, like I was there just to entertain him. Doing my best to ignore all that, all the roiling disaster inside my skin, I pressed on.

"We have gigs on the calendar. We can still be Dasa without being *us*."

"You think so, Sarah? Do you really?" He punched the garage door. Standing to one side, he hardened himself into a statue. Into pure, untouchable marble with unspeakably sharp edges. "Because I might, I *might*, you see, have some trouble singing love songs to a lying, cheating—"

"Don't you dare call me a whore," I snapped.

His smile ever more brittle, Dave said, "I was going to say 'bitch.' But that was illuminating, thank you."

Grabbing my bag, I made myself walk toward the car. It felt like a walk of shame. Like the whole world's eyes were on me. Judging me. Without Dave staring me down, I stared myself down instead. I didn't recognize myself anymore. I wasn't a good person. I wasn't a good girlfriend.

Just then, Dave forgot propriety and yelled down the drive, "And so you know, your C7 sounds like shit!"

I slammed my car door and cursed when I dropped my keys. Fumbling for them, I finally lost it and really cried. Hideous gasps wrenched through me. I could hardly breathe. Every time I tried to take a breath, it seared my throat and caught on a new well of sobs. Everything tasted sick and salted and I hurt. Everywhere.

How could anything good ever come from something this awful? Shoving the keys in the ignition, I backed out of the driveway without looking. A pickup truck blared its horn at me, and that only made me cry more. I could barely see the road, but I had to get out of there. As far from Dave as I could get.

The worst part was knowing that it was mostly my fault. But in my head, I'd had this idea that we could break up and it would be bittersweet. Like we could salvage the band, and our memories, and maybe even our friendship. Instead, it came out messy and vicious. Maybe everything hadn't been perfect with Dave, but it was good. He was good and I still loved him. There wasn't a switch to turn that off. I hadn't walked into the garage feeling everything, then out brand-new and feeling nothing.

It was so confusing; even with Will waiting on the other side, I was shocked at how raw I felt. One part of me wanted to turn around and beg Dave to take me back. We'd shared so much. Three years was such a long time. And yet, in one ugly conversation, it was like we had sandblasted them out of existence.

There was nothing left now. Everything was in ashes, and I didn't know what to do. I could run to Will, and I would. Maybe the awful mess I'd made of my heart would be healed.

I had no idea how I got across town without crashing into something. Everything was a blur of tears, but I made it to Jane's all right. When I rolled out of the car, Jane must have spotted me from the window. In a burst of speed she usually saved for grabbing the last slice of pizza, she bolted down the walk.

"What happened?" she demanded, throwing an arm around my shoulders. She sounded ready to go into battle. I only wished there were something she could slay. It would make her feel better, and me, too. But there was nothing. Nothing but the disaster I'd engineered myself.

Trying to wipe my face, I managed to croak, "I finally made up my mind. I broke up with Dave."

Steely, she asked, "Did he hurt you?"

Oh God, it was just like Jane to jump to the worst possible conclusion. Shaking my head, I swore. "No. No. He didn't touch me."

"Good." Wrapping an arm around me, she led me into the house and straight to her bedroom.

In the garage, a circular saw whined. The sound came again and again, screaming punctuation for the storm inside my head. While Jane mopped me up, I sat miserably on her bed, listening to the saw scream, then silence.

Throwing away a handful of tissues, Jane offered me the box and sat heavily beside me. "Do you want to talk about it?"

My throat closed. Apparently, my body wanted to shut down completely. My head disagreed, rolling the breakup like a movie reel, over and over, the worst parts playing the slowest. With a hiccupping sob, I said, "He hates me. I didn't want that."

A soothing hand on my back, Jane looked over at me. "You can't control how other people feel, Sare. But maybe this is for the best."

"I don't see how." My sinuses pounded, my head, too. The saw cried out again, and I fought the quivering in my lower lip.

"It's a clean break. None of that messy let's-be-friends crap. Nobody said that, right?"

With a miserable laugh, I shook my head. "Not even."

"Then good. You made up your mind. And now there's no room for you to back up on it. It's over with Dave. Now you move on."

"I didn't expect it to be like this. I thought I would feel better after I did it." Though I hadn't been keeping her in the loop, I did have to admit—just so it made sense: "I had a talk with Will the other day."

In response, Jane raised an eyebrow.

"There's something there," I told her. "I know you think he's not capable of that, but I'm telling you, he is. And he's going away in the fall, Jane. If I don't find out what that is *now*, I'll never know."

For a moment, Jane said nothing. She rubbed my back, gentle circles that gave her time to think and, at the very least, continued to soothe my upset. Dark eyes darting away, she took a deep breath, then sighed. "This is what I'm afraid of."

Knotting my hands together, I said, "Okay?"

"The one thing that worries me is this." Jane had never sounded more serious, and it made me uneasy. "You had one major issue with Dave. After every show, he walked away from you to flirt with everything that moved. If a girl came up to him to talk about quote unquote music, you just didn't exist."

I was confused. Both of those things were true. But where was she going with this? "I know."

Jane widened her eyes. "Will Spencer is a verified manwhore. It's not just flirting with him, and you know it."

"You think I should get back together with Dave?" I asked her, stunned.

With one last pat on my back, Jane stood up. Her voice was gentle, not usually her strong suit. I could tell she was trying to be careful with me.

But as she trashed a handful of tissues, she looked me over and said, "No. Of course not. What's wrong with your relationship with Dave has always been wrong with it. And maybe Will is the perfect rebound."

"There's a 'but' in there."

Nodding, she said, "Yep. And the but is, you need to put yourself first. You're smart. And you're talented. So fucking talented, Sarah. You don't *need* anybody to make music with you. You don't *need* a guy to make you special. Running back and forth from guy to guy isn't going to solve anything.

"If you want a boyfriend, that's great. But it's time for you to realize that anybody that you're with is *lucky* to have you, and they need to step it up accordingly."

She was so passionate. So sincere. Was she right? I didn't know. Not yet.

But I was about to find out.

THIRTEEN

That night, I sat on the edge of my tub and ran the water as hot as I could stand it. With my pajama pants rolled up, and steam swirling around me, I slowly dipped my feet into the tub.

Hissing, I waited for my skin to adjust to the burn, then finally relaxed. Soaking my feet was something I usually shared with Ellie. She was the one who started it. After grueling dance classes, she liked to sear away the ache. Tonight, though, she had an extra performance, and I needed some quiet time.

My fingers skated across the screen of my phone. I hesitated, then touched the messaging icon. Heart thrumming madly, I typed my message slowly. And then I thought long and hard about whether I wanted to send it. I felt like Jane was standing right behind me, arms crossed, eyebrow raised. I heard her voice clearly, reminding me that I needed to make *myself* happy. So what did I want? What did I actually, truly want?

It was like standing on the edge of a cliff. I could back away from the edge. I could make up with Dave. If he apologized, I could, too.

Things would be the same kind of normal they'd ever been. I could hide in the sweet, steady warmth of his arms and never come out again.

No, I told myself. I couldn't.

I could stand here all alone. Or I could decide that it was time to jump. So I hit send.

Tag, you're it.

No last time I checked u were figuring stuff out, Will replied.

Last chance. Last chance to abandon the intoxicating, terrifying possibility of Will Spencer. My fingers flew, and I hit send without shame. I know. And I did. Broke up w/ Dave this morning.

Srsly?

I'd never lie about that. So tag. You're it.

Swirling my feet in the water, I watched the screen with dread and anticipation. What if this had all been a game for him? What if he'd played it with other girls? My heart swore he hadn't. I wanted to believe it, but now I needed proof.

The heat from the water crept through me. Sweat gathered on my brow and beneath my shirt.

The seconds ticked by, and my murmuring echoed in the bathroom. It wasn't praying, not exactly. It was more like an incantation. *Please, please don't let me be wrong about this. Please don't.*

A chime announced Will's reply. I'll talk to Trish.

When? I asked.

Soon, he said. Very soon.

When I got back to school on Monday morning, Will and Tricia still looked very much together.

I refused to let myself hate Tricia, because out of all of us, she was the most innocent party. That didn't mean it didn't feel like a deep swallow of acid to watch her lay her head on Will's shoulder. It was a knife through the heart to see her nuzzling close to him at his locker. She had exactly what I wanted. And she seemed to fit against him almost as perfectly as I did.

A couple of times, I turned around to see Will watching me. Because I didn't want to believe I was out on a limb by myself, I convinced myself that he didn't look happy. In fact, he looked like he was starving—he had a wide, wounded expression that I couldn't forget, even when I tried.

I'd looked at the edge of the cliff, and I'd jumped. But now I felt like I was freefalling, unsure if anyone would be there to catch my fall. And it felt more and more likely that Will wasn't going to. So he deserved to be miserable, I thought. I tried to comfort myself with a dark sense of victory. Will had never been the guy who pined, who cared, who thought twice about a girl. I had to move on. I had to put myself first, as commanded.

I walked as far away from Will and Tricia as I possibly could. I found a nice, quiet corner down by the wood shop where I could eat my lunch in peace. It was the last place anyone expected to find me. I learned to enjoy the rich cologne of sawdust and mechanical heat. If I never saw Will, I never had to suffer.

In avoiding Will, I avoided Dave, too. And it appeared he was avoiding me right back. There wasn't even a ghost of our relationship lurking in any of our old spots. We were just *gone*.

The only good thing to come from misery was songwriting. "Scrambled Eggs" became a ballad titled "Everything." It got harder and richer. When I disappeared into it, it was the perfect escape. For the first time, I felt like I was completely naked in my lyrics. I spilled everything out, so honestly and so relentlessly that just singing through it to adjust the key could make me cry all over again.

Spring rushed into full bloom. In days, little green shoots became daffodils and tulips. The birds came back. Sitting outside, enjoying the sunshine and the solitude, my phone finally rang again. Dave's ringtone, a bar from one of his favorite Dasa songs, startled me. Dread filled me. He wanted his stuff back. We needed to work out the band breakup. My thoughts raced with all the things he might say.

"Hey, Dave." I tried my best to sound natural.

"Hello, Sarah," he said. His voice was soft. Tentative, like the first time we'd met. "I hope I'm not interrupting."

Sweeping my hair from my face, I sat all the way back. I gazed into the pale green leaves just starting to bud above me. They were still so thin that light poured through them. Their delicate, vulnerable veins stood out in delicate shadows. "No. No, I was just working on some stuff. No big deal. What's up?"

The line went quiet. Then Dave cleared his throat. "I was wondering if you were going to come to the garage this weekend."

Surprised, I sat up warily. "I . . . wasn't planning on it. Did you need me to?"

Though I couldn't see him, I could picture his face perfectly. I knew it almost as well as my own. His blue-gray eyes were probably looking to one side, his lips pursed as he worked through what to say next. If I had to guess, I really wouldn't have been surprised if he was rubbing his throat with one hand. He did that a lot when he didn't know what came next. It was like he was massaging the words out of himself.

There was a rustling sound as he shifted the phone, probably from one side to the other. Then he said, "You usually do. And you were still working on lyrics the last time we talked. How are they coming?"

Just then, I wanted to see Dave more than anyone in the world. It was shocking how painful it was when the numbness wore off. I talked too fast, afraid I sounded desperate.

"They're done. I think they're really good, but I don't know." My voice broke. "Without you, I just don't know."

Exhaling softly, Dave said, "Look, Sarah . . . I said some things I really regret."

"Me too," I replied.

He cleared his throat, and it was better, really, that we had this conversation on the phone. Maybe if we'd been face to face, it would have been easier to avoid the hard stuff.

I couldn't help but wonder if I'd made a mistake. If not in breaking up with Dave, then at least in the way I'd gone about it. Was this a sign that Dave wasn't ready to give up on us?

Then he spoke again.

"I also said some things I meant. I don't know what I want right now, Sarah."

Weighted, I sank back in the chair. And I nodded, because it wasn't a pleasant thing to hear. But at least it was honest. "Fair enough."

"I don't think you do, either. But I miss playing with you."

"I miss that, too," I admitted.

"So, then, let me ask again. Are you coming to the studio this weekend?"

"Don't leave a bitch hanging," Jane demanded, plowing through a veggie burger of epic proportions. "What did you say?"

Shrugging, I picked through my cheesy fries. "I said yes."

The table shook when Jane slapped it. Way overdramatically, she cried out, "What!?" like she'd just found out that I had sold both my kidneys to a con man or something. Flopping back in her chair, she shook her head at me. "You're going backward."

Sometimes, I wanted to throttle her. "He didn't say he wanted to get back together."

"Do *you*?" Jane arched a brow.

Impatient, I flicked a bit of real, actually-made-from-cow's-milk cheese onto Jane's vegan plate. Admittedly, a jerkwad maneuver. But she wasn't making it easy to be sensitive to her needs. "No. The important thing is—"

"The precious music. I know, you keep saying that."

Even though Jane and I got along really well, sometimes she got too strident. It was like she didn't know how to stop being the hammer. When she saw a problem, she had to crash into it at full speed. Trying not to sound peevish, I said, "You don't have to like it. It just is, okay?"

Waving in surrender, Jane delicately slid her plate to the side. "Okay, fine. It just is."

"Great," I muttered.

"Sooo . . . have you talked to Will?" Jane asked.

For the first time, I didn't want to talk about it. I didn't want to dissect it, and I didn't want to hear anyone's advice. The sound of his name left me reeling, but not in a good way.

Things were so screwed up and so confusing. Days had passed and nothing. Now, I wasn't sure he was ever going to have a talk with Tricia. It was entirely possible we—*I*—had mistaken a moment for something more.

When Will and I were together, I had no doubts. In his arms, his lips on mine, I knew we were meant to be. But Will hadn't taken the one step that would put us together. I couldn't make him. And honestly, I didn't want to.

Jane leaned in. "Well?"

"It's up to him now," I said.

"What was the point in breaking up with Dave if you weren't going to take Will for a spin?"

Darkly amused, I stirred my drink. "What do you care? You think Will is a douche bag."

"I'm judgey," Jane informed me. It wasn't a surprise, but it was funny to hear her admit it. "I judge everybody. What do I know? Okay, I know absolutely everything there is about film history that's worth knowing. But seriously, I don't date. But you . . . you actually seem to like interacting with other human beings on a personal and romantic level."

It was my turn to snort at her. "Okay, Jane-Bot, whatever."

"Seriously." Jane patted my hand against her cheek. Sincerity rolled off her in waves. There was no sarcasm in the rise of her eyebrow, not a single hint of a smirk on her Sensational Scarlet lips. It was all Jane, entirely engaged and real with me. "Are you okay?"

I didn't even surprise myself when I said, "I am."

That was fine—Jane was plenty surprised for both of us. Her eyebrows pulled yoga poses: disquieted feline, perturbed goose. "Are you really?"

That was enough of that. Sure, I'd waffled a lot lately. And no, it didn't look like things were going to turn out the way I'd hoped. But I'd made a decision, and I felt good about that. It was a complicated emotion.

Patting her fondly, I told her, "Everything will be fine. If it doesn't work out, oh well. I tried. I don't want to be fifty and wondering what-if."

"Let's be fair. Nobody wants to be fifty, period."

The atmosphere felt so much lighter all of a sudden. It was easier to smile. To underscore that, Jane flicked a sweet potato chip in my direction and went back to her sandwich.

I arrived at a realization: I was the one in control.

I took a deep breath and typed slowly. I wanted to make sure autocorrect didn't morph my text into something bizarre and incomprehensible. Leaning against my car, I watched Will toss a ball in the air, then swing at it with a low, lazy shoulder. There was a reason he wasn't on the school team.

It was a warm Saturday morning, but the batting cages were fairly deserted. Another symptom of small-town living: it's never a shock to look out your car window and see someone you know. When I caught a glimpse of him as I drove to the music store, I pulled over immediately.

It was the week before graduation, and most people had better things to do. There were parties and campouts, last trips to the amusement park. It was strangely touching to find Will alone.

His black T-shirt clung to his chest. Every time he swung the bat, a slice of pale skin appeared at his waist. Though it was nothing but a hint of his back, I got swept up in the rush of seeing any part of him that usually remained hidden.

With a held breath, I hit send. fyi, you're still the once and future it.

Will let the bat fall. His shoulders lifted and fell with a sigh. The text had arrived. Black brows knitted, he pulled his phone from his pocket. I took a shallow breath, wondering what would happen when he realized it was from me. A dark, terrified thrill ran in my veins.

When he read the text, he lifted his head immediately. Unguarded, Will wore a look of raw need. For a long moment, he stood there, reading the text over and over again. I watched him hesitate, trying to decide what to say in return.

It was like my nerves were waking again. Adrenaline shot through me. That magnetic pull began, urging my wanton body to get closer.

To touch. To hold and taste and have. Fantasy splashed through my thoughts, urging me on. I could kiss him there—I could trace the rise of his ribs with my tongue. He'd whisper something wild; I would smear a kiss across his skin and cast my eyes up. Meet his and dare him to bare more for me.

Hands trembling, I sent another message before he could reply. I see you.

Immediately, he lifted his head. Sunlight slanted across his face. Blue eyes illuminated, he turned. His motions were sharp. His gaze keen, until he caught sight of me. Considering me through the fence, he approached slowly. Chain link separated us, the thinnest barrier.

"You on the visitor's list?" he joked quietly. He devoured me with longing looks, tugging on the fence between us.

"I'm not breaking you out," I replied. Unlatching the gate, I slid inside. "I'm breaking in."

The crack of wood on leather echoed down the row.

Will considered me, his pale eyes unreadable. "I haven't talked to Tricia yet."

My heart sank, but I reached for the bat. Picking up a ball, I weighed it lightly. When my sisters and I were little, our dad would spend an occasional afternoon in the backyard, pitching to us. I don't think he expected any of us to become professional athletes, but he wanted us to be well-rounded.

I tossed the ball in the air and swung. Bat connected with ball, the bright, rich sound of wood against leather echoing between me and Will. Leaning over, I reached into the bucket for another ball. "I know you haven't."

"I don't want to ruin her graduation," he continued.

How thoughtful of him, I thought somewhat bitterly. But what about me?

With a lazy swing, I tossed another ball in the air and fired it at the end of the lane. "That's fine."

My quiet must have unnerved him. He slipped closer to me, his hands straying into the space between us. Like he yearned to touch me, but didn't dare. Shoulders angled, he watched as I knocked another ball into the distance. "I want to be with you, Sarah. You know that."

Tossing the ball into the air, I watched it arc and fall. The red stitching had long since faded. Its casing, once white, was gray. And it still felt good to knock it right down the cage. My shoulders didn't burn, and I wasn't out of breath. Inside, I was dying, but I refused to let it show.

"Prove it," I said.

With that, I sent a line drive into the dirt, dropped the bat, and walked away.

FOURTEEN

In our time apart, Dave had revamped the garage studio. His workbench remained, but it was newly organized. A pegboard held all his tools. The long rows of nearly refurbished guitars had disappeared.

The space was just as sharp as Dave was, in his new, clinging jeans and shirts cut to follow his broad shoulders and narrow waist. A line from an old Hole song flitted through my head: he'd made himself over. Suddenly, he was Hollywood hot, super comfortable in his celebrity skin.

Trying to take it all in, I said, "You've been busy."

Dave pushed a hand into his hair. It sprung between his fingers, streaks of summer gold. "I've had a little free time to play with."

Turning slowly, I tried to absorb everything that was new. He'd pushed the couch against the far wall. The long counter in the back of the garage was clear. Now it held music stands and pencil cups. Alligator clips clung to the top of a corkboard. The song lists we usually put together on scraps of paper were all neatly pinned.

"It looks nice," I said.

As if confessing, Dave exhaled heavily. "I e-mailed the studio; they have time on their calendar next week if we want to finally record a demo."

Tension I didn't realize I had drained from me. Looking at the garage again, it came into perfect focus. This wasn't just some cleaning up and rearranging. He'd taken a long, hard look at what had gone wrong. And he'd done everything he could to fix it. To move *forward*.

"I locked in the rate," he added when I was quiet too long. Edging toward me, he slipped into orbit around me. It was like he wanted to reach out, but didn't dare. "So if next week is too soon, we can do it whenever."

"Thank you," I said. I meant it with a depth that just a couple of words couldn't convey. It came from the marrow of my bones and from the deepest part of my heart, from the same place songs were born, an unnamable place that still—I had to admit—belonged to Dave.

Nodding, Dave moved closer still. "I've been thinking about the harmonies for 'Scrambled Eggs.' Trying to work them out. I don't have the music, though."

Finding a smile, I caught his hand. Turning it in mine, I smoothed it between my palms. So familiar. The scars and the calluses, the worn crease of each finger. His hands were so beautiful. Will was the one who'd left things hanging, so I didn't try to deny what lingered. With Dave, I felt a sense of peace. Of rightness.

"It's called 'Everything' now."

"I like it," he murmured.

Quiet, I tried to see the future again. I tried to catch just a glimpse, see where this was all going. Who was future Sarah? Who was she with? What was it like? But I still couldn't see the answers. Now more than ever, I realized that imagining a future with someone meant nothing. I could make up fantasies all day long. What mattered most were actions.

Dave tugged me closer, wrapping his arms around me. "I can chill after our gigs, too. I didn't know it bothered you that much."

Though Dave's arms were safe and familiar, I missed the spark I felt when I was close to Will. Things were still unsettled. Though I wasn't quite ready to sever the connection I felt to Will, I was starting to consider it. Muffled against Dave's chest, I asked quietly, "Can we sit and play some songs?"

"Absolutely." Dave brushed a rough kiss against my hair and let go. Trailing toward the couch, he picked up his guitar and waited for me to follow.

When I settled, he still stood. Plucking a few notes, and tuning one of the strings, he smiled down at me. It was an anxious smile, laced with shyness and hope. Coaxing a beautiful flourish from his guitar, he asked, "Know any Iron and Wine?"

Just like that, it was like we were all the way back to the beginning. Warmth filled me, spilling over inside me and painting an unstoppable smile on my lips. Fingers danced across guitar strings, drawing honeyed notes to swirl around us. Seeing his face again, remembering his face again . . . it felt good. We moved together, our lips parting, harmony lacing together effortlessly.

The song ended too soon. When the last notes trailed away, I didn't want the spell to end. Neither did Dave. Was it possible that the connection we had when we played together could translate in other ways? He moved closer, our weight distressing the old couch and tipping us toward each other. With a quick, downcast look, Dave clutched his guitar.

Then, he said, "We should concentrate on the music right now. Get ourselves sorted out."

At first, the suggestion shocked me. But I appreciated that he was willing to be careful with me. With us.

Nodding, I said, "Okay."

When he looked up, he seemed transformed. I remembered the round-faced boy I met on the first day of high school. But he wasn't there anymore. Dave had grown up since then.

"All right," he said, readying his fingers on the freeboard. "What key is 'Everything' in?"

I told him. His voice slid into my song.

This time, I didn't have to jump. Together, we fell.

It was a long, wonderful way down.

When I finally left Dave's garage, a pleasant tension played on my skin. It bothered me all the way home, and all the way through my last bit of homework before the school year officially ended.

Slumped at the kitchen island, I kept humming, ignoring downward-sloping aggregate demand curves in favor of brand-new music with Dave.

The landline ringing shattered the relative quiet. Exactly two people called the house line regularly. The first was Mimi Sally in Tucson. The second was Grace, away at college. Plucking a quarter off the counter, I flipped it as I answered. Heads said it was a Grandma call. Caller ID said it was my sister. I chose to believe caller ID.

"Hey, Gracie," I said smoothly. "Did you sense I was being attacked by a graph?"

"Is Mom there?" Grace asked. She sounded weird.

Immediately, I was on edge. I could tell something was wrong. She skipped the ritual teasing, which was never a good sign. A worse sign was her asking for Mom. While they got along fine, Grace was more of a Daddy's girl. The only time she wanted to talk to Mom first was when something needed fixing.

Pacing down the hall, I said, "I don't know if she is or not. I'm looking. Is everything okay?"

"I just need to talk to Mom," Grace said, more firmly.

If she'd sounded a little more like herself, I would have given her hell for biting my head off. Or pointed out the million reasons why she should talk to me first. One, I was an excellent listener. Two, I was an impartial judge. Three, I was her baby sister, and it had been a long time since we'd caught up, and I was worried about her. But it just didn't feel right today.

I was weirdly relieved when I found Mom in her office. She was pretending to work, but when I came around her desk, I caught her watering digital zucchini on Facebook.

"Found her," I told Grace, then handed the phone to Mom with a shake of my head. *That's right, I caught you*, my feigned disapproval said. Then, quietly so Grace wouldn't hear, I told Mom, "She sounds upset."

Taking the phone, Mom patted me on the back to shoo me away. "Thanks, Noodle."

My voice still low, I jerked a thumb toward the door, the universal symbol for *I'm heading out*.

Now that I'd freed myself, it was easy to ignore the rest of my homework. It's not like it wouldn't still be there when I got back. My brain needed a rest and some caffeine.

Slipping behind the wheel of my car, I rolled all the windows down and turned the radio all the way up. I never listened to my own music when I drove. Instead, I liked to pump pure, frothy pop through the speakers.

Before I realized where I was going, I had already turned down the right combination of streets. From my house to Will's, without a single thought. It wasn't hard.

Our neighborhoods were separated by a woody park, and money. My house was nice enough, but as I wended my way toward Will's, the porches grew columns and the walks sprouted brick and landscaping.

Will's house loomed in the distance. Weathered red brick and ivy, it stretched out beneath tall trees, presiding over a velvety lawn. It had sections, angular and visible. As if it wanted very much to have an east and west wing, and might someday if it would only wish on the right star.

I'd absolutely meant it when I told Will that it was up to him now. I wouldn't be knocking on his door or calling to beg for his attention. But my subconscious hadn't gotten the memo. How else had I ended up cruising past his house, misery slowly flooding my skin?

Slowing, I glided past his house. I couldn't look away. It was like he was a flame, and I was a stupid, stupid moth. Suddenly, though, my heart leapt. Tricia's car was in the driveway.

Touching my Bluetooth, I told it to call Will.

"Hey, Sarah. What's up?"

Carefully neutral, I said, "Not much. What's up with you?"

"Hanging with Tricia." He sounded matter-of-fact. "Are you busy later?"

Over and over in my head, I told myself I had no right to be jealous. I made my choice, he'd made his. My heart refused to listen. Each beat turned my blood to acid. As I inched past his house, I stared at it, hard. Like somehow I could see them from the outside. As if I'd really want to.

Forcing myself to hold on to that neutrality in my voice, I said, "I'm not sure. I might have plans."

"You might?"

"Yes," I said. Then weakness bled through, and I added, "But you can call and find out for sure later."

"Great," he replied. "Will do." Then the line went dead.

I was stupid. So stupid.

Grinding both hands on the wheel, I stomped on the gas. The acid spread to my stomach. A bitter taste rose in my throat, and I swallowed against it.

The phone rang.

It was Dave. Of course it was, with his uncanny ability to sense when I was stressed or sad. Nothing could be easy or clean or simple. The constant push and pull couldn't ever let up. I considered letting it go to voicemail. On the third ring, I answered—guilty.

"Where are you right now?" Dave asked.

"Just driving around. What's up?"

"The studio called. They had a cancellation and can get us in for an hour or two this afternoon to lay down our vocals."

"Perfect," I exclaimed.

Sounding a little surprised, Dave said, "It's not too soon?"

"Absolutely not. Let me swing by home to grab some stuff, and I can meet you at the studio?"

Excitement bubbled up inside of me and pushed my bitterness over Will aside. Three years of hard work had finally paid off. Dave and I were finally going to record in a proper studio. This was a real beginning. The first step to a future where music was a profession and a calling.

And Dave, the heart of the band, the guy who had been there since the beginning, would be there at my side.

FIFTEEN

After our recording session, I turned down Dave's invitation to go celebrate. I didn't know how to explain to him that I wasn't in a celebrating mood. I should have been. And deep in all the complicated mess that was my heart, I was proud that we'd finally cut a real demo.

Even though my musical chemistry with Dave was as strong as ever, I couldn't stop myself from thinking about Will. But it felt like a birthday with one balloon and no cake. Somehow incomplete; somehow very, very lonely.

Surprise interrupted the introspection, because when I got home, there were two unexpected cars in the driveway. I went to the front door, and it swung open. My stark best friend shot me a knowing smile.

"So who's a hot-ass rock star?" she asked.

I laughed and slumped against her. "How did you know?"

A voice rang out from the kitchen. "Mom has a big mouth and so do I."

I tripped, nearly taking Jane down with me. "Gracie?"

My eldest sister stepped into the hallway, a pint of Ben & Jerry's in each hand. Shaking them, she raised her brows expectantly. "Is this happening or not?"

It had been months since I'd seen Grace. She'd been away at Loyola the entire year. It was too far away for her to come home for most breaks. The last time we'd seen her was Christmas, when she'd flown in with her boyfriend, Luke, on Christmas Eve. But by Boxing Day, she was gone. It sort of left us feeling like it hadn't happened at all.

In spite of her sick obsession with higher mathematical functions, Grace was the magic in the holidays around our house. She was the one who loved trimming the tree. She was the one who insisted we still needed stockings—Mom, Dad, and the stray neighborhood cat included.

Throwing my arms around her, I hugged Grace. She still smelled like lavender. Her hair was silky as ever. I hadn't realized just how much I'd missed her until that very moment. When I finally let her go, I pulled back to get a better look at her.

She wore clothes I'd never seen before. And there was a new shape to her face. She was still Grace, for sure. But she looked neater. More refined. It took me a minute to realize that she looked a lot like Mom.

"What are you doing here?" I asked her, handily stealing the pint of Chocolate Therapy in her left hand. Tossing it to Jane, I dived for the silverware drawer. Teaspoons weren't going to cut it. I hauled out the big tablespoons, one for each of us. "Not that I'm not glad you're here—I am!"

"I can't move into my graduate housing until the end of summer," she explained. "My landlord wanted me to pay three hundred dollars more a month for a short-term lease."

Jane made a disgusted sound. "There has to be a law against that."

Always fair, Grace shrugged. "Maybe there is. It wasn't worth it to me to fight it. I missed this place. And the monkeys in it."

With a wink, she nudged me, then peeled the lid off her Cherry Garcia. Unlike her savage little sister, she delicately spooned her ice cream into a porcelain bowl.

"What about Luke?" I asked, wondering about her very efficient long-distance boyfriend. He was studying biological oceanography at MIT–Woods Hole.

Waving her spoon dismissively, Grace said, "Home is closer than Loyola *or* Cal-Berkeley. We're going to meet up at the end of July for our anniversary."

"Four years," I told Jane.

"Impressive."

"But really dull, comparatively." Grace went from casual to cut-throat, skipping all the gentle, prodding questions. We were sisters. She didn't have to be polite or delicate with me. "Because I heard somebody's already living the rock-star life."

"It's just a demo," I demurred.

Crinkling her nose, Grace said, "I'm talking about someone's two boyfriends."

For that, I shot a look at Jane. She was an absolute lunatic, acting like I had been holding court and enjoying a harem full of boy toys. Dipping my spoon into Grace's ice cream, I settled into one of the island stools.

"Uh, no. I acted like total trash and kissed another guy while I was still dating Dave. Then I broke up with Dave and found out the other guy didn't actually love . . . I mean, like me."

It was funny the way Grace got defensive of me when I was the one bashing myself. Very sternly, she abandoned her dessert to lecture me. "Is he stupid?"

"Maybe," I said. "Does it matter?"

Grace's defensiveness changed targets. "He's obviously stupid if he doesn't think you're great. But you know what? Stop being hard on yourself."

"Don't you think I should be?"

"No," Grace said firmly. "There's nothing wrong with reevaluating a relationship. You started dating Dave when you were fourteen. You grew up. You're a completely different person now."

"No kidding," Jane said.

Never one for banter, Grace started tidying up after herself. Her ice cream wasn't even half-finished. Moving comfortably through our kitchen, Grace wiped and tossed and rinsed like she'd never been gone.

That was one thing Ellie and I both missed about our sister. Her borderline kitchen OCD was our gain. We never had to do dishes when Grace was home.

"Anyway," I said, because it was nice to have somebody objective in the mix for once, "I think the friends thing is going to work with Dave. I mean, witness: demo reel ice cream."

Tossing a sponge in the sink, Grace turned to lean back against the counter. "So why don't you sound like you're happy?"

Leave it to Grace and her analytical mind to call bullshit. Including catching her little sisters in the midst of semi-delusional lies. The ache started in my chest again, and I put my spoon down. "It wasn't what I expected."

"How so?"

It took me a minute to explain the boring, technical details of recording. How each person recorded separately in their own booth, then each instrument separately. To Grace's credit, she looked riveted. And when I finally finished up the explanation, she was completely ready for me to explain what was actually wrong.

"The thing about Dasa is, you know, I'm at my best when I perform *with* Dave—"

"Bullshit," Jane coughed into her hand.

With a prim look, Grace silenced her. "Enough." Then she turned back to me. "Go on."

"Well, recording isn't *with*. You have to record separately, right? And he wanted us to record a song I wrote. Which was weird, because I wrote it when we broke up. And sort of wrote it about the other guy. Besides all that, it's *my* song. He's been making fun of it since I started it, and I didn't want to share."

Sympathetic, Grace curled her arms on the island. "You outgrew him as a boyfriend. Is it possible you outgrew him as a musician, too?"

That question surprised me. It struck hard, and left me feeling weak. Was that possible? Still reeling, I said, "I don't . . . I don't know."

"I do," Jane said, still plowing through her carton.

Then it hit me. Will had known, too. He'd told me so, his back to my back, beneath the wavering light from the pool. If that was his whole purpose, to push me on—to push me up—maybe I could stop feeling bad about the parts of him that I hadn't gotten. Just as I thought it, my phone bleated.

Another shock consumed me. It was Will, which was surprising enough. But the text itself left me breathless.

want to run away together?

SIXTEEN

It was a joke, but also an invitation to meet. Conflicting emotions ran through me. I was thrilled to hear from him, but just a moment earlier he'd had me feeling like a fool. So I replied, but not eagerly. I refused to look like I was desperate and jumping at the chance to get some attention.

Family night first, txt u later?

Ok, he replied.

The family night excuse wasn't a lie. With Grace home, we had to have family dinner. She hadn't seen Ellie on stage in a couple of years, so we caught one of the evening performances at the theater. After that, we had to get dessert and sit in our living room and catch up.

Shortly after midnight, I stood on my front porch and texted Will that it was time if he was still interested.

OMW, he said. And he didn't lie. We didn't live all that far apart, but I was surprised at how quickly his black Miata pulled up in front of my house. There might have been a time when I would have bounded down the walk. Not anymore. I was playing it cool, and I took my time to get to the street.

Sliding in beside him, I smiled as I buckled the seat belt. "My sister's home from college."

"Cool," he said. Throwing the car into gear, he sped down my street. He drove much faster than he needed to, and he looked upset. The furrow of his brows cast shadows over his pale eyes. Leaning back in my seat, I watched him. I waited for him to say something.

As we sped along, it became more and more obvious that he wasn't going to. Annoyance brewed inside of me. I didn't appreciate getting called out in the middle of the night for . . . what? An angry, silent drive? As much as my fingers itched to touch his hair, to curl behind his ears, the rest of me really wanted to go home.

Rather than wait for him to deign to speak, I asked, "Did you break up with her?"

"Yeah, I did."

I paused for a moment, unsure of what to say.

"How did she take it?"

Will cut a look at me. "I don't want to talk about her."

My throat tightened a little. Everything about him confused me. I wasn't happy after I broke up with Dave, either. It was a sad and ugly day. But I hadn't run to Will and stomped around and refused to speak and somehow expected him to make it all better. Leaning against the door, I peered out at the sidewalk. East River flew past, shadowy and gray in the dark.

"What are we doing?"

Jerking the wheel, Will pulled into a playground parking lot. Cutting the engine, he sat there, staring at the brightly colored swings and slides in front of the car. The swings swayed with ghostly motion. It was after midnight, and the playground looked haunted and desolate.

Will unsnapped his seat belt, but he didn't move.

I was starting to lose my patience. "Say something, Will. Say anything."

"No," he said flatly.

I turned to him. I felt like I'd been punched in the chest. I wanted to catch my breath, but I couldn't draw one.

"This," Will said finally. He thumped his head against the headrest in frustration. If he'd been a different kind of guy, he might have punched the dashboard. Instead, all his anger was directed inward. "This is so fucked up."

I couldn't believe what I was hearing.

"If you didn't want to be with me, then why did you text?" I demanded.

"Graduation is ruined," he said. It wasn't cruel when he said it. He sounded desolate. Wounded. Finally looking at me, I saw it all in his eyes a moment before he said it. "I couldn't invite you to my graduation party, I couldn't ask you to be my date for the prom, because to the rest of the world we're *nothing*. That trip to Marblehead, I wanted to take you. I wanted it for us."

Now baffled, I struggled with my seat belt and said, "Then why didn't you?"

"Because she was graduating, too. Because we're friends. Because it seemed too complicated to change everything when I'm about to leave for college soon. Because I'm an idiot, I don't know."

He was slipping away. It was a fight to keep space between us, but I fought all the same. "I get that, but I'm not—it's not okay for you to take your anger out on me."

Pressing his hand to the window, his fingers skated the glass. "I know."

Wary, I said, "Do you regret it?"

"I regret everything," he shot back.

Everything?

Tears welled in my eyes.

"I'm in love with you, and I wasted years standing two feet away from you," he raged suddenly. "Four years of high school, girl after girl, I kept chasing and catching all over again because it was never right. They were never the right fit."

Love? It was love? I'd been asking myself that since the very first kiss. It had felt so scary and so hard to figure out. Was love supposed to be comfortable and safe and warm and sweet? Was love supposed to be painful and intoxicating and terrifying? Was love supposed to keep you up at night, craving more? I never found an answer that satisfied me, but I thought I was starting to understand.

"Will," I said softly, reaching for him.

"Don't," he said. The raw, undisguised emotion in his voice startled me. "Because I wasted all that time. I wasted all of *our* time. It kills me to realize how many times I didn't get to kiss you. How many nights I didn't know you were supposed to be mine. I know that now, and it's wrecking me."

I burst out of my seat belt and fell onto him. Catching him by the front of his shirt, I kissed him. I kissed him hard, and it wasn't sweet or spiced. It was salted, with tears and heartache. Touching him, my flesh finally woke. All the thoughts that had been frozen by uncertainty melted at once.

On his lips, I murmured frantic whispers. "I love you. I love you, Will. I love it when you get philosophical, and I love your sly sense of humor. I love how *good* you are. You're so good, Will. You try to hide it and I don't understand why, but I want to find out.

"I want to write my name on your back with my fingernails, and try to braid tiny braids into your hair even though it's way too short. I want to write songs about you. I want you to tell me everything that you think when it's three o'clock in the morning and you can't sleep. I want to keep your secrets, and I want you to keep mine. But I don't want you to be my secret anymore—I want the world to know about us. No more hiding, no more whispers. I want to do everything out loud with you. Everything."

Stunned, Will softened beneath me. The angry fists of his hands unfurled. They touched my shoulders, but tentatively. Like he was afraid if he searched further he might discover I was nothing but smoke. That I would disintegrate and he would be left there holding nothing.

"I have to leave in the fall," Will said, broken and barely voiced.

The enormity of the moment overwhelmed me. Sitting up a little, I framed his face in my hands. We really did know each other innately, on another level. We didn't look *at* each other, we looked *in*. If he could see my eyes, he'd know I meant every word. And a million more that I couldn't even speak. Without Will, I didn't think I could take another breath.

"So?" I said.

I brushed my thumb against his lips, my gaze inexorably drawn there. But I made myself look up. We were more than our bodies. More than the unmistakable want that danced between us when we touched. I made myself bare in front of him in another way, my eyes wide open and every part of my heart on display.

Quietly, desperately, he pressed into my touch. "Sarah . . ."

"You belong to me. I knew that the first time we kissed. I'm yours, Will. And you're mine. And that's all that matters."

Will kissed my thumb. Then my hand. Drawing me closer, his gaze didn't waver. He voiced one last dissent. "It's over with him?"

I swore it again. "Will, I'm yours."

Now that we could be with each other, I wanted to be with him every hour of the day. But it wasn't enough to just sit in each other's company. Because Will had once surprised me with the meeting beneath the pool, I was determined to find someplace just as special to show him.

Everything in the school's theater was out. He already knew where the catwalk was. My house wasn't an option, because meh, it was my house. It was full of parents and sisters, and that weird outdoor cat that people kept feeding even though it wasn't ours.

When inspiration struck, I stopped dead. The date muse had finally reached down to grace me with her gifts. It took a few days and two favors from Jane to get everything in order. But I knew it would be worth it.

I texted Will to meet me at the old botanical garden after dark. In the shadow of chestnut trees, I watched for his car in the gravel parking lot. The familiar grinding of tires on stone excited me much more than it should have. The sleek lines of his Miata reflected moonlight and the hazy green streetlights above.

When he parked, I bounded toward him. He was barely out of the car before he had me pressed against the door. Looping my arms around his neck, I rose up to meet his kiss eagerly. The current between us switched on. It hummed and pulsed, our heat pushing away the warmth of a near-summer night.

Reluctantly, I broke away. I had to press my fingers between our lips to ward him off. Laughing, I brushed my nose against his. I felt full of starlight, spilling over with it as I gazed up into his silvery blue eyes.

"You have to wait," I said.

"Haven't we waited long enough?" he asked teasingly.

Since I'd blocked my lips, Will dipped to my throat instead. He strung a chain of searing kisses there, following the maddening race of my pulse. His hands skimmed beneath my shirt. Smooth fingertips swirled ornate patterns against the small of my back. Somehow, he made even a lazy brush of thumbs against my waist feel wickedly delicious.

Catching his hands, I wriggled from beneath him.

Using my best, most flirtatious smile, I said, "I'll make it worth your while."

That perked him up. One black eyebrow arched high, he tugged me closer. Nimble and sure on his feet, he spun us around. It was a split second, but a split second when I felt every inch of him pressed against me.

"Follow me," I said. I knotted our fingers together and led him into the old abandoned botanical garden. We passed a *No Trespassing* sign that was weathered gray and black. The arch of ornate iron at the entrance felt like we were stepping into another world entirely.

A lush, tangled jungle spilled out in front of us. Ivy scaled the fences and most of the trees. A glossy green carpet, it spilled over the neglected walkways, which had never been paved.

"Let me guess," Will said. "We're going to meet the apothecary that lives in the woods. She's going to make a potion to stop time for us."

With an incredulous laugh, I looked back at him. "Where do you get this stuff?"

He answered with a playful shrug. His eyes were so keen in the dark. I could tell he was trying to figure out why I chose this place.

Jessa Holbrook

What my plan was. He failed, completely. There was no way for him to guess what waited for us when we ducked through the alley of overgrown willows.

Surfacing through the delicate green veil of leaves, I stopped. Watching his face, I waited for him to take it in. For surprise to register. I wanted this to be just like that moment I'd had down in the boiler room, when I realized what he was showing me.

A gazebo trailed gracefully toward the sky, confident in its place in the middle of the sitting garden. With Jane's help, I had hung a white sheet on the side of it. Battery-powered white lights sparkled on the ground, illuminating a path on the lawn. I'd laid out a quilt and some pillows. Bags of microwaved popcorn waited to be torn open and poured into the outsized bowl I'd liberated from home.

"What—" Will started, but I pressed a finger to his lips.

"Shh. Sit down, get comfortable."

Because once he did, I could switch on the laptop and projector I'd hidden in a fall of clematis. I had three hours of battery power for both, so I hit play and hurried to sit on the quilt with Will. Light poured from the projector, and the sheet became a movie screen. Tingling in excitement, I turned to study his profile.

His lips were parted in surprise. Wonder played over his features, smoothing some of his sharp angles. There in the dark of the botanical gardens, heavy roses hanging their heads around us, he was *beautiful.*

Without words, so much passed between us. I still felt urgent beside him. Like my flesh needed his, all dewy and ripe. My head was dizzy with the realization that *I* was the architect of this moment. I didn't have to wait for him to give me what I wanted. This was my fantasy, and if I wanted to touch him, I could. And I would. But first, I wanted to savor him. Affection tempered all that need and want now, a fledgling bud of something sweet to complement the spice.

130

It had been easy to fall into his arms. It grew harder to stay out of them. I wanted to brush his hair back from his face. My fingers longed to trace the dark slashes of his eyebrows, the thin and knowing tilt of his lips. But now, I wanted to put my ear to his lips; if he'd whisper his universe to me, I'd listen to it all.

Rubbing a hand down my back, Will let the previews play for a few minutes before he faced me. Light reflected off his clear skin, colors from the screen dancing like a kaleidoscope across his face.

Finally the movie started, and Will dissolved into laughter when he realized what I had picked. *Clash of the Titans* splashed across the sheet, the fabric adding wavering curves to Liam Neeson's already questionable costuming.

"It was this or Disney's *Hercules*," I said, snuggling closer.

Pressing a kiss to my temple, Will pointed out, "*Percy Jackson.*"

With a smile, I glanced up at him. "Oh, good one. Maybe next time."

I slid closer to him, hip to hip. My shoulder curving into his. A quiver ran the length of my spine when he gently twisted my hair out of the way. I wanted to be shameless. Suddenly, heat coursed through my veins, and I *wanted*. I wanted him to mark me, to leave some evidence of him that I could touch in the morning. The thought came from nowhere, or from some darker part of myself I had never met. I was still mostly untouched, but my body didn't care. Tingling and sensitive, every inch of me was awake and aching for Will.

I knew he felt it, too. His fingers curved, pressing into my back. They traced it restlessly, each stroke broader, more insistent. I wasn't going to strip in the middle of the botanical garden. I wanted to, though, each time his touch slipped the hem of my shirt to graze across bare skin.

Will put his brow to my temple, shuddering with a long, exhaled breath. Beneath the tinny, raucous sound of CGI battle, I heard Will whispering. I couldn't make out his words at first. It sounded like a prayer, a rosary whispered against my curls.

Then aloud, so loud it seemed to echo off the broken-down statuary around us, Will said, "Are you really mine, now?"

My throat ached to tell him the truth. That I'd been his since the moment I kissed him in the boathouse. We were indelible, written on each other's skin. It was true—there were so many things we had to face.

He was going to college; I was staying here. Our future paths seemed completely unlikely to collide unless we forced them to. But I wanted to force them to. I wanted to surrender to this. I didn't answer his question, not out loud. Instead, I pulled his mouth to mine and answered with a kiss.

That was better. That was the truth.

SEVENTEEN

The last week of school arrived, and the halls were controlled madness. Only two teachers bothered to assign homework. The rest surrendered, understanding that nobody was there to work anymore. The seniors were already done with their classes.

That meant no Will in the hallways.

I hadn't seen him since our date in the botanical gardens, almost a week ago. His family had surprised him with a celebratory graduation trip to Florida. That meant we had to make do with rushed cams and texts. I hated every second without him. I told Jane that we were together—it was official, the end—and dared her to make something of it.

Trying to cull the last of my personal stuff from my locker, I turned to see Jane winging her way toward me with an expectant smile. She'd done something new to her hair, razoring the blunt edges of her bob to make it seem even more geometric. It didn't bounce when she walked—it sliced, gleaming and dark and incredibly cool.

When Jane saw my face, worry tempered her smile.

"How's grand romance, your majesty?" she asked.

"Swoon-worthy," I replied. Then, with a frown, I tossed more random stuff into my paper bag. "Did you have this much crap in your locker?"

Jane watched me haul out yet another thick stack of loose notebook paper. I tried to sort it, but after I flipped through, I realized it had to come home with me. Scraps of music mingled with class notes I never needed again.

Reaching past me, Jane pulled out a Styrofoam cup full of bent staples. "Um, no. I didn't have this much crap in my locker. Dude, what *is* this?"

"Trash." I took the cup and dumped it in the brown grocery bag at my feet. "They're from helping Mrs. Adler grade her homework. Don't even ask—it's not worth the breath."

With a shrug, Jane moved on. She peeled a photo-booth strip with pictures of the two of us off of my locker door and tucked it into her shirt. She thought she was funny, but she was giving that back. She wasn't all that keen on taking pictures. Hauling her into the photo booth at homecoming was my victory, and those pictures were my spoils.

"All right, I've been thinking," she said.

"Uh-oh."

"This is our last summer in high school. Our last year together before we go off to college and get questionable tattoos and have even more questionable hook-ups—"

"Because what is college for?" I asked.

"Getting the nasty out of your system," Jane filled in. "Anyway, I want us to do something together. You know, something that will last. Something we can be proud of, and look back on and . . ."

Amused, I closed my gutted locker's door. "Oh em gee, is hardcore Jane Dubinsky getting all sentimental on me? Isn't that my job?"

Jane picked up my trash bag, rolling her eyes. "I'm going to make a short film, and I want you to write the music for it."

My teasing stopped instantly. Jane did a lot of short films, but usually, they were "experimental." Like, twenty-second clips of the same plastic bag swirling in the wind. She stole the idea from an old Kevin Spacey movie, and I never really got the point.

Slinging an arm around her, I bumped against her and smiled when she bumped back. "So what's it about? A lonely salt shaker that gets emptier every time somebody uses it?"

"Oh bite me," she said. "As a matter of fact, Snarkaholic Rex, we're making a movie about East River. *Our* version of it. The story of our home. That way, when I'm giving TED talks and you're the musical guest on SNL, we can point at it and say, *This is where we came from.*"

Tears sprang up, an unexpected well of emotion. I stopped us dead in the middle of the hall and threw my arms around her.

Jane nudged me off fondly.

"You never did tell me how movie night went, by the way."

"It was perfect."

"So that's that, right? Summer fling time?

Closing up a little, I shook my head. "No, it's more than that."

Jane made a little noise that sounded like judgment. But she was nice enough to keep it to herself, just this one time.

"Why would you think it's just a fling?"

"How could you not?" Jane asked. She seemed genuinely baffled. "He's leaving for college in the fall."

She was absolutely right, of course. He was headed to St. Philip-Windsor College, an elite private school, about four hours away. As he described the campus, I had imagined him on the quad, shirtless and playing ultimate Frisbee.

I'd been failing to mention that immutable fact. We both had. After all, Will's epiphany came packaged with the realization that we had lost years, and we only had months before we'd be separated again. I'm not sure how I'd so thoroughly convinced myself not to talk about it, though. Because once Jane said it, it felt frighteningly, loomingly clear. Will would be leaving—sooner rather than later.

"Sare?" Jane said. "You okay?"

I nodded, though I knew it was a lie. Will and I couldn't keep pretending that we had all the time in the world.

Two months. Eight weeks. That wasn't enough.

Propping my cell phone on my guitar case, I sat down in front of it. Carefully framing myself against the background, I settled in. Behind me, a massive bronze sculpture swirled toward the sky. It was a piece called *Two Lovers, At Play* and anybody who grew up in East River would recognize it.

It was the centerpiece of the Arts Garden near the museum. In elementary school, it was an annual field trip. We'd look at the latest exhibition inside, then eat our sack lunches in the garden.

Many a game of tag had been won in the shadow of *Two Lovers, At Play*. And in sixth grade, we all suddenly understood that *lovers* had a slightly naughty definition. After that, our game morphed into kiss tag, much to the teachers' frustration.

So when I sent a cam request to Will, I wanted to make sure that he could see the statue clearly. Excitement raced through me. Clutching my guitar, I almost laughed in delighted relief when Will's face suddenly appeared on the small screen.

"Tag," I said. "You're it."

For a moment, he looked confused. Then, his pale gaze narrowed, and I could tell he was studying the scene behind me. He lit with realization. A wicked smile curved his lips, and suddenly he was moving.

"I see you there," he said. Scenery wavered behind him as he walked through his house—his family room with built-in bookshelves, ceiling to floor, then his kitchen, all gleaming granite and stainless steel. "Thinking you won't get caught."

Strumming a teasing chord on my guitar, I leaned toward my phone. "I'm not going to get caught. I'm more clever than that."

"We'll see," he said.

The lights went out on Will's phone. For a second, I thought I had lost him. Then the sound of the garage door ground to life. Light blanked the screen, and then suddenly, the picture moved again. It wobbled, too blurred to make sense. I heard him open a door, and then the rev of an engine.

A sting of hot sweat touched the back of my neck. My plan had been easier to enact than I thought. He really was coming to find me.

The video flipped, and I found myself staring at the ceiling in his car. I could only see Will's elbow from time to time. Sitting back, I started to play. Not my own songs, but music that he would recognize. First, the James Bond theme, in a Cali-surf style that made it sound urgent.

"Better hurry," I teased. I wasn't going anywhere, but he didn't know that. "Your time is running out."

"I'm halfway there, girlie girl."

Laughing again, I replied with a few folksy bars of Macklemore's "Thrift Shop." The arrangement was all Ed Sheeran, and it made Will laugh like a loon.

"Uh-oh," I said. "There's a crowd gathering. I might have to run."

Will's distant voice replied. "Run as fast as you want. I'll always catch you."

Segueing into a standard blues riff, I played it through a couple of times. Then I started making up lyrics just to mock him. My heart pounded faster by the moment.

Will didn't live that far from the museum. He was getting closer, but because all I could see was the ceiling in his car, I had no idea how close he actually was. It was like the thrill and adrenaline of being chased without running a single step.

My fingers skipped down the strings, a faster blues progression than I intended. "There's a pretty boy on the road," I sang, trying not to dissolve into laughter. "And he's coming for me. Got his engine running, 'cause that boy is built for speed."

Will was laughing, too. With an amused groan, he said, "Never do that again."

Halfway through another verse about shifting my gears, hands grabbed me from behind.

My shriek was genuine, my fear a shock. It lasted a split second. Long enough for Will to tip me back against his knees and to lean over me. He plastered his hands over the guitar strings to silence it.

"You're it," he said triumphantly.

Jittery from the adrenaline rush, I reached up to twine my arms around his neck. "Not yet. You know the rules."

He sank down behind me, then pulled me back against his chest. His lips tasted so sweet, an extra buzz in their caress. Letting my guitar slide from my lap, I turned in his arms. On my knees in front of him, I stroked my hands over his shoulders. His smooth, sculpted collarbone slipped beneath my thumbs. I felt him swallow, felt the streak of breath in his throat.

Right there in my hands, he was alive. I felt like a god, like all this belonged to me. Like he took those breaths just for me. A heady mix of desire and invincibility made me brave. He was mine, and I could do whatever I wanted. Take whatever I wanted, feel his skin on mine, if that's what I wanted—and I did, desperately.

Shifting my weight, I pushed him back. I climbed the length of his body, straddling his hips and bending over him. My hair fell around our faces. It shielded us from the rest of the world. It made a dark, quiet place where we could escape, even in the middle of the Arts Garden. Tugging his lower lip with my teeth, I broke away suddenly.

"Wait a minute, how did you sneak up on me? You're still in the car!"

Will grinned. Threading his fingers in my hair, he stroked and twirled until he was hopelessly tangled in it. "My *phone* is in the car. *I'm* here with you."

Drunk on his smile, I sank down for another kiss. "Extra points for being clever."

His hands swept up my back, and he pulled me down the rest of the way toward him. Lying on his chest, I felt the beat of his heart. I rose and fell with his breath, and there was no space between us at all.

All at once, I was aware of him. Of his body, its hard planes pressed against me. The denim and cotton that kept me from his skin frustrated me. Maybe Will wasn't the one who was running fast—it must have been me. Because I wanted to push the shirt from his shoulders and touch his bare skin. Feel his skin against mine, follow my hands and find out where they would take me.

Reading my mind, Will caught my wrists and held them tight. "We have to stop doing this in public."

A flash of need struck me silent. Now he was deity, claiming me and keeping me. My fingers flickered in response; my body arched closer to his. If we were alone, someplace quiet and private, I could have him—all of him. He could have me.

Only one thing held me back from agreeing with him out loud. Jane and Grace had gotten into my head. I didn't know how far I could go with Will if this was just a fling. Avoidance only worked for so long. I couldn't keep lying to myself, seeing only the perfect and ignoring the flaws. He was leaving, and I didn't know if he planned to look back for me. That hurt, and right then, I didn't want to hurt.

Straining against his hands, I fought for a lush kiss, and won it. Slicking past his silken lips, I let myself forget again. We *were* in public, kissing in the shadow of *Two Lovers, At Play*, I could give myself up to it. There was only so far things would go here, in the Arts Garden. We still had plenty of time to talk.

Secure in that realization, I murmured Will's name and melted into bliss.

EIGHTEEN

To get started on the film, Jane declared that we needed to get creativity fuel. By that, she meant boxes of oatmeal cream pies, bags of Pirate's Booty, and Red Pop. Possibly the most disgusting combination in the universe, but it was tradition, and it worked for us.

She pushed our tiny cart down the snack aisle of the Red Stripe. It was a weird little grocery smack in the middle of our neighborhood. An old brick building among the vinyl siding, it had been there long before our houses were built.

Based on the desiccated shape of the apparently immortal owner, I suspected it would be there long after our houses were gone, too. It was the Market of the Damned, but Doritos were always two for one, so who could stay away?

Certainly not Jane and me. We'd gone from one snack to a growing mountain of them. With grabby hands, Jane threw in two more bags and smiled at me. "Noms."

Incredulous, I said, "I'm going to go get the Red Pop. And nothing else. Try to control yourself."

Glazing over, Jane pushed the cart on down the aisle. In a zombie monotone, she announced, "Need . . . Ring . . . Dings . . ."

With a mountain of processed garbage already quivering in the cart, the last thing she needed was Ring Dings. But I knew better than to get in her way. Jane was going to do what she wanted. No input needed, no advice regarded. And when she was sick as a dog at three in the morning, she'd be gracious enough to let me say I told you so.

I checked my phone as I headed toward beverages. I was so caught up in scanning my Instagram feed that I didn't realize the drinks aisle was populated. With popular people. Specifically, with Tricia and her best friend, Nedda.

By the time I raised my head and realized who was there, it was too late to bolt.

"Oh, hey, Sarah," Nedda said suddenly. Her voice was sticky and thick, too sweet for the situation for sure. "Doing a little light shopping?"

Guilty, I couldn't quite meet either of them eye to eye. They'd come to our gig. Invited us to party with them. Gotten Dasa the prom gig. Basically, Tricia Patten was the nicest girl in the entire freaking universe, and now I felt six feet lower than the dirt at her feet.

"Just getting some soda."

"Oh," Nedda said. "I thought you might be shopping for somebody else's boyfriend."

Everyone knew. Of course they knew. I wanted to slap Nedda for bringing it up, but the fact was, I'd been a jerk.

I'd been a sneaky, underhanded jerk to Tricia of all people, who had never been anything but nice to me, all through high school.

"Knock it off, Nedda," Tricia said, proving my point ably.

Surprised, Nedda looked from Tricia to me, then back again. Snatching up her purse, she said, "I need Funyuns," then stalked off.

My heart lurched into a random pattern, the confrontation over before it started. Or was it? Adrenaline raced through me, and it felt like I should say something. But what? Watching until Nedda disappeared, I finally turned to Tricia and took a deep breath. "I owe you an apology."

"Okay . . ." she said. She sounded more curious than anything else.

"I'm sorry for the way things started with Will." My throat tried to close, but I kept forcing words through it. My awful inner self still wanted to deflect. To explain and blame, to tell her I didn't know they were still dating. To *lie*, if it would only make this easier. None of that mattered, though. I had done plenty of wrong, and I had to face my part in it. "I never intended to hurt you," I stammered. "But of course I understand that intentions don't count."

"Huh."

I'm not sure what I expected. It would have made sense if Tricia had taken the opportunity to lay into me. Or to press a needling finger right into my guilt. If she'd screamed, or raged, or moved to hit me. Instead, she lifted a four-pack of artisan root beer off the shelf and put it in her cart.

"Will and I had been friends for a long time," she said, her voice quivering slightly. She didn't sound angry, so much as wounded. "When I first asked him out, he told me that he loved me. As a friend. And if I wanted to add benefits to that, he'd be crazy to say no. But I was the crazy one—to think I was the last girl he'd be with."

An ache spread in my chest. I wanted to hug her. Comfort her. Instead, I kept my hands to myself and murmured, "I'm so sorry."

Tricia shook her head. "I was stupid. You can overlook a lot when your friends are the ones behaving badly. Before I asked him out, I thought it was kind of . . . funny, I guess. That girls just couldn't say no to him. That he went from one conquest, to the next, to the next. That everybody fell for him and got their piece and it was all good."

Internally, I winced. But it wasn't news to me that Will had more experience than I did. It was practically chiseled into the school trophy case. Most Conquests in a Single Season: Will Spencer.

My throat closed up, but I took a step closer. "I'm really, really sorry."

"Look, I blame him," Tricia said. Then her expression hardened. "But you should be careful. I thought I was different. You probably think you're different, too. Will Spencer was one of my best friends, and he still cheated on me. He's never going to change, Sarah."

Like a shard of glass, that buried itself deep. It was unreachable, and agonizing. I *was* different. The both of us felt it. We both said it. Right?

I closed on myself a little, building a shield out of crossed arms. "I just wanted you to know that I'm sorry. You've been incredibly good to me, and I should have been kinder to you."

Tricia's expressive face said so much. She was quiet, thoughtful. And deeply, deeply hurt.

"Personally," she said, summoning a forced smile, "I think he just hates to be alone. One girl's never going to be enough to fill him up. Not me, and not you."

I didn't know what to say. Did I agree? I didn't know. But I knew I wasn't about to argue with her. Tricia touched my shoulder gently. If she noticed my flinch, she didn't acknowledge it. But she did meet my eyes. In her delicate voice, she said, "Good luck."

It wasn't cruel. It was simply matter-of-fact. She said it and walked on, cloaked in thoughtful dignity. And I think that's why it bothered me so much. She could have been vicious and hateful—and I would have deserved it. But she had known Will incredibly well.

It scared me that she offered me a warning. She must have really thought I needed it.

And while I stood there wondering what to believe, my phone chimed. Will had good timing—or maybe bad. I wasn't quite sure.

so u know, ur busy all night tomorrow night w me.

My pulse quickened. Curling around my phone, my fingers danced across the screen. He really was like a drug. Tricia's words still echoed in my ears, but I couldn't wait to see him. I didn't know what he had planned, but I actually ached to find out.

Where are we going? I asked.

It's a surprise, he said. Trust me.

NINETEEN

With nightfall coming, we drove down the old river road outside of town. Before the highway, everybody took this road to get to the beachy cottages that lined the water. It was just far enough away that you could say you went somewhere with the summer, but not so far that you had to refill your gas tank until it was time to go home.

With the top down, my hair was a wild mane. It swept around my face, twisting and tangling as we sped into the dark. There were no streetlights this way. No bright, illuminated signs. In fact, a few miles out of town, it turned into forest. Flashes of moonlight on water danced between the trees and the sweet scent of pine filled the air.

About an hour later, Will pulled off the main road. At first, I thought he was just going to park on the shoulder so we could walk to the water. But the bounce and jolt of tires on gravel told me otherwise. We took the hidden drive slowly. The lighter stone pathway looked almost liquid in the dark, like we were cruising along a river of our own.

Finally, Will pulled to a stop. Cutting the engine, he came around to open my door. Taking my hand, he led me carefully along the rough path to a cabin nestled in a stand of weeping willows. The headlights dark, the car silent now, everything took on an otherworldly shape. Summer frogs chirped all around us, the whisper of crickets filling the spaces between.

Wood smoke lingered in the air. Pungent and rich, it seemed to swirl with a cooler, cleaner scent. It took me a moment to realize it was the smell of fresh running water. Though the path hadn't been sure in the dark, I could tell we were close to the river here. Closing my eyes to shut out all the dim light, I heard it. The swift, smooth rush of water carried with it a chorus of night sounds.

Producing a single key, Will unlocked the cabin and stepped aside to let me walk in first. As soon as I did, I realized he'd already been out here today. There was a fire banked low in the stone hearth. Glass bottles shimmered in a pail of half-melted ice. I laughed when I picked one up and realized it was root beer.

Will tossed me a church key, then leaned back against the door. "I still owed you."

"Yes, you did," I said with a smile. "Are we breaking and entering?"

"Nah," he said, his gaze trailing my face. "My family owns it."

"It's nice," I said. I opened a root beer and started to toss the cap into the fire. Instead, I slipped it into my pocket. The glass was cool on my lips as I took a sip, the soda lush and spicy. Moving through the cabin, I took in all the little details. The living room was just big enough for a couch. A tiny table with two chairs sat behind it.

French doors opened onto the river. From here, I saw starlight on the current. It danced like fireflies, chasing and chasing, never stopping. If I took half a step, the light shifted and I saw Will reflected in the glass behind me. His gaze followed me, burning even in the dim light.

"It's not as nice as the cottage I had at Marblehead. But maybe we can do that next year. Winter break, maybe?"

Turning, I leaned against cool glass. The cabin was so small, it would only take a few steps for us to meet in the middle.

He looked so pristine. So absolutely perfect. His thin white button-down clung to his chest, the collar open to reveal a beaded chakra necklace encircling his throat. It was a flash of color against his skin. It matched his jeans and brought out the blue of his eyes. Shadows played up and down his body, and he knew I was drinking in his details. He leaned his head back against the door. Raised one foot to press against it. Thumbs hooked in his jeans, Will was utterly comfortable being contemplated.

A dark thrill came over me. If everything went right, I'd get to see all of him. Summer and swim class meant I'd seen nearly every inch of his body.

Cut and perfectly angled, his back was as tempting as his chest; his strong arms matched the muscled length of his thighs. And with or without jeans, it was obvious he had a world-class, quarter-bounceworthy ass. But now I'd find out where that dark streak of hair beneath his navel ended. If that heavy curve in his jeans was backed up by an impressive erection.

Six-months-ago Sarah would have been too squeamish to even think about something like that. Now, I *wanted* to know—even if it made me squirm to admit it, even to myself.

With a sip of root beer to fortify me, I tried to stand there as comfortably in my own skin as he did. I think I managed it. I felt good in my black eyelet lace. Its halter-top showed a little skin, but the color left some mystery. I loved the way it moved. Will's gaze traveled down the flared lines and lingered on my bare thighs.

A blush rose on my chest, slipping up my throat and touching the tips of my ears. No one had ever looked at me the way Will was looking at me now. Most of the time, I was the girl that people's eyes slid past.

My sisters got the refined beauty in the family. I was rougher, my hair untamed. My hands were too big to be elegant. I wasn't tall enough to be willowy, but I was too tall to be petite.

Under Will's slow consideration, to my own surprise, I felt sexy. I felt worthy—crazy irresistible. I became aware of my own power, my own heat. He wanted to get to everything I hid beneath my dress. When he dragged a hand over his mouth, I knew it was watering. He probably had plans for me. Slipping his tongue into me, maybe his fingers, too. What's more, I wanted him to. I wanted him to gasp for me. To beg for me.

I didn't realize it at the time, but he'd made me feel exactly the same way that first night in the boathouse. No wonder I ended up flirting with him. No wonder I pushed him back and kissed him first. Being with Will stripped away my inhibitions. He made me forget to be afraid.

"You know, St. P-Windsor's only four hours away." Will shifted, his foot slipping off the door. Tension jangled my nerves, but I loved him so fiercely right then. Swallowing the lump in my throat, I pushed off the glass doors to make my way to him.

Heat pooled between my legs and my skin begged to be bared. If I tugged at the ribbons on my halter, it would fall away. All my bare skin would be his to kiss, to touch—to lick. Nipples hard behind thin, silky fabric, they stung in anticipation. The tremble in my belly translated to a thin, shimmery ache beneath my lacy lingerie.

Already, I could imagine how dark Will's hair would look against my skin. What I longed to find out was what his mouth would look like, plush and swollen and worshipping the curve of my breast. Sinking lower. Disappearing between my thighs—

But I was the one in control here. My body had to follow my mind. I had to know that Will and I weren't just talking about the future, but that we were going to *have* one.

Clutching the root beer so hard my knuckles went white, I said, "You might feel differently when you get there. You're going to meet so many new people."

"They're not you," Will replied.

"They might be hot."

His voice rougher, lower, Will took a step. "But they're not you."

"We don't have the best track record," I said. I berated myself for reminding him that we hadn't been free to get together when we first got together. But I couldn't avoid it, could I? As nervous as I was to have this conversation, it had to happen. I couldn't keep going with Will unless I knew we were going somewhere permanent. All that uncertainty knotted me up and I couldn't relax until we pulled those knots free.

Will took another step. "That only happened because it was you."

He looked at me and I saw he really meant it. I felt like a cage had opened. Like I had suddenly flown free. Will and I had a future, one that he was already planning for. He loved me, and I loved him, and all at once, I let all my doubts go. Light, so light I wasn't sure my feet touched the ground, I took another step toward him. Enough serious talk, I teased him softly, "Or maybe it was the root beer."

He nodded at the bottle in my hand. "How is it?"

"A little warm," I replied. I was right; it was only a few steps for both of us to meet in the middle.

I offered him the bottle, but he shook his head. Taking it from my hand, he set it aside. Then he slipped his fingers into my hair. There was a subtle possessiveness in his touch. Just a way that he pulled me to his chest that screamed ownership. It wouldn't have mattered if we were in the middle of Grand Central Terminal—his touch stripped the rest of the world away.

The subtle blue of his eyes shifted. Dark lashes fell as he leaned in. When he kissed me, it wasn't tentative. He dipped past my lips, his tongue swirling hot against mine. Low, hungry sounds rolled in his throat and his fingers twisted in my hair. Chasing the sugary sweetness of the root beer from my mouth, he slicked into me.

We had kissed so many times before, but this time, there was intent. I felt the chase in my blood. It didn't matter that I was already caught, that I'd already pledged myself to him, that my chest still pounded with anticipation. Each slip of tongue was a drug. It made me run fast; it stole my breath. Banding an arm around my waist, Will dipped me back.

Off-balance, all I could do was beg for more. And I did beg, offering up my mouth again and again. My hands flew up the back of his shirt. Though my nails were blunt, there was enough of an edge to them that I could rake them along his fine shoulder blades.

The sound he made when I did that was unholy, and incredible. Then, we were moving, completely in sync. We stepped at the same time, drifting past an open door, into a cooler, quieter room.

Moonlight spilled through the window. It traced Will in silver as he backed me up against a wide bed. So many emotions flickered across his face. A brow lifted, his lips parted in murmured wonder. All I could think as I sank into the crisp linens was that he was beautiful. Not handsome, beautiful. Some divine artist had freed him from marble and breathed life into him. This moment, and every moment with him, was beautiful, too.

Spilled across the bed, I reached down for him. Will caught my hand and pressed a kiss into the palm. Then, he grazed his lips against the inside of my wrist. It felt like a brand against the tender skin there. For a brief, blazing moment, I thought nothing could feel better than that kiss against my wrist.

Then, instead of sliding up to cover me, Will brushed his hands against my knees. His palms raced up my thighs, parting them gently. When his touch disappeared beneath my skirt, I gasped. This wasn't the way I had imagined it. For some reason, I'd thought I'd direct him, and he'd follow faithfully. Now I realized he had his own ideas. And I had no hope of guessing his plans. I couldn't have even guessed the details—like the foreign pleasure that swept over me when his slightly rough cheek brushed the inside of my thighs.

Never would have guessed that feeling his hot breath through my panties would blank my mind quite so completely, either. I was terrified, my hands twisting in the quilt. I wasn't having second thoughts. It was just a great unknown, and I needed a push. One last look back before flying. Pushing onto my elbows, I carded my fingers through his hair. I just needed a kiss. One more kiss—I might have whispered that aloud.

Will pushed forward, skimming the curve of my lips with his. But he didn't linger there. He left me stunned, dragging my own lower lip through my teeth. Because the next thing he kissed was the curve of my knee. His mouth did linger there, as if it were the most perfect knee he'd ever seen. As if he couldn't keep himself from nuzzling it.

My breasts felt full, constrained by too many clothes. My head swam; it was too full, too. Nervous longing played through me. I wanted, even if I didn't know exactly what. To me, it was simply more. More of his mouth. More of his fingers skating up my thighs. Then suddenly, beneath the silk edge of my panties. His bare skin on mine shocked me and I gasped.

Even against the bed, my hips swayed. I arched beneath Will, then sank back again. I had no idea what I was doing—then I realized, maybe I wasn't supposed to.

There was a difference between being safe and having faith. I trembled, but I wasn't unsure—I didn't know what would happen, but I was excited to find out. Every first time was a leap into the dark. What was important was that this time, I wasn't leaping alone.

Will brushed his nose against my thigh. Drawing a breath against my skin, he shuddered. Murmured something appreciative, flicked a look in my direction. Watching my reaction, he slicked his fingertips, grazing and tracing—teasing. They were close, almost inside me but infuriatingly far away. I wanted to reach down. I wanted to guide his hands to places only I had touched, but leap into the dark or not, I was too shy.

"Will," I murmured, plaintively. Restless beneath him, I combed my fingers through his hair. Nails grazing his cheek, my thumb strayed too close to his mouth and he tasted that, too. He sucked the tip of it, even as he stroked his own thumb along the curve of my clitoris. I curled tight, my toes, my spine, and whimpered in pleasure.

Will Spencer, bastard.

He knew *exactly* what he was doing to me. Playing my senses with lazy flicks of tongue, he dared me to do something about it. It wasn't cruel; in fact, it was quietly gallant for such a player. In a voice meant for my ears alone, he asked, "Yes?"

The world stopped. It hung suspended, quivering and full of possibility.

Above the bed, a window opened to the night sky. It was cloudless, black, and pierced with a million points of light. Our breaths fell heavy in the dark; the bed beneath us creaked. My toes pointed, they stroked restlessly against his hips. That was before.

"Yes," I whispered back to him, and together we sank into the exquisite after.

TWENTY

People said you had to suffer for your art. I had to admit, it was easy to wrench a song out when everything was a disaster. But even though I loved the music I wrote when I was in dark places, what I wrote after my first night with Will was *extraordinary*.

They didn't feel like my songs. More accurately, they didn't sound like anything I'd written before except for "Everything." I *loved* these songs. They soared with rich, complicated melodies. The guitar work was some of my best yet.

I dipped into my savings account and paid for two more hours of studio time. I was going to spend the next couple of years eating nothing but ramen, but I had to have my own demo.

With the mic in front of me and Dasa behind me, I soared. When I sang my own songs, when I played my own music, recording was a rush. Take fifteen was as exhilarating as take one.

Even the engineer noticed a difference. When I packed up my guitar and headed out at the end of my second hour, she stepped into the hall to catch me.

"You're going places, girl," she said.

Though we'd had a lot of local success as Dasa, I couldn't remember anyone saying anything like that to me personally, ever. The attention had always belonged to Dave. Dave was the star. But now, a new, tentative foundation spread beneath me. All the lingering worries that I needed the band to succeed began to fade.

I was so drunk on my new music that I turned up outside Will's window three nights in a row with my guitar. His manicured backyard was perfumed with summer lilac. There was just a single pool of light to stand in. So I planted myself there and texted Will to come to his window. He shared the nascent west wing with nobody; his parents' room was on the far east end of the house.

Even his silhouette at the second story window thrilled me. Stowing my phone, I played through my new songs one by one. I kept everything sweetly muted; if he wanted to hear the words, he'd have to come to me. I'd sing them right into his ear.

The minute he hit the back door, I knew to put my guitar down. He'd sweep across the lawn and crash into me. Picking me up, he spun with me until we were both dizzy. Then slowly, he'd let me slide down his body until our lips met.

We stole seconds in his bedroom and my music room. We found out that you can't get very far in the back seat of a Honda Civic. On the other hand, the warm hood of a Miata in moonlight was the perfect place to get a little dirty. It cooled, but we didn't.

On the Fourth of July, we drove to the next town over to watch fireworks on the river. Jane, stepping in as best friend ever, covered for me so Will and I could spend a few whole nights together at the cabin. We always had root beer and solitude. One night, we spread a blanket beneath the stars, stripped to the skin. But sinking into bed with him is what I liked best.

When I rolled over in the morning and found him scrambling eggs in nothing but his boxers, my heart leapt again. I didn't want to go home; I didn't ever want to wake up alone again. Slipping behind him, I wrapped my arms around his waist and rested my cheek against his back. We fit together so beautifully that it genuinely ached to let go.

Only one thought marred our summer days and nights. It was already hard to spend the day with him, then have to return to my house when it was done. How was I ever going to survive when it really was miles between us, and weeks before I'd see him again?

Will talked me into filling out an early admissions package. It was increasingly clear that I had to start thinking about myself first. With the new music I was making, and my new outlook on life, that was fine. U of M in Ann Arbor was only about an hour from Will's college, which would put us a lot closer together if I went there. And it had a great music program.

Since I'd never put much effort into planning for college (I hadn't saved a whale or invented a cure for an infectious disease or started volunteering at the age of three), there was no way I'd get into schools like Juilliard or Yale. But UMich was a possibility, and the proximity would be nice. Will was convinced that my music was good enough to get me in there early, and with a scholarship. I didn't know about that, but his confidence always felt so good to hear.

When we got tired of answering probing application questions, we would take breaks. Sometimes to drive. Sometimes to pick things out for his dorm room.

I had to stop him before he bought discount sheets. Casting furtive looks, I carefully peeled open one of the nicer packages and made him fondle the goods.

"See?" I told him. "You can buy the ten-dollar sandpaper, or you can get these. Start out with something nice, Will. You know you're not going to wash them until you come home at Thanksgiving."

Cornering me in the bedding aisle, Will pressed me against the shelves and kissed me. He stroked his hands down my waist, over my hips. And he laughed against my lips, a low, wicked sound. "I'll have to after you come visit."

"Bad!" Scandalized, I dared to dip my fingers down the front of his jeans.

They only skimmed the waistband of his boxers. His loosely tucked shirt kept me from touching any skin at all. Apparently that was close enough. He pressed against me, his interest evident in a hard, hot shape against the crook of my thigh.

One kiss away from really inappropriate, we were interrupted when a woman wheeled her cart into the aisle. She stopped dead. A sticky toddler in the seat craned around to look at us. I could practically hear the music screech to a halt as she shot us the dirtiest look imaginable.

Instead of simply backing out of the aisle, she attempted a three-point turn instead. All the better for her to hiss at us as she retreated.

"This is a family store!"

When she finally tottered around the corner, I burst out laughing and buried my blushing face against Will's shirt. We grabbed the better sheets and hurried to check out. We both thought it would be best to escape before we got arrested for indecent exposure at the East River Target.

It didn't matter where we went. Wherever we were, we were alone. I kept waiting for the buzz to wear off, but it never did. I caught my breath every time I saw him.

Every single time he came to my door, or looked out his window, I caught myself hoping: look at me, see me, love me. And every single delirious time, he did. Swirling into my house after a day with him, I didn't try to stop singing. My lyrics or somebody else's, music spilled out of me as I swayed through the halls.

When I returned home from our trip to Target, a light was on in the kitchen. I padded down the hall to find Grace sitting alone at the island. She wasn't eating—or reading, or looking out the window. She just sat there, staring at the butcher block. I'd never seen her sit so still.

When I came closer, I realized her eyes were rimmed with red. Big displays of emotion weren't Grace's style. She had always been more comfortable quantifying and qualifying things. She liked it when she could measure and sort, when she had complete control.

Touching her shoulder, I apologized when she startled. Somehow, she'd had no idea I'd walked into the room until I reached for her. Slipping closer, I lowered my voice. A quiver broke the pretty line of her lower lip, and my heart wrenched in my chest. "Sis, what's wrong?"

"Luke won't be visiting this summer." She said it coolly. As if she was just passing on a message. "Actually, he won't be visiting again."

"Oh, Gracie," I said. "I'm so sorry. What happened?"

I leaned against her shoulder because sometimes, she didn't want hugs. It was hard not to smother her in my arms. When Ellie broke up with her partner last year, she curled on her side in the couch and used my legs as a pillow. Hours passed with me handing her tissues and combing through her hair.

Grace shifted her weight ever so slightly. She pressed back against me, her version of wallowing. "I knew something wasn't right. He kept missing our Skype dates. I'd get one text for every four I sent."

On her behalf, I felt betrayed. "Are you kidding? How hard is it to answer a text? It takes maybe two seconds."

"Don't you dare make fun of me, but I calculated the rate of return. The gap between the time I sent him a text, and when he finally replied. As of last week, the average was two days, the mean was three, and the margin of error . . ."

I couldn't help it. I threw my arms around her. Pulling her head to my shoulder, I kissed her hair and held her so tight. My poor, reasonable, regimental sister's heart had broken. It was a terrible moment of realization.

Petting her, I asked, "So could you calculate the trajectory and speed I'd need to throw a rock to hit him in the head from here?"

Instead of chastising me for being childish, Grace sniffled on my shirt. "A rock is too small. Use a bazooka."

"I'm so sorry," I told her. I let go with one hand and one hand only. Stretching to snag the box of tissues from the counter, I slid them in front of her. "Did he have an excuse for all this bullshittery?"

Grace stilled. A painful smile cut the corners of her lips. It was a macabre expression, one that left her dark eyes desolate. Her voice tinged with anger, she snatched a tissue from the box. "Oh, that's the best part. He's in *love.*"

"What?!"

Swiping at her face, Grace turned to me. "He says it started by mistake. The North Atlantic is just so lonely."

Rage bubbled in my belly. There had been a time when we'd teased Grace about all the time Luke spent on research vessels. *How long before he mistook a manatee for a mermaid? Were there even manatees that far north? Would a harbor seal do the trick?* But those were jokes. Never once did we think that he'd fall for an actual human woman, or fall into her bed. Berth. Bunk. Whatever it was they had on ships.

"Are you kidding me?" Whistling under my breath, I handed her a new tissue. She'd shredded the last one in record time. "How long has this mistake been going on?"

Closing her eyes, Grace drifted away. It was like everything drained out of her at once. Her anger, her sadness. They were all pushed down by a thin layer of ice. She probably needed the numbness just to answer that question. Her lips barely moved. The answer slipped from her, bleak and almost inaudible.

"A year. So when he was here at Christmas, he was already sleeping with her."

Where Grace was frost, I was fire. I wanted to snatch back every conversation I'd had with him. I wanted to reverse time and reclaim every single thing we'd given him—up to and including Grace's heart.

Trembling with anger, I said, "And he had the nerve to drink our eggnog."

"Last Thanksgiving," Grace said sharply. "When he came out to Chicago for my college family dinner? Sleeping with her. At Tam and Becca's seder! The whole time, he was sleeping with her. An entire year, and I had no idea. Why didn't I notice?"

"Because you trusted somebody you loved. There's nothing wrong with that."

A shuddering breath overtook her. Hiding her face in her tissue, Grace shook her head. "I feel so stupid. And so embarrassed. Bragging to everybody about how we were making long distance work. That people who couldn't just weren't committed enough."

My throat closed up. I'd never thought she was bragging. She was just Grace, cataloging the data that put her relationship with Luke in the upper percentiles for success. Now, for every time Ellie and I had whispered *very effectively* at each other, I hated myself. And, I have to admit, I began to doubt myself a little.

Because I'd believed in Grace and Luke. It was because of them that I was able to laugh while picking out sheets for Will to sleep on four hours away. Their relationship, which had seemed so perfect with the video calls and late night texts, had taken the fear out of my future with Will. I'd believed that it was possible because I personally knew someone who was making it work.

Only now, I didn't. Now I realized somebody could smile and look me in the face and talk about how great my sister was . . . and the whole time be cheating on her. It was a shock to look back at the holidays. Luke brought really thoughtful presents. He'd helped in the kitchen. He'd asked us questions about our lives and acted invested in our family. He'd laughed and smiled at Grace, and the whole time . . .

No wonder Grace hadn't seen it. None of us had.

What could I say to make it better? Short of buying an intercontinental ballistic missile off Craigslist and aiming it straight for Luke's fat, cheating head—I had nothing. Nothing but hugs I wasn't sure she wanted, and tissue she kept destroying instead of using.

Leaning over her, I kissed the crown of her head. Smoothing a hand down her hair, I said, "This sucks. I'm sorry, too, because it's just going to keep sucking until one day, when you realize it sucks less."

"When?" she asked plaintively.

"I don't know." With another kiss, I squeezed her. "But you know what? You'll get through this. You're smart, and you're strong. Something better is waiting for you."

"That's the worst part."

"What is?" I asked, filled with dread.

"I don't want something better. As stupid and sick as it is, I still want *him*."

Grace slipped to her feet. The look on her face brought me to tears. It was like someone had scraped out every bit of my big sister and left nothing but a shell behind. She haunted the hallway, gliding toward the stairs and onward to bed. She seemed so fragile. So insubstantial.

The kitchen felt empty, now. The pale light from the stove seemed to struggle to light the space around me. It was like the room had surrendered with Grace.

I couldn't help but feel guilty, because I knew Tricia had gotten that same horrible call. Because of me. Is this what she'd looked like that day? Had she gone home to her sister and cried while she tried to be brave?

Shoving those thoughts aside, I busied myself cleaning up confetti tissue. It didn't matter that Will was going away. We weren't doomed to the same fate. Yes, we'd gotten together under terrible circumstances. But I'd done my best to make up for it. Will was sorry, I was sorry—and we were different.

Weren't we?

One Sunday morning, Will climbed to my window and lured me out at dawn. The grass still damp under our feet, he led me to the woods that separated our neighborhoods.

The "woods" wasn't much in the way of wilderness. The trees were just thick enough that you couldn't see the fenced backyards on either side of it. Mostly, it was a shortcut that little kids used, their worn dirt paths marking the way. Sweet, trilling birds greeted the sunrise with unusual melodies. My hand fit in Will's perfectly as we walked deeper along the path.

"There's rain coming," Will said.

We both smelled it in the heavy air. It was evident in the scarlet streaks the morning sun made across the clouds. Though there was no danger at all, I pressed closer to Will. I curled my arms around one of his, and kissed his shoulder. "Red sky by morning, sailor take warning."

Sharing a secretive smile with me, Will said, "Still holding on to that whole wisdom thing, Athena?"

"Forever," I replied.

Then, he stopped me with a kiss. Just a taste, a promise for more later. And when he pulled back, he turned me to face an unexpected clearing in the woods. The brambles and thorns wound around the trees now instead of spilling across the ground. A thin carpet of grass blanketed the ground, the blades glittering with dew.

"Call me crazy," Will said, taking a step into the clearing. Pulling me with him. Unexpectedly, he sank to the ground and pulled me into his lap. He gathered me in his arms, his cheek rough against my hair. "But I thought you'd want to see this."

It took me a moment to realize what I was looking at. Then, all at once, the light changed. Subtle shadows traced the ground, revealing rings of mushrooms. Creamy brown, no bigger than my pinkie nail, they looped and whorled in the thin grass. Spider webs wove along the ground. Dew hung on the gossamer threads, catching the light like diamond chips.

Enthralled, I murmured, "How did you know this was here?"

With a roll of his shoulder, Will buried his face against my hair. "I woke up and I needed to see you."

"I like how this starts," I said.

Will rewarded me with a kiss. Then he tightened his arms around me, warm and possessive. "So I started to get in my car, but then I saw the old path. Something told me, *Will, go that way.*"

"You know, that's how people in horror movies end up dead," I joked.

Snorting, Will nudged me. "I wasn't looking for a cat. I didn't tell anybody I'd be back. And most importantly: I didn't run through here in bare feet and pajamas."

Amused, I twisted in his arms. I fit so comfortably in them. Noses brushing, I couldn't stop glancing down at his lips. But since he'd lured me out before brushing my teeth, I managed to resist. "All kidding aside, Will, thank you."

"For what?"

How could I explain it? Meeting his gaze, I lost my breath. But I managed to speak all the same. "For knowing I'd want to see this. For being amazing. For loving me."

"You make it easy, Sarah."

Will wound one of my curls around his fingers. His studied expression swept over my face. All the teasing softened to emotion. The clearing became a quiet chapel, a sacred place for just the two of us. These were the moments I never tried to describe.

How could I possibly explain the way my blood changed course to match Will's? No one else would understand the fragile weight of the air when Will's bravado melted to reveal his heart beneath. So I never explained. I just lived in these moments when they came, and clung to them once they'd passed.

When the last day of our summer came, I sat in my front window and remembered those kisses in the clearing. The silvery perfection of his smile captured in the glass of the diving window. The sulfur still hanging in the air as we made love beneath a sky full of fireworks. The warmth of his body next to mine as we filled out my college application together.

I wrapped those memories around me like a cloak. It was still August, the hottest part of summer, so it didn't seem fair when the black Miata turned down our street. It wasn't a car meant for packing up and going anywhere. It trailed heavy in the back end. The passenger seat was crammed so full of stuff, the window looked more like a picture frame. Just seeing his car loaded up that way made me want to cry.

"So this is it," Grace said.

She'd walked so softly that I hadn't heard her come up behind me. Concern etched her brow. Clutching a mug, she hovered close to the hallway instead of coming over to me.

Hopping up, I said, "I'll see him in a couple of weeks."

Grace offered a painful smile. Then, without another word, she turned and walked away. As bad as I felt for her, I sort of wished we were kids again so I could pull her hair and threaten to tell Mom. I was nervous enough about the future. Sometimes it felt like Grace was deliberately trying to make it worse.

I wanted to be a good girlfriend. I didn't want to be angry. Or upset, even though that's how I felt. This was the last time I'd see Will for a while, and I wanted to send him away happy. Happyish. After a few more breaths, I was either calm or hyperventilating. I threw open the front door and bounded down the walk to meet Will.

"I'm stuck," he said sheepishly.

Approaching the window, I leaned in and laughed. Somehow, he'd gotten his seat belt tangled with a nest of computer cables. Those cables snaked into the tightly packed block of *stuff* that filled the car. Some of it was obviously furniture. Some of it, clothes. But the rest? Who knew. It was a crazy Picasso of a pack job.

With a teasing smile, I said, "Don't get any ideas." Then I leaned over him, right through the window. I felt his breath against the curve of my breast as I tamed the cable beast. The car door dug into my ribs. Halfway to dizzy, I finally managed to unsnarl him from his own trap. Sliding back out again, I opened the door and stepped back with a flourish. "Ta-da."

Almost as soon as the door opened, Will was out of it. He engulfed me in his arms. Newly aware of his scent, I buried my face against his shoulder.

Tears rose up, violent and certain. I twisted my fingers in his shirt and blindly sought a kiss.

I kept making deals with myself, or the universe: one more kiss, and I can let go. One more whispered I love you, and I can wave and say goodbye. It was never one, and I didn't think I could do it. The only thing that centered me was the tension coiled in Will's body. He clung to me just as desperately. It felt like he wanted to wrench us both to pieces.

"We'll Skype every night," he promised. When he pulled his head back to look at me, I was stunned to see tears in his eyes, too. His pretty mouth contorted; he was better at holding things back. He was trying to be strong, for both of us.

I nodded vehemently. "Facebook, Instagram, Twitter, texts, I'll be there."

"Nobody's on Facebook anymore," he said, trying to joke.

In reply, I hiccupped a sob. I thought it was going to be laughter, but instead, this awful sound rolled out of me. Like a strangled wail, it hung heavily between us, a dark and desolate sound.

"Hey," he said, catching my face between his hands. "Don't cry. Don't cry, okay? We aren't breaking up. There's nothing to be sad about. You can't fight destiny."

Because he said it, it was true. For that brief, bright moment, I was unafraid. I saw us on the other side of this—the two of us traveling the world. Stealing kisses in the shadows of ancient monuments, waking up on the banks of famous rivers. That's what waited for us, our destiny. The two of us, together.

Then the light went out. Will swept me up in another kiss. Instead of spiced, it was salted. The passion in it was dark, nothing but despair. It was a kiss that said goodbye in a thousand terrible ways. Then suddenly, I was cold. Will tore himself away from me. Deliberate. Desperate.

With one look back, he tried to say something. All that came out was a faint, mourning whisper. His lips shaped the three words, but nothing more.

"I love you, too," I said, my voice broken.

The edges of his strength crumbled. Revving the engine, he didn't pull out so much as race away. The tires screeched against the pavement. Burned oil lingered in his wake. Wrapping my arms around myself, I stared at the distance growing between us, his car growing smaller. I kept on staring at nothing when he turned and disappeared from sight.

I stared into the mocking blue sky as the ground gave way beneath me. Sinking to sit on the curb, I tried to make myself so small. Like maybe if I could just fold myself up tight enough, it would stop hurting.

Now that he had gone, I let myself go. Great, jagged sobs tore through me. When I closed my eyes, they only got worse. Because when I closed my eyes, I couldn't summon a single beautiful memory. They lingered just out of reach, taunting me with their happiness.

"Come back to me," I whispered. But it was too late. Will—my Will—was gone.

TWENTY-ONE

It looked like my music room had exploded.

Paper covered every available surface. Approximately nine million Sharpies in various colors spilled across the floor like rainbow shrapnel. Jane had not one, not two, but *three* laptops linked together.

I sat perched in my favorite chair with my feet tucked neatly beneath me. I didn't dare put my feet on the ground. One wrong step and I would destroy my best friend's storyboard.

"I'm shooting for twenty-five minutes," Jane said.

"Is that including credits?"

"Probably?" Then she shook her head. "No. I'm going to do a clean reel with B-roll footage."

I dutifully scrawled that answer down on my iPad, though I had to admit I didn't know what any of it meant.

My stylus swirled across the tablet screen.

Just as I scribbled in *opening and closing credits separate*, a blue bird icon popped up.

Dorm life is definitely better with good sheets. #sleepinglate

He'd only been gone six days, and he was already waxing philosophical on dorm life? So cute. Since Jane had gone to that weird headspace that was "figuring out the shot list," I sent a quick reply.

Lucky sheets. #jealous

Instantly, Will replied. Lonely sheets. Then, to illustrate just how lonely they were, he tossed in a link to a selfie.

Sprawled back on a narrow twin bed, Will gazed right into the camera. The insane, icy blue of his eyes popped against his pillow. He touched a fingertip to his cheek. Lush lips turned down in an exaggerated frown—he tagged it #missingyou. It was the perfect comeback.

"Wait, wait, wait!" Jane exclaimed.

Startled, I held up a hand. "I haven't moved!"

She paced just inside the living room. Every step ruffled the sheets on the floor, which made me weirdly nervous. I kept waiting for them to fly out of order. Then what would happen? Bolts of freak lightning from the sky? An epic, seizured meltdown?

Jane pulled her hair back and scanned for something in particular. Then, she lunged. I actually flinched, which made me laugh.

The blue bird bubbled to the top of my screen again. I stole just one glance at it while I waited.

Hey, Athena, wanna go for a tour?

A link taunted me. Splitting my attention between Jane and Will, I touched the screen to load the picture. At the same time, I looked back up at Jane. "What are you doing?"

"I want to establish this with postcard pictures," she said. I was completely lost, so she explained, "You know, all the scenic things that they put on the brochures and stuff. Come to East River—it's not as lame as you think."

"Ohhh, like the Arts Garden."

"Exactly!" Jane stepped over her storyboard, then stopped abruptly. One foot hung in the air, like she was playing an arcane version of Twister that only she understood. "And the botanical garden, and the Pattens' boathouse."

She was so distracted that I peeked down at Will's latest picture. He'd gotten out of bed and pulled on a green St. P-Windsor sweatshirt. His hair stuck out at odd angles. From the jaunty tilt of his smile, he was just fine with that.

A funny little pang opened in my chest. It was ridiculous to be sad that he was wearing a new shirt. Completely insane to be jealous that other girls were going to get to see him in all his rumpled glory. But I felt it all the same.

He was handsome all of the time. It's just, there was something especially irresistible when he had a case of bedhead first thing in the morning. Though for him, first thing in the morning was two in the afternoon for me.

The room got too quiet. A little too late, I realized that Jane had said something and was waiting for me to reply. Swiping the picture off the tablet screen, I said, "Sorry, what?"

"Don't even," Jane said. "I will literally kill you with my own two hands and bury you at the quarry if you turn into *that person.*"

A blush colored my cheeks. Putting the iPad aside, I wrapped my arms around my knees. "I know, I know. The one who gets a boyfriend and disappears. I'm not, I promise. I just miss him. I'm trying to get used to it."

Bright, Jane said, "I have an idea that will make you feel better."

I leaned forward. "Yeah?"

"You could commit to a project with somebody awesome."

I laughed. "Man, I don't know. Where would I find somebody like that in East River?"

With a great step over her storyboards, Jane bounded from the room. Already halfway down the hall, she called back. "Try looking in your kitchen. Bitches like that are starving artists. They're probably going to decimate this whole container of hummus."

Quick as I could, I texted Will. With Jane. Tour rain check? Will make it up to you tonight.

In a testament to my deep and abiding love for Jane Dubinsky, I left the tablet behind without waiting for a reply.

After my shower that night, I hopped online while I squeezed the water out of my hair with a towel. It usually took forever to get it dry enough to sleep on.

That meant I had plenty of time for a tour of St. P-Windsor. Rather than contacting Will on Twitter, I sent a private message. It was one thing to flirt and tease in public, but I wanted some alone time with him, even if only digitally. Skimming my fingers over the screen, I shot off a message into the dark.

I return triumphant, with my rain check.

Hey, he replied. BRT, 2 min. Skype?

I answered by opening the app. Setting my status to away, I waited for Will to appear. A little bleat caught my attention, a message coming in over chat. Touching the screen to bring it up, I felt a leaden weight in my belly. It wasn't Will. It was Dave. He didn't say hello. There were no pleasantries. A single line popped up, clipped and business-like.

Checking gig calendar, are we still on for later this month?

My fingers hovered over the screen. Once it was obvious that I really had moved on to somebody else, that there had been somebody else while we were still dating, Dave had gotten a little weird. Our texts were supposed to be about business now, and they were. But there was a definite frost that rimed them.

Our calendar had been empty for most of the summer. I'd been splitting my free time between Will and writing music for myself. The longer the silence spread between us, the more uncomfortable it got. So I stared at Dave's question for a long time before finally answering. It was a get-out-of-Dasa-free card. He offered it up bloodlessly.

It should have been easy to take it. I even typed out **Maybe we should cancel so they have time to replace us.** For some reason, I just couldn't hit send. In my mind, I saw Dave's face so clearly. Shadows crossed his beachy good looks. He probably had his lips pressed into a tight, pale line.

Dave almost never wrote music entirely on his own. I had songs that were mine, but with the exception of a few experimental ambient tracks he put together on his keyboard, the only music Dave had belonged to us both. It was unfair to cut him off like that. He had always fronted like he was the talented one, the star quality—but I was starting to realize that perhaps he needed me even more than I thought I'd needed him.

Glancing over my desk, I stopped to look at some of the leftover paperwork from my Michigan application. I skimmed the sheet, a partial CV that listed all my performance experience. All of it, every single bit of it, was something I'd done with Dave.

I changed my response.

Yep. Looking forward to it. You?

The reply didn't match my question. **Great, thanks. TTYL.**

Before I could type anything else, Dave went offline. My stomach felt oily sick, but I shook it off. It made sense that things might be a little strained right now. It would be fine, I decided. Once we got on stage and got back to the music, it would be smooth and easy like it always was.

Peeling the towel from around my body, I tossed it toward the bathroom. Stripped naked and still damp, I actually let out a little peep when the connection tone in Skype blared to life. Blushing, I sat down quickly. I arranged the screen so Will saw me from the shoulders up and accepted his call.

The video stuttered. The screen was too dark; I heard people talking and laughing in the background. Suddenly, the video brightened. A blur of motion filled the screen, replaced a moment later with Will. His hair was still a mess, and his face was flushed pink. It looked like he'd been out running or something.

"There you are!" I exclaimed. I was relieved. Though I'd had to rain check him, I was afraid things would get too cool or too fun for him to catch up with me later. Even the BRT hadn't erased that anxiety entirely. Now I could relax and settle in with him.

A little out of breath, Will pushed his dark hair off his forehead as he settled in. "Yeah, sorry about that. There's a club fair out on the quad, I was checking it out."

At the same time, I was checking *him* out. With glass between us, he couldn't see me straight-up objectifying him. A wicked thrill ran through me. It zinged beneath my skin and sweetened my blood. Apparently, my body didn't care that Will was four hours away. It wanted a taste of him while his skin was still flush and earthy with sweat.

"Find anything?" I asked, my toes curling a little.

He shook his head, the picture finally stabilizing. Behind him, I could make out a desk and a computer. It was the most generic dorm background possible. "Eh, I don't know. I was mostly window shopping."

The picture flickered, the connection threatening to fade. I embarrassed myself by moaning out loud. "No, don't go away!"

After another patch of static, Will reappeared. "I don't know what the deal is. I have five full bars."

I wrapped my arms around myself. Fully exposed to the air, I was a little chilly. My wicked thoughts warmed me from the inside, but they did nothing for the outside. Standing up, I covered the camera with my hand for a second. "That's just me, hold on a sec."

"Where are you taking me?" he asked.

Shameless, I replied, "To bed."

"Oh, I didn't know it was that kind of Skype."

With a laugh, I shot him down instantly. "Sorry, sailor."

Now that he'd mentioned it, I couldn't help but wonder. Will had seen me stripped to the skin before, but I wasn't about to give him a sexting show. It was one thing to be alone with somebody I loved. Putting on a striptease all alone in my room? I'd never done anything like that, and the idea made me slightly embarrassed. A random, sing-song thought wound through my head: maybe not *today*, but maybe *someday* . . . ?

My blush deepened. Picking up the tablet, I held it at an angle that captured my chin and my nostrils, but definitely not my bare skin. Carrying Will to bed, I dropped into my soft summer blanket and tried to tug it around me. "Okay, all settled in. Can you see me?"

With a lilt in his voice, he seemed to rake his gaze all over me. "Well, I see some of you."

"I just got out of the shower," I explained.

Will pointed down, asking playfully, "Pics or it didn't happen."

"No pics," I snorted. "No Snapchats, no video. Sorry."

He glowed with a smile. "Gotcha. Ask again later."

At once, I was exasperated and amused. And it was just like he was in the room with me. While I couldn't *touch* him, everything else was the same. The joking, the easy flow of conversation ... we still had that. My body was on a slow burn, acting like it had a chance to twine around his tonight. The ache between my thighs urged me to bare skin so he would come closer. My brain helpfully reminded it that he couldn't. Careful to keep myself covered, I slid out to lie on my side in bed. Propping my iPad against a pillow, I settled in.

"You promised me a tour."

"That's right," he said, standing up. "I did. Sorry, okay, so this is the dorm room." He waved the phone around so fast, I caught nothing but smears of color. "My roommate's *not* here right now. He's at Robot Boxing, and that tells you everything you need to know about Antwon."

Propping my chin in my hand, I watched as Will plotted his path. He carried the phone out in front of him. No longer in the shot, Will narrated the hallway while I tried not to get queasy from all the shaky-cam.

"This is the hall I live on. The RAs decorated all the doors before we got here. There's a robot for Antwon right there. And for me, a pair of tennis rackets."

They looked more like fat, white mittens—but it was the thought that counted, right? Twisting my hair over my shoulder, I laughed softly. "You want to know what's funny? I mean, I know you played tennis and golf at East River. But if I were cutting out construction paper to represent you, that's the last thing I would have put on there."

"Do tell," Will said, carrying me on down the hall. I caught glimpses of whiteboards already filled with notes. People's feet clopped by in flip-flops.

I tried not to get distracted by the scenery. "I mean, you were class vice president. Why not a flag? Or a stock chart, since you're a business major."

"A red Solo cup," he countered, turning the camera to face him. He grinned, tossing his head back. "You know that's my actual rep."

Rising above, I informed him, "Maybe, but inaccurate. Root beer bottles would have worked better."

Will blew me a kiss, then turned the camera into the hall again. Approaching the elevator doors, he flashed me toward a room I couldn't quite see. "Laundry over there."

Once he said that, I made out the sounds of dryers rumbling. They hadn't been at school all that long. It made me wonder who already had a whole load to run. Maybe there had been a soda accident or something. A girl laughed, her voice muzzy, disappearing into the mechanical hum.

"How long are they allowed to stay?"

"Who?" Will asked. The elevator dinged, and he stepped inside. "Next stop, the common room. And my tiny, tiny mailbox. You should send me things. It's empty and sad."

Nodding toward people I couldn't see, I said, "I will. But the girls. I thought I heard a couple girls in there."

Brows knit, Will peered at me, baffled. "I don't follow."

"Isn't there a curfew?" I asked. It was awfully late. "When they have to get off your floor?"

Will shook his head. "No, uh-uh. I mean, I can't have guests longer than four days in my room, but that's about it. We can all visit anyone at any time."

"Oh," I said.

My surprise didn't show, because Will pressed on. "In fact, I think you'd love my next-door neighbor. Her name's Hailey. She plays the guitar, too."

Wait, wait, wait. He was in a co-ed dorm? Somehow, I felt like I should have known that. He should have mentioned it; it shouldn't have come as a surprise. All those girls living in the same building with him, just doors down, mere steps away . . . I couldn't help but remember what Tricia had said. One wasn't enough. Two wasn't either. Now he had a whole dorm full, right down the hall. Right next door. Doing their laundry in short-shorts and worn-out T-shirts. Panic closed my throat.

It would be so easy for him to pick and choose. And even if he didn't go looking, would he say no if they came to him? It wasn't like I was the first girl to throw myself in his path. Would I be the last?

I tried to keep my voice light when I said, "That's cool. Acoustic?"

"Yeah. But she's not as good as you are," he reassured me. "You kick ass."

How completely fantastically amazing, a girl with a guitar right next door. Two steps away. From my Will, who already knew her well enough to know her name, and her guitar, and how well she played it. So, so awesome.

I plastered on a smile. I wanted my tour, and I wanted my time with Will, and I wasn't going to let a sudden case of envy ruin that.

"Where are we now?"

"Common room, ta-da," he said.

He turned the phone away from his face. Slowly scanning the room, he pointed out the TV area and something that looked like a book corner. Pool table, foosball, and so many people in thin shorts and T-shirts, draped everywhere. In short order, he showed me the café, the mail-nook, and before I knew it, we were outside.

It was sunset there. The brilliant colors streaking the sky actually reflected on his face. He turned, and he was painted in gold and scarlet, and in that moment, I forgot. I forgot to be jealous, or to be worried. I forgot the distance from East River to St. P-Windsor. I forgot everything, because I remembered all over again—I was in love with Will Spencer.

He caught the expression on my face, even from so far away. Bringing the camera closer, he looked right into it, as if he could find my eyes through the screen. Nothing had changed except our proximity. I had all the proof I needed because he smiled at me, so softly, and said, "Hey, I love you, too."

It was so easy to believe him. I had no idea how hard it was about to get.

TWENTY-TWO

"I love the senior parking lot," Jane practically sang at the top of her lungs.

I loved it, too. We got to park closest to the doors, with our own numbered spots. I'd won number twelve in the lottery, so basically, I pulled directly into homeroom on the first day of school.

The usual first-day excitement was different this year. We'd finally made it to the top. We didn't have to worry about being the new kids anymore. No more were we the looked-down-upon. We were the pinnacle, the people who got to define the tone for the year.

And for us, it was the start of a long party. Though we had classes, most of us were down to electives. As long as a nothing catastrophic happened, we were graduating.

Plus, we already had a good idea where our GPAs put us in the class ranking. The AP-taking-half-credit-marching-band people still had a year to duke it out over who'd get the 4.55 valedictory prize and who'd bomb into salutatorian with 4.54444. For the rest of us, we'd banged out most of our required credits and turned senior year into pre–college frosh by taking classes that interested us.

My schedule was packed with contemporary teen fiction, music, music theory, and music education—just out of curiosity. I wasn't super-great with little kids, but it was a satellite class. That meant five days a week, I'd leave early to go play my guitar for fourth graders.

Senior year was set to be the perfect, no-stress, all-glory year. Especially because my early-action package was already in the loving hands of Michigan's admissions office. I planned on putting in regular-decision applications to NYU, University of Chicago, Berklee College of Music, and St. P-Windsor—but if I had Michigan, I'd know soon.

I had a good feeling. I didn't know why.

Slinging her arm around my shoulders, Jane hauled me into the school with a deep, ecstatic sigh.

"Ahh, nothing like the smell of fresh floor wax and breakfast burritos in the morning."

"You're so damaged," I said, laughing.

We headed for the senior cafeteria. Our school had a big central kitchen, with two cafeterias on either side. In theory, it was supposed to speed up the lines. What it had effectively done was create a class schism.

Underclassmen were banished to the *bad* side, defined by the fact that the gym doors opened onto it. When they were propped open, the underclassman side took on the odor of eau de jock strap *and* mystery meat.

Juniors were allowed to eat in the senior caf, but only on the outskirts. The squeaky tables that framed the carpeted holy land, but didn't impinge on it.

Now that we were seniors, Jane and I headed for the inner-circle tables. All of the tables were made of the same cheap faux-panel and plastic, regardless of location. And the blue carpeting was, frankly, disgusting. None of that mattered. This was our twelfth-grade-given right, and we were claiming it.

As we strode in, Simon hopped up and waved his hands over his head. The art people were already congregating on one side. It was weird how much one summer could change people. Round faces had taken on angles, our clothes were more together, and a couple of the guys suddenly had broad, broad shoulders.

Jane stepped onto one of the chairs and sat on the table in the middle of it all. "One hundred eighty days till freedom, my people!"

We all cheered and didn't care who heard it. Sitting on top of Jane's feet, I sprawled back against her knees. Though all our usual cliques had coalesced, the edges were looser than usual. As different as the pops were from the jocks from the arts, we had senior year in common.

Drifting into our orbit, Emmalee pretended she didn't see Simon. Instead, she crouched next to me. "Hey, can I bug you?"

"Absolutely," I said.

"We're doing a senior blast to raise funds for all the girls' athletics," she said. "We were thinking about hiring your band, are you still doing that?"

With a smile, I nodded. "Absolutely, of course. Why wouldn't I be?"

Shrugging, Emmalee said, "You know, just with the whole Will thing, I mean . . . everybody knows . . ."

"That you should lock up your boyfriends around Sarah?"

We both jerked our heads up at the same time. Kara Coleman stood a few feet away. She was one of the beautiful people—and

Nedda's little sister. Apparently, she was carrying Nedda's grudge into the next generation at ERHS.

The weird part, though, was how she said it so matter-of-factly. She didn't sound malicious. It was like she thought she was joking. Like it was an accepted facet of my personality: Sarah Westlake, boyfriend poacher.

Emmalee shooed Kara along. "Move along, lady. If you wanted Dasa for the ritual Key Club initiation, you should have gotten here first."

"Or I could just wait until your back is turned and make a better offer."

It happened so fast, I didn't have time to say anything. I didn't even have time to blush. I was mortified, but the moment passed before I had to confront it. Who was Kara to incidentally slut-shame me with a smile?

Squirming in my own skin, I smiled uncomfortably. Rationally, I knew that everybody was too excited about the first day of senior year to notice my mini-drama. It still felt like all eyes were on me. Worse, I had the impression that the flow of gossip all summer had diverted around me . . . because it was *about* me.

Jane leaned over, smooshing my cheeks between her hands. "S'up, buttercup?"

"I was just telling Emmalee how she owns me now. I'm going to be her guitar-monkey."

"Oh, excellent choice," Jane told Emmalee. "This is a high-quality, hand-crafted, Etsy-grade guitar-monkey. She's guaranteed to bring you many hours of pleasure and delight."

With a laugh, Emmalee stood up. "You guys are so weird."

"Thank you!" Jane tossed her head back, basking.

To me, Emmalee said, "I'll e-mail you later with the details, okay?"

"Sounds great," I told her.

And though I smiled, and laughed, and fell into conversation with my friends, Kara's words lingered.

Dany Kilpatrick was an incredibly adorable sophomore art geek.

With fire-engine-red hair and way oversize black glasses, she seemed like she was still in the process of growing into herself.

Some days, she wore Birkenstocks, and some days, combat boots. She had the potential to be a smoking hot pottery goddess at East River—for the time being, she was still constrained by cute.

Literally bouncing down the hall, she caught me before I veered into the senior cafeteria. A thick stack of metal bangles jingled on her arms. A gentle cloud of patchouli wafted from her skin, somehow sweeter on her than it was on the stoners and burnies.

"Hey," she said, shifting her weight from foot to foot. "Hi, hi. I'm Dany, you don't know me . . ."

With a smile, I said, "I do, actually. You did the red lacquered head at the art show last year. That thing was awesome; it gave me nightmares."

Suffused with color, Dany clasped her hands together. "You are so sweet, thank you!"

"Yeah, no, it was great. I really liked it." It was stupid, but I felt so magnanimous. Like I was doing the supportive senior thing right. Or something.

"Okay, then, well," she said, rocking back on her heels. "This is kind of a weird question, so . . . you know, slap me if I'm completely out of line."

"Go ahead," I said indulgently.

Squinting one eye at me, Dany seemed to shake herself apart. Then she came back together in an instant, her focus laser-like and intense. "You and Dave Echols broke up, right?"

That was the first touch of her needle against my ego bubble. Slowly, I nodded. "We did. Yeah. Why?"

"I think he's so great," she gushed.

I hesitated. "Okay?"

"So talented, I mean, most guys who play the guitar are kind of douchey about it. He's just so authentic and intense and dedicated, you know? Of course you know! You know him so well, and, I mean, I heard that you broke up with him to date Will Spencer, holy crap. I mean, no judgment, you have to live your truth. Fearlessly pursuing and all that. But for me personally, Dave is just . . ."

Squeezing her hands into fists, she shook them. It was like there were words out there for what she meant, but she just couldn't find them. This was weird. She was weird. The whole thing was weird.

Now trying to escape, I nodded and took a step away. "He really is great."

"Wait," Dany said. She lunged at me. For a split second, I thought she was going to hit me. Instead, she grabbed both my hands and squeezed them. "I'm doing this all wrong!"

"Doing what?" I was almost afraid to find out.

Dany dipped a little. For a brief, horrified flash, I was afraid she was going to kneel in front of me. I don't know why—the theater people did stuff like that all the time. And she was just enough over the top that I didn't put it past her. Thankfully, all she did was clutch my hands to her chest. Which was also weird.

"I just want you to know I honor your place in Dave's life. And I respect you as a woman and as a sister artist. So I'd like your blessing."

Stupidly, I said, "For what?"

185

"To ask Dave out," Dany replied. Her eyes were so wide and green and earnest. She blinked at me like a little forest creature.

I said the first thing that came to mind, which was both stupid and utterly fitting. Something right out of Jane's absurdly sprawling fantasy novel collection. Somehow, I even said it sincerely.

"Go with grace, my good kinswoman."

Dany left two coral kiss prints on my cheek and insisted on putting her contact info into my phone, but, thank God, that got rid of her.

One period before the end of the day, I was so ready to head home. The morning's exhilaration had worn off, and lunch had completely tweaked me out. All I wanted was to get through independent study, get Jane, and then get the hell out of Dodge.

I wheeled out of the orchestra room and crashed right into Dave. Rebounding off his chest, I was startled before I realized it was him, and flustered after. He looked strangely great in a new scarlet Polo. The color suited him; he looked smooth and regal, like he was walking through the masses, but somehow stood apart from them.

I finally managed to say, "Jeez, I'm sorry, I didn't see you."

"What's this about playing for the athletics banquet?" he demanded. There was no softness in his eyes. They were the same shade as a storm on the horizon. His jaw was squared and stiff, like he was grinding his teeth.

"I think it's actually just a party," I started.

"I don't care what it is," he said. "Gigs like that are a *band* decision. We both agree, or it doesn't happen."

The words struck me like a slap. Never once in three years had we ever worried about saying yes to anything for the band.

Too baffled to be defensive, I said, "I didn't realize you'd have a problem with it. I can go tell her no right now if you want me to."

He jerked, looking away from me. In his jaw, a muscle pulsed. It was the briefest flash of anger. I guess he managed to beat it down, because when he looked back at me, he shook his head no. "I want it. But things are different now. Remember? You wanted them to be different."

Yet another pang of guilt flickered in my chest. "No, you're right. From here on out, we make band decisions as a band."

"What if I already had plans?"

Confused, I pulled my backpack onto my shoulder. "I don't follow."

"Maybe I had plans," he said. "Maybe I had a date. I'm just saying."

People streamed around us in the busy hall, laughing and talking as if we didn't exist at all. It made it hard to find the Dave I knew in all the chaos.

I didn't think we could be more awkward than we were in that moment. So, I decided to find out for sure. Putting on a way more casual face than I felt, I said, "Funny you should mention dating, though. Dany Kilpatrick cornered me at lunch today. Wanted to know if you were available."

Instead of relaxing, Dave stiffened. "What did you tell her?"

It felt like a trick question. Shifting my backpack from one shoulder to the other, I shrugged. "I said you were great, and she should ask you out."

Looking past me, Dave sighed. Then, with a forced smile, he said, "In any case, it's not really your business. So . . ."

"Okay," I said flatly.

I don't know why it hurt my feelings when he said that. It was incontrovertibly true. Dave's personal life was no longer my business.

"You still have access to the calendar," he said. "Just update it whenever. Let me know when it's on there."

"You bet," I said.

The bell finally rang, putting an end to this miserable non-conversation. Hurrying down the hall to my last class, I pulled my phone out. I fired off a quick text to Will—all it said was 1st day back missing you so much. Then I ignored the uncomfortable, barbed ache in my chest.

TWENTY-THREE

With Jane's help, I set a custom ringtone for Will.

Now when he called, my phone purred, "Hey, Athena."

I was almost embarrassed to admit to myself how much it turned me on when I heard it. I couldn't help it. If I heard that whisper, it meant time with him. Long hours talking to him, or watching as he walked me through his life at St. P-Windsor.

One night, he took me to the sciences building. It was a sprawling, gothic hall, with sharp peaks and angled arches that didn't welcome you to its doors. They warned you that you weren't prepared for what waited inside. After dark, the doors still unlocked, it accepted visitors in its shadowy corridors.

"You can't be scared," Will laughed. He took the stairs two at a time. "You're four hundred miles away from the monsters in Strickland Hall."

"You lie," I told him. "You're wrong. They can come through the phone lines."

Making his eyes wide, Will held his camera in front of his face.

With a slow zoom in, he laughed maniacally in the background. It was completely ridiculous, and yet, a thrill of terror washed over me.

"Please don't make me hang up on you."

His lunatic expression melting to one of amusement, Will winked. "Your wish is my command."

I lay back in my bed, my laptop cuddled in the crook of my arm. Its warmth and light bathed my face, mirroring the sensations that swirled through me. Catching up with him after my evening shower was turning into a nightly habit.

With the time difference and our respective schedules, our long calls almost never started before eleven at night. Though I was running short of sleep, it was worth it to have the time alone with him. I tried less and less hard to hide myself during each call.

Will had a great view of my bare skin. My hair pulled up, I bared my throat and my shoulders. The towel slipped slow, showing off way more than a sweetheart neckline; the curve of my breasts cast deep shadows of cleavage. I was almost tempted to take a screenshot for myself. I felt lush and gorgeous and ripe. From the way Will's eyes tracked my every move, he must have thought so, too.

"By the way," I said, as his footsteps echoed down an eerie hall, "Mom and Dad are okay with me driving out for your homecoming weekend. I thought it might be a problem, but Mom convinced Dad it was okay."

With a grin, Will said, "Have I mentioned I love your mom?"

He turned down a narrower hall. It really was terrifying. Carrying the phone into an unlocked room, a strange glow illuminated the edges of the screen. Tension mounted; I heard something liquid and bubbling. The hum of an unfamiliar machine. And then suddenly, something white and floating and obviously dead filled the screen.

I shrieked.

Will laughed. Instantly, he sounded sorry as he turned the camera to face himself. "It's okay, Sare. It's okay. I'm sorry."

My heart pounding, I demanded, "What the hell is that thing?"

The picture shifted. Lights went on, chasing shadows away in an abrupt, blinding flash. A chair screeched on the floor, and my perspective changed. With Will narrating, he panned his phone slowly along a bank of aquariums. "It's the physio lab. The professor keeps anatomical specimens in here. There's fetal pigs—that's what I showed you—along with cats, rats, cow hearts . . ."

A little nauseated, I pulled a hand down my face. "Ew. Seriously, Will?"

"Sorry," he said. I softened, as I could tell he meant it. His sincerity came through, even as he left the lab. Voice low, he murmured as he headed out of the building. "Hailey did the same thing to me when she was here studying last night. I thought it would be funny."

I was getting used to all the Hailey mentions. Sort of. Sometimes she popped up in his videos. It wasn't for long. She just photobombed, waved and said hi, then disappeared. Her face decorated the background of half his Instagram shots. I told myself there was no reason to worry about Will making a friend, even if it made me feel uneasy.

Didn't he text me as soon as he got up every day? He sent long e-mails from his English lecture. All day long, texts came in. Check out this gargoyle in the chapel. And I found a tiny wishing well, see? And Have to read *Scarlet Letter* again. This is proof there's no God. There were videos, and our nightly calls. His Instagram account was packed with different shots of campus, tagged specifically for me. He even threatened to start a Tumblr.

Seriously, Will couldn't have done more to make sure I was included in his day. I was probably just tired from lack of sleep. And lonely, because even a hundred videos couldn't replace one good hug.

Rolling onto my stomach, I curled my arms and rested my chin on my hands. "I'm glad you took me there. I'll just have nightmares for a week, is all."

When Will returned to his dorm, his room was quiet; it turned out Antwon had better things to do most nights than to come home. When Will sprawled on his now-familiar couch, I shifted my position, too.

Will's eyes went wide. "Sare?"

All I had done was sit up. Putting the laptop on the edge of my desk, I sat up and let my towel fall. My skin tightened, both from exposure and from the rush I got from his expression. It wasn't a full-body nude by any stretch, and the only light on in my room was the pale flicker coming from the computer screen. But there was enough flesh and illumination that a sharp hunger filled Will's eyes.

"Promise me no screenshots," I said, defensively crossing my arms over my chest.

I caught a glimpse of myself in the local video window. It felt heady and powerful to realize that I thought I looked nice. I'd never considered the possibility that I might be objectively sexy. It was always Will's reaction that let me make that leap. When he looked at me, I *was* sexy.

Raising an eyebrow, I prompted him, "Promise?"

Hilariously, Will crossed himself. "I swear on my life."

"Okay, you flash me so we're even."

His video feed blurred. For a second, I saw his desk lamp and his ceiling. Then the picture righted itself and there he was, stripped to the waist. He turned his phone vertical and propped it on a shelf nearby. His smooth, sculpted chest fed down to the narrow streak of his waist.

His pants hung low, revealing the slightest curve of his hip. A shadow of dark hair, just hidden from sight. Tight denim outlined a hard curve behind his zipper, and a flush washed over me. I made myself look at the rest of him.

He wore jeans, but his feet were bare. I don't know why that stirred me up, but it did. He looked so comfortable in his skin. Lanky and long, his shoulders like fine Italian-cut marble, I realized just a second too late that instead of taking the edge off missing him, this sharpened it. What I wanted was for him to reach for his button and peel everything away. But I wanted him to miraculously be at my bedside while he did it.

"Much better," I said, my voice thin.

His gaze traveled over me. Even from a distance, I felt its heat on my skin. A blush tingled as it rose on my chest. Could he make out the color-shift from so far away? He had to see the way it lifted everything. I felt the ghost of his hands on me, the phantom trace of his mouth in places it had once explored. Between my breasts—between my thighs.

A slow, hungry smile touched the corners of Will's lips. He was no more naked than he would be at a game of touch football. Comfortable, he scrubbed his fingers through his hair and teased. "So where are we going with this?"

"You've arrived at your destination for the night," I replied. Then I dropped my pillow in front of the camera on my computer.

Across the miles, I heard Will cursing under his breath. He made me brave, but I wasn't that brave. Or crazy. I wanted a lot of things. A Fender Stratocaster with a hard case. Blueberry pie for breakfast every day. A million dollars so I could make it rain—but that didn't mean I was going to get them. Or that I should.

Rolling off the bed, I grabbed my robe. I tied the belt, and then double, triple checked it before I pushed the pillow out of the way again. I was once more completely decent, and a little thrill still lingered.

"So what you're saying is that you're a tease," Will laughed as he sprawled back. He was decadent with his body. Shameless. Then again, I could walk out of my house on Saturday morning and see shirtless guys all up and down the street—mowing lawns, going for a jog.

"You got plenty," I told him, amused.

Lazily rubbing his own collarbone, he nodded. "I figured. It's for the best. I don't know if Antwon is coming back tonight, and I'd hate to start something I couldn't finish."

The flush in my cheeks turned to a sear. Though I'd started by flashing him, I hadn't thought about it all that much. Just a few short weeks ago, I never could have imagined getting naked on camera at all.

Hell, two seconds ago, I was sure that was as much as I was willing to show. But it niggled in my head that Hailey was two doors down. If Will didn't want to wait, he didn't have to.

Suddenly, I was seriously contemplating more. My base animal self certainly wanted more. I ached all over, missing those moments when we were closest together, remembering how it felt to kiss him, become tangled up in him, move together as one.

"We could try it," I said finally. The words felt like honey on my lips.

Even with the occasional glitch in the video, I could tell Will was interested. He all but vibrated from it.

His skin was taut, too. Muscles rippling as he moved, his edges were sharper, more defined. His face, too. The narrowness of his eyes told me he was thinking about it. The flick of his tongue between his lips told me he wanted it. The feeling was mutual.

Dragging his lower lip through his teeth, Will leaned forward. "I know somewhere I can take you. Not tonight. Saturday?"

A tightness filled my chest. It stole my breath as I leaned forward, too. We had promised to find a way to be together even when we were far apart. And though it had been easy to ignore our physical needs at first, it had been just that: ignoring them. They may not be at the forefront, but they vibrated through me just beneath the surface. They certainly hadn't gone away.

I kissed the pad of my index finger, then pressed it to the camera. "It's a date."

TWENTY-FOUR

At the Eden, things were very much not the same with Dave. A form-fitting Henley replaced his usual crisp, preppy plaid. Instead of soft, clinging jeans, he wore a skinny pair, and gone were his generic boat shoes. Instead, he sported a pair of black Chucks. The ragged hems of his jeans dusted the crisp white laces, teasing in contrast. His blond hair was freshly cut, with a bit of spike to it now.

He moved comfortably, throwing his head back to laugh as he talked. He slipped his hands into the back pockets of the jeans, loose-limbed and relaxed in his own skin. Apparently, now that he was allowed to flirt with anyone he wanted to, he did it before the show, too.

The smallest part of me was surprised that he didn't acknowledge me. But the reasonable parts beat that into a paste. We weren't together anymore. He didn't have to help me set up. I was completely capable of sound-check on my own.

It was even all right that mingling before the set, he stayed on one side of the stage while I lurked on the other.

At a table on my side of the stage, Grace, Jane, and Ellie sipped at their drinks as they waited for the show to start. Having them there made me nervous. Though I usually had a bolt of adrenaline right before performing, this was different.

Tonight was a wild card, our first performance since the breakup. I had no idea what to expect. And I hated that. That was the one constant with Dave—I always knew what to expect. I always knew that performing would be amazing; I always knew that we would laugh afterward. Now all of that was gone.

When the lights switched down, I steeled myself and stepped onto the stage. Too many bodies and burned coffee perfumed the air. Though it was a bar, most of the hardcore drinking happened upstairs where the dance floor pounded away with bright lights and electronica.

Pulling my guitar strap over my head, I watched Dave bounce in place a couple of times before taking the stairs up.

All at once, he stood beside me. And it *was* beside. He could have had blinders on, the way he stared out at the audience as he pulled on his guitar. The piney scent of an unfamiliar cologne clung to him. It was like standing up there next to a stranger.

Producing a set list from his case, he taped it to the inside of his mic stand. "It's the usual set," he informed me.

The house lights shifted, casting red behind us and bringing the audience glare down to shadow. It wasn't a particularly packed night. Most of the tables had someone at them, everyone still talking over their drinks. The buzz wouldn't stop, and we didn't expect it to. But tonight, it made it harder to concentrate.

"Thanks for coming out tonight," Dave said, strumming a few chords to get his guitar in tune. "I'm Dave Echols. This is Sarah Westlake, and we're Dasa."

Polite applause smattered through the crowd. The bartender chipped away inside the ice bin, some unexpected percussion.

Skimming the set list, I was glad we hadn't put together a new one. No matter how off we were, these were songs we'd sung a thousand times together. A lot of those performances had been right here. The playlist was familiar as a favorite pair of tennis shoes. Worn, comfortable, reliable.

As Dave introduced our first song, I struggled with the sudden weight of emotion. This might be our last gig at the Eden. I remembered how punch drunk we were the first time we talked our way in to play. That whole experience glittered in my memory, a field of perfect stars on a moonless night.

As we started playing our first song, an upbeat piece, I suddenly realized how sad I was to leave this all behind.

The stage was hot. It always was. There was a restaurant kitchen on the other side of the wall. The lights weren't gentle, either. We segued into another fast number, and I had started to let go of all my thinking when it was time for the third.

It was a ballad Dave and I had written together after we'd gone to see some bad art movie because we thought it was something we were supposed to do. It was miserable, three hours of French people posing to death in black and white. Except for a single red glove, the only flash of color in the whole picture.

Afterward, we'd tried to discuss it. We wanted to be those people who strolled through the night, richer and deeper, conversing like true artists. But I broke down first and admitted I had no idea what the red glove was supposed to mean. Dave dissolved into laughter, his blue-gray eyes dancing. He didn't get it either.

The next Sunday, we started writing a song called "Red Glove." It was all about two people who pretended to be above it all, when all they wanted to do was fall. It was the first song we wrote where Dave led, and I embroidered with sweet, pure harmonies. For a piece written by sixteen year olds, it still felt meaningful.

As we hit the chorus, I looked to Dave. Our eyes met—he'd forgotten to stop looking at me, too. The scarlet light glowed through his golden hair. It traced the fine lines in his face, gathering in a dimple that only appeared on certain notes.

The cool distance he'd been keeping melted away. Rough and raw, his voice tumbled over the notes. The vibrato hung between us, buzzing on my skin.

Our very pretty, practiced song transformed. There was new heat on the stage, coursing between us. An edge of desperation flowed through the lyrics. It had always been there, but Dave was consumed by it tonight.

The talkative audience hushed a little. Did they feel a change in the air? It suddenly seemed like sacred space. Out of nowhere, I felt split in half. I missed this. I missed Dave.

We had the stage for two and a half hours. After the final song, Dave invited the audience to buy copies of our CD at the bar. Instead of wading into the crowd the way he usually did, he disappeared down the hall to the bathrooms.

Left alone to gather my equipment, I moved in a daze. Fingers numb and head stuffed full of cotton, I fumbled the simple latches on my guitar case several times before getting them lined up and locked.

My skin itched. I longed to scrub myself raw, everything clean and new. A scalding shower where I washed my life back to normal sounded so good. Since both sisters and the bestie were in attendance, though, that shower seemed impossibly out of reach.

"Grace went to buy a CD," Jane told me.

Winding up the battery packs, I tossed them in the club's equipment crate. "She doesn't have to do that. I can make a digital copy for her."

"I know. But I went to grab some footage of people buying CDs, and she decided she needed one, so . . ."

"That's sweet," I said finally.

"It is," Jane agreed.

She watched me, unable to hide her curiosity. Though she was doing her best not to ask anything out loud, her expression shouted. Had I noticed the heat with Dave? Was I feeling okay? The answers were yes and no, in that order. Since she hadn't voiced her questions, I avoided replying.

"I don't think I'm up for House of Tokyo after this," I said to fill the quiet.

It was a teppanyaki place not too far from my house. The showmanship wasn't great; I think I could have made a better onion volcano than most of the guys on the grill there. But it was fun, and silly, and out of the ordinary for all of us. We'd planned to stop for dinner after the show, but now the last thing I wanted was a long, drawn-out meal.

"If you want to talk . . ." Jane said, letting her voice trail off.

"I'm really tired," I told her. It was true. Then, to offer an explanation, I said, "It's been a while since I played a full set. It took a lot out of me."

Shuffling along the edge of the stage, Jane nodded. "Okay, sweetie."

That annoyed me. It felt like she was coddling me, and I wasn't sure why. Yes, the performance had been unexpectedly emotional. Yes, I felt kind of stripped in front of half my family and my best friend. Still, I wasn't made of glass. I wasn't so easily breakable.

Before I could call her on it, Dave came out of nowhere. He hopped up the stage steps and tapped me on the shoulder. With a jerk of his head, he said, "Can I talk to you in setup real quick?"

Setup is what we called the dingy office where the club's manager let us lock our stuff when we weren't playing. It was plastered with yellowed posters from bands gone by. The place smelled faintly of cigarette smoke and old, sour coffee. It was my least favorite part of the Eden, but that's usually where we got our cut of the receipts.

"I'll be back," I told Jane and followed Dave down the hall. To him, I said, "Are they trying to get us to wait until next time to get paid again? We told them before that it wasn't gonna happen."

Reaching back, Dave caught my hand and tugged me inside the cramped office. There was no one in there. Just the two of us, pressed into a tight space. Crowding me against the wall, Dave let go of my hand.

He wasn't touching me at all anymore, but I could feel the heat from his body, transferring to mine because he stood so close. There was something darker in his eyes, too. Not dangerous, just wanton. His gaze never slipped from mine. I felt undressed by it, that same sting and connection we had on stage spilling out into our lives.

"What's going on?" I asked. I hated that my voice went fluttery and soft.

Planting a hand against the wall, right next to my head, Dave said nothing for a moment. It was like he was reading me from the inside out. In a strange way, it felt like he had just noticed me for the first time. An old, dormant flicker of infatuation rose in my chest. It was physical, I told myself. Just physical, a screwed-up body-response to a really emotional performance.

"I know I wasn't alone out there," Dave finally said.

A flash of tongue touched the bow of his lips as he paused. Why was I staring at his lips? I shouldn't be staring at anything but the screen of my cell phone, waiting for Will's call.

Swallowing hard, I put a hand on Dave's chest and pushed him back gently. I couldn't help the way the music sometimes made me feel. But I was 100 percent in control of the way I acted. "It was a good show. That's all."

Brushing his thumb against my chin, he studied my lips. Then he said, "I'm not giving up on you."

Rather than let me respond, he leaned in close again. For a second, I was sure he was going to kiss me. The air was electric, and he felt wild and alive so close to me. But instead of touching my flesh with his, all I felt was his breath. It skimmed over my mouth, and he lingered there for a split second.

Then, he was gone. Out the door before I could say a word. Flustered, I slumped against the postered wall. My heart pounded against my ribs. I felt horrible, but I couldn't pinpoint why. I hadn't mixed my signals. I hadn't done anything to give him the impression that things had changed between us. We connected when we sang. We always had.

If Dave had decided there was some hope in a lost cause, that was his problem, not mine. With a few deep breaths to center my thoughts, I headed back to find Jane and my sisters. Odd impulses shot through me. I felt like a marionette, taking big, exaggerated steps.

Coming back into the club, I found my mini-entourage huddled together, whispering to one another. Grabbing my guitar case, I hefted it off the stage. The exhaustion had lifted. Now I had too much energy and nowhere to burn it. So, lightly as I could, I bounced up to them.

"Think I'm up for dinner after all," I told them. "I'm starving."

I slipped away from the table between the "making fried rice" and "throwing shrimp at the ladies" portion of the show. My hands trembled as I secreted myself in the hallway by the bathrooms.

The only thing that would make me feel better was a chance to talk with Will. It had been two days since our last real conversation, and I needed to hear his voice. I dialed his number and waited, thumping my head faintly against the wall.

When the line connected, a girl's voice answered. "Will Spencer's phone, how may I direct your call?"

A wicked, vicious hook twisted in my belly. I thought I recognized the voice. I'd heard it often enough, popping up in the background when Will sent videos or talked to me on Skype. Forcing myself to sound neutral, I said, "Hey, Hailey, is that you?"

"Oh my God, are you psychic?"

I noticed the slightest slur in her voice. It made me want to reach through the phone to throttle her. I admit, the reaction was completely overblown, but I needed *Will*. And I needed *Will* to be the one who answered his phone when I called. Not some girl who may or may not be drunk. Gritting my teeth, I said, "No, it's Sarah. I just recognized your voice."

Suddenly gushing, Hailey sounded like she was moving through a crowd. "That's so sweet, you recognized me. Will's right about you. So seriously smart."

Good. I was glad that Will talked about me. It would have been nice to know he talked about how incredibly sexy I was, and how he couldn't live without me. But for the moment, hiding in House of Tokyo while my sisters applauded the knife skills of our chef, all I wanted was to talk to him. Immediately.

"Thanks. Crazy question, is Will around?"

"I'm looking for him," Hailey replied. Her voice went muffled for a moment, that weird place between too loud and too soft that happened when you tried to talk under the music but over a crowd. Then she came back, "I know he's around here somewhere."

Chest growing tighter by the moment, I ducked into the bathroom. Some cold water on my face would help. It would chase away the unbearable heat that swept over me. I hated the way my voice echoed off the tile, making me sound empty and distant.

"You know what," I said, cranking the tap open. "Just do me a favor and have him call me when he can. Anytime, I'll be up."

Laughter erupted on the other end of the line. I heard a roar of voices in the background. It sounded like a party chant, but I couldn't make out the words. Dipping one hand into the water, I patted it against my throat. I wanted to be angry that he was at a party, but it was Friday night. There was no reason for him to be home. He knew that I had a gig tonight. I didn't want him sitting around in his dorm room, lonely and bored.

But a mad little bit of my brain wanted him to realize that something had happened, and I needed him. I wanted that psychic connection we seemed to have to kick on. Where was he? Why didn't he know I needed him?

"Hailey," I said, louder.

"Sorry, it's crazy here," came the reply. "As soon as I find him, I'll let him know, okay?"

I couldn't bring myself to thank her. Or to say goodbye. I just hung up and put my phone on the mirror ledge.

Staring into the glass, I tried to wash away the red splotches that stung my cheeks. And I tried not to wonder why he was out with Hailey. Why Hailey had his phone. And where he was in the middle of a party, when no one could find him.

Because I'd met him at a party. I couldn't help but be reminded—I'd met him at a party, when he was supposed to be with someone. And he'd ended up with someone else completely. Wrenching the water off, I snatched my phone and hit the bathroom door a little too hard.

That was different, I told myself viciously. You were different. Are different.

I'd heard those exact same words from Will's lips, not so very long ago. Why was it suddenly so hard to believe them?

TWENTY-FIVE

Will didn't call me back that night.

He didn't call the next morning, either. I tried to busy myself with a new song for Jane's movie, but nothing came out right. A single chord put me right back in that smoke-stained office with Dave. Everything else sounded sour and distorted. Since music was part of the problem, I couldn't escape into it.

That meant I had to resort to cleaning. Anytime things were really messed up, I liked to straighten. Physically organizing things was the only way I could feel like my emotional life was in some kind of order.

Turmoil meant I was going to wipe down the ceiling fans and scrub the crown molding with a brand-new sponge. The good china, the set we only used at Thanksgiving and Christmas—it was so soothing to pull down all twelve place settings and wipe each gilt-edged piece individually.

For 345 days of the year, I was a perfectly normal person. I kept my clutter to a minimum, wiped up my spills, and took the trash out before it tipped over the edges. The other twenty days, spread randomly throughout the calendar? I danced just out of reach of OCD. Today I felt compelled to break out the vinegar and old newspapers. It was a two-story house. We had a *lot* of windows.

Climbing onto the stepladder, I pushed curtains out of my way. The picture window in the living room was tricky. It was extra-wide, and it had no panes. One little streak in the middle invariably meant starting over. I attacked it with relish.

Padding through in slippered feet, Grace stopped with her cup of tea. She peered up at me, watching as I alternated between vinegar and newsprint. The glass squealed with each stroke, a sound that drove Ellie crazy. Clearly, it didn't bother Grace. She sipped and watched, watched and sipped. Finally, I looked down at her.

"Are you that bored?"

With a shake of her head, she sat on the arm of the couch. "No, I just think it's interesting."

"What?"

Setting her tea on the end table, Grace folded her hands in her lap. Her hair fell in soft waves around her face, remnants of last night's braids. Dark eyes thoughtful, she trained them on me as she weighed her words. Grace was always deliberate. This was no different.

Finally, she seemed to nod to herself. "You and Ellie are so much alike. Except when you're upset. I like to clean away the pain, too."

Being that she was immaculate all the time, I was surprised. What was left to clean when her apartment and her room were always so perfect? But it was sweet for her to find a similarity between us.

She was right—I would have never considered us alike. Except in the usual ways; if we stood next to each other, people knew we were sisters. We had the same coloring and the same crooked smile. But that was on the surface.

Attacking a few white-ringed spots, I said, "Yeah. Ellie likes to break things. She's the yin to our yang. Or the other way around. I don't know."

Her voice buttery soft, Grace asked, "Did something happen last night?"

A lot of things happened last night. Performing as Dasa was weird. Dave's personality facelift was uncomfortable. Hailey answering Will's phone sucked. Then, waiting up until four in the morning for Will to return my call, for nothing . . . But I wasn't sure I wanted to confide that in Grace.

"It's just stuff," I told her. "Senior year, the band, Jane's movie. It's a lot."

Grace stood and looked around. She peered down each hall, precisely, then came back to me. Putting a foot on the bottom of the stepladder, she put a hand on my back. "Don't get mad . . ."

I stiffened. "That's the worst way to start a conversation if you don't actually want somebody to get mad."

Quietly, Grace glanced around again. "Ellie overheard you talking to Will about . . . um, how do I put this delicately?"

The picture window was about to get streaked. I put my vinegar bucket down and turned on the stepladder. With my best dark look, I pretended I wasn't trapped there. I was, unless I wanted to knock Grace out of my way. Depending on what she said next, knocking her down might have been an option.

Lifting my chin, I said, "Just put it however, Gracie."

"Fine." Pressing her lips together, Grace drew a deep breath. "She heard you making a date to get naked on camera with Will, and far be it from me—"

"What the hell?"

There was no way I was going to stand there for *this* conversation.

Lifting one of her hands, I stepped down and seriously considered bolting for my room. But why should I bolt? I hadn't done anything wrong. It was my nosy, gossipy sisters who were on the side of fail this time.

Grace held out her hands to me, like she expected me to take them. "Sarah, sis, it's okay! We're just worried! Did he upload some of the pictures? Is that why you're so frantic to reach him?"

"Who says I'm frantic to get ahold of him?" I demanded.

"You talk when you text," Grace said. I must have looked baffled, because she demonstrated. "Hey, Will, did Hailey give you that message? Hey, Will, could you give me a call? Hey, Will, I need to talk to you. Hey, Will . . ."

"Shh, shush, zip it," I said. My cheeks flamed. One, because what kind of first-grader was I, that I talked when I texted? And two, because my sisters had taken a tiny scrap of inaccurate information and spun it into something completely shady.

"You can talk to me," Grace said. She was so earnest. So incredibly earnest. I still wanted to hit her.

"There's nothing to talk about," I told her. Snatching up sheets of newspaper, I rolled them into balls to use on the windows. "We haven't done anything like that yet. That's not why I want to talk to him."

"Is there something I can do? I really am a good listener."

She kept standing there, perched like a sparrow on a windowsill. She seemed tiny and delicate. Telling her to buzz off felt cruel. There was just enough sincerity in the air around her, and I was still so upset and confused, that I broke. I'd finished half the downstairs windows and didn't feel any better. Maybe dumping it in Grace's lap would do the trick.

"Dave hit on me last night after the show, okay? It freaked me out, and I wanted to talk to Will."

"Oh," Grace said, surprised. She must have had a no-sexting-the-Internet-is-forever speech all prepared. When I busted out with something completely different, it gave her pause. Finally she said, "He didn't have his phone? With the time difference, he should have still been up when we got home."

Once I'd started, the rest came spilling out in a rush. "He was up! He was at a party. I know that because his next-door neighbor *Hailey* answered his phone. She said she couldn't find him, but she'd pass the message on."

Grace blinked at me. If she'd had pearls, she might have clutched them. "Is Hailey a girl?"

"Of course she's a girl," I yelped.

"I wasn't sure!"

"I told her to have him call me. Anytime. No matter what time, but he didn't. And he hasn't answered my texts this morning, so I'm freaking out just a little bit, Grace. Just a little bit. Do you have any idea how many windows this house has?! It's a lot!"

Slumping, I was exhausted and relieved. At least it was out; at least I wasn't the only one with all this garbage in my head, even if I had just dumped it all over Grace the Doomspeaker. Okay, that wasn't fair. And I felt really bad thinking it, because Grace abandoned her tea instantly and bundled me into her arms.

I didn't want the hug, but it was so weird that she was giving it to me that I gave in in spite of myself. My chin bumped uncomfortably against her shoulder. I felt like a little kid. Like she'd just picked me up after I fell off my bike or something.

With a soothing croon, she petted my back. "Oh honey, I'm so sorry. I don't know why they can't control themselves when they go away . . ."

I pulled my head back and squinted at her. "He's not Luke, Grace."

A more familiar expression appeared on her face. This one was just a little bit patronizing. That older-sister-knows-best face, where she shook her head ever so slightly, pitying me because I just didn't understand yet what she knew to be the truth. "Everybody's different, it's true."

Backing out of her arms, I shook a finger at her. "No. No. What Luke did was skeevy and disgusting. I'm still actively hoping a walrus sits on him. But that's Luke. That's not Will."

"I hope that's true—"

"Don't."

White-hot rage flashed over me. She'd been creeping around behind me for weeks, listening for signs of trouble. It was almost like she wanted things with Will to fall apart. If they did, then it justified her suspicion. She could prove she tried to protect me. Even, perhaps, she could find some justification for Luke's behavior if Will was just as much of a dog. If all men cheated, then she might feel less damaged.

Too bad for her, she wasn't going to get that from me. Or Will. Snatching up my bucket of vinegar water, I pulled myself up to my full height. "We're not talking about this. Because there's nothing to talk about. I'm not mad that he hasn't called me back. I'm worried. About him. Because I *trust* him."

As if shedding an unwanted coat, Grace backed off. "Okay. Your life is your life. You're the one in control."

"You're damned right I am," I snapped. I sounded so fiery, so furious, that I thought Grace believed it.

I only wished I did.

Since I couldn't wash windows in peace, I retreated to my room. Dragging my laptop into bed, I slipped slowly into crazy-person mode. First, I pulled up Will's Twitter account. He'd last updated it at nine o'clock his time, which was ten my time, so just before I'd called. His last message, mysteriously, said OTP COME SEE ME OTP. No tag. No reply. It made no sense.

I plugged it into a search engine and got an urban dictionary definition that meant either Will had started to care really, really deeply about getting two TV characters to kiss, or I had the wrong definition. Back to Twitter, I dug through his friend list. A couple of other people had the same message on their timeline, at the same time. And then, nothing.

Maybe it was a party password. But wouldn't a party have pictures? With a few quick clicks, I called up Instagram and even the sad little Facebook account that Will never updated. The last thing on his wall there was Packing for college, going to miss my girl. Wistful, I stared at that for a few minutes while I tried to examine my life and my choices.

Was I really worried about *him*?

My head made a good case for worry. What if he was hurt? But my heart knew that he was fine. He'd been partying. No doubt, he was sleeping it off somewhere. I didn't want to let myself wonder, even for a second, if he was sleeping it off somewhere *with* someone else.

But wonder I did. Why did Hailey have his phone? Why was she—now that I was scrolling through his Instagram with a more critical eye—in all of his pictures?

With her sun-streaked hair and her freckled nose, even I had to admit she was cute. Almost every picture featured her pulling a face or striking a pose. In some shots, she had feathers dangling from her hair. In others, a peacock blue streak dyed right in. Glitter sparkled from her skin; her clothes were casual pop star, and fit her perfectly.

She looked like *fun*. The kind of girl that a semi-reformed party-boy would love.

Heart sinking, I slapped the lid of my laptop closed. I couldn't keep looking at this. Instead, I pulled up the camera on my phone and sent Will a video message for once. I did my best to sound sort of okay. I wasn't, but I didn't want him to think I was completely unbalanced.

With the camera blinking at me, I hesitated. Then I finally just said what I was thinking.

"Hey, Will. It's, like, three on Saturday. I haven't heard from you, I hope you're okay. Something weird happened after the gig last night. We can talk about it when you call. I'm missing you so much today. I'm so glad your homecoming is soon. I miss your face, and the rest of you, too. Call me. Love you. Bye."

Rolling out of bed, I ducked my head so I wouldn't have to face myself in the mirror. I was more than a little ashamed of myself. I just felt powerless to stop it. Will had been so good about staying in contact until now. The sudden drop-off combined with constant reminders of another girl in his life was the perfect storm of long distance anxiety.

A long, hot shower would clear my mind. Unfortunately, with all three sisters back in the house, a short hot shower had to do. I scrubbed my skin pink and nearly broke my neck when I heard Will's voice saying, "Hey, Athena" from the next room. I grabbed the towel, but didn't take the time to wrap it around me.

I lunged for my phone, answering it with shaking hands. I couldn't help but judge myself as I answered. "Will! I was starting to get worried!"

"Just got your message, what's up?"

His voice sounded sleepy and warm. Soft, like flannel—like he was still in bed. Was it in his bed? A sour taste rose in my throat, but I forced it back down. "I tried to call last night. Hailey answered . . ."

"Yeah, she was holding my phone for me," he said.

I wanted to ask *why*. I wanted an explanation for him being gone all night, for his weird tweets. For the reason he wasn't waking up until three in the afternoon. Instead, I laid my towel on the bed and sat on it.

Shivering a little, I curled into myself. If I asked any of that, I might not like the answer. That's not what I wanted. Or needed. I just needed Will to be there and for everything to feel right again.

My quiet went on too long, because Will said, "You there?"

Swallowing down all my anxiety, I nodded. "Yeah, I am. I just had the worst night. Dave's not acting like himself, and the gig was . . . strange."

With a muffled *hmm*, it sounded like Will rolled over. "Was he a dick?"

Suddenly, I didn't want to tell him. I didn't want him to think I had led Dave on. It was so generous of Will to be cool about the band. In his place, I'm not sure I would have been that chill. So I shook my head. "No. He was professional. The chemistry was just off."

"You dumped the guy," Will said reasonably. "I'm not surprised."

"True."

"Call me an asshole, but I'm actually kind of glad."

Knitting my brows, I curled my toes anxiously against the carpet. "You are?"

I heard bedsprings and Will sitting up. His voice tightened, probably with a stretch. "You're my girlfriend now. I don't want him getting any ideas."

Another wave of guilt rose in me. That was my opportunity to tell Will exactly what had happened. I even opened my mouth to do it. I don't know what held me back. Probably fear. I was a coward, I could admit that. Everything felt so tenuous between us, I didn't want to test it. As much as I wanted answers, I was terrified of losing him.

So what I said instead was, "You know I'm all yours."

"As long as he knows it, too."

Eager to get past this topic, I leaned over the edge of my bed. Water dripped from the curls that had escaped the loose bun on the top of my head. Each crystalline drop caught the sunlight as it fell, a little bit of ordinary beauty to distract me. "He does. But there's something I *don't* know . . ."

Amused, Will asked, "What's that?"

Quoting his Twitter account, I said, "OTP come see me? What's that all about?"

Will laughed. It sounded so good to me. Rich and sweet like honey, soothing me from the inside out. At least, until he followed it up with an answer.

"Omega Theta Pi. I'm rushing."

TWENTY-SIX

The first thing I told Jane was, "Do not laugh at me."

While she arranged her face, I peeled the breading off an onion ring and popped it in my mouth. Most people thought vegetarians were so healthy. Those people had never experienced the deep-fried wonder that was the Garden Fry at our favorite hangout, Planet Veg. Mushrooms, onion rings, french fries, green beans—yes, fried green beans. They were delicious.

Jane reached for the platter. "I'm not laughing at you."

Slumping on the table, I dropped my head. I could barely look her in the eye. I knew she wouldn't laugh. But I also knew that on the inside, she'd be howling. Waving a crispy bean like a baton, I moaned, "Will's joining a frat."

Jane didn't laugh. She choked. Her face turned pink and she beat her chest until she caught her breath. Shaking her head slowly, she took her time. She took a drink. Then, after setting her glass back down, she asked, "Are you really surprised?"

My mouth dropped open. "Yes!"

Mirroring my expression, Jane blinked at me. "Why?!"

"Because he's smart!" I exclaimed. Then I lowered my voice, because the people around us didn't care and I was getting shrill. "Smart guys don't join frats. They're for meatheads and legacies and people who go to college to network the old boys' club instead of getting an education and . . ."

Jane raised one eyebrow by increments, until it disappeared beneath her bangs. "Stop when you get to something that doesn't apply to Will."

Glowering, I said, "Let me repeat. He's smart."

"Okay." Jane reached across the table to take my hand. "Personally, I find the Greek system emblematic of a privileged attempt to inject classism into an inherently classless society—"

I crossed my eyes at her. "Spare me, Margaret Mead."

"More like Karl Marx," she shot back. Then she went on. "But even I don't think you have to be a certifiable idiot to join one. Like you said, they're all about networking. Meeting the people who will get you jobs later in life. Oh, and also? Tons of beer, life off campus, and a party in your backyard twenty-four seven. Will Spencer is exactly that guy."

Bristling, I took my hand back. "He's not."

With a sigh, Jane sat back in her chair. Awash in resignation, it was like she was waiting for me to come to my senses. When I didn't, she spread her hands. "He was a jock all through high school. His mommy and daddy bought him a sports car for his sixteenth birthday. He was on both homecoming court and prom court, and he's going to a school that costs forty thousand dollars a semester."

I narrowed my eyes.

"Oh, and also? He decided to pledge a frat. Case closed. Party animal graduates to frat brat, news at eleven."

Clasping a hand to my forehead, I tried to force back the ache that sprang up at my temple. Those things were true, absolutely. But that's not how I saw Will. I didn't think it was the way Will saw himself, either. Jane was right, though—nobody was making him rush. He was doing it because he wanted to.

"I just . . . There's, like, this innate thing inside me that got nauseated when he told me that. Like, it somehow changed my opinion of him the tiniest bit."

Plucking a mushroom from the tray, Jane nodded. "Sorry, girl, but Will hasn't changed. If you'd said he was joining Greenpeace, or decided to drop out and open a grow-op, then I'd be like, Bessie, take the reins!"

"Then why am I surprised?" I asked plaintively.

It was something I'd been wondering since I got off the phone with Will. My preconceived notions about what it meant to join a fraternity weren't helping at all. But I'd visited a lot of campuses last fall, and Greek row always had two things in common: incredibly ornate mansions that screamed wealth, and a healthy garden full of red Solo cups on the porches. Or the lawns. Or both.

"You're still wearing your rose-colored infatuation glasses," she said.

My feelings for Will were deeper than infatuation. But Jane was right. I'd still been walking around in that glowy state, where everything seems perfect and nothing bad can ever happen. It was a hard crash to reality to realize that I didn't know *everything* about Will. That he could surprise me. Disappoint me. Even hurt me.

Biting the mushroom in half, I let the earthly flavors fill my mouth. Silverware screamed on china; other people's conversations filled my ears like the buzzing of bees. A heaviness filled my chest. Or, I think more accurately, a lightness left me. I wasn't floating two feet off the earth anymore.

Filling the quiet in our conversation, Jane dragged a fry through ketchup and said, "Just promise me that no matter what happens, you won't go running back to Dave."

I was stunned. Getting back together with Dave hadn't ever crossed my mind. Not even a little. But it was like she opened the smallest door when she said it.

One bump in the road with Will didn't mean I'd go running back to my ex. And that's all this was, I decided, a bump. Things would get better. Everything would be fine. I'd see Will soon for homecoming, and we'd reconnect, and all would be well.

"That's not an option," I told her, and I meant it. I really, truly did.

Because I needed some air and to chase the sound of other people's voices out of my head, I went back to the botanical garden.

The remnants of our private movie night there were long gone. But the ghosts of us, together, still lingered.

Sitting on the lawn, I crossed my legs. With my phone tilted to avoid the sun, I shot a message off to Will. I hated how carefully I felt like I had to word things. The last time we were here, it was perfection. I was drunk on freedom and love and the teasing spark of exploration. We played together; it all happened so seamlessly. Now it was all work, lined with doubts. My fingers felt heavy as I finally typed out my message. I wanted the joy back. I wanted it to be easy again.

can we talk for a few?

Though I didn't watch the clock, I felt seconds ticking away. I tried not to think about Grace and her rate of return with Luke. I'd never understand her charts and graphs anyway. It was best if I kept my thoughts about me and Will separate from everybody else. Though some small part of me wondered if that was the problem all along.

The more I reflected, the more I realized I'd never spent time with Will and his friends. I'd never been part of his social circle. That public face, I'd seen from a distance all through school. That's how he managed to sneak up on me at Tricia's party. It wasn't that long ago that I was incredulous to find out there was more to him than pretty, rich, and popular. It seemed like I'd known him for decades, but in reality, it had only been months.

Finally, Will replied. too much to txt?

Swallowing at the knot in my throat, I nodded even though he couldn't see me. Phone call would be better. Face time would be amazing.

Another minute slipped away. Instead of texting back, Will called. His ringtone purred at me. It twisted a sharp finger in my heart. The video we'd taken that clip from, Will was so bright and happy and thrilled to be talking to me. Now, apparently, he didn't have time for video.

"Hey," I said, answering.

"Hey back, what's up?"

Though it was the middle of the day, I heard what sounded like yet another party in the background. It wasn't quite as raucous as the one from Friday night. Still, it was obvious it was warming up. Girls laughed, and guys roared their approval. At what, I had no idea. Rubbing a hand against my chest, I tried to smooth away the ache beneath the bone. "Not much. Missing you, as usual."

"Yeah, me too," Will said, somewhat distracted. "I can't talk too long right now. I just wanted to make sure everything was okay."

It was all falling apart. Just like Grace had said it would. I rolled back on the lawn. Throwing an arm over my eyes, I blocked out the sun and stopped up my tears. "I was wondering about the fraternity thing."

A hum came over the line. I couldn't tell if it was Will or just all the sound around him. "What about it?"

"I didn't know you were going to join one, for one."

"That's not how it works," Will said patiently. "Right now, I'm rushing. It's gonna be a couple of weeks. Spending a lot of time at the house with the brothers, doing mixers, fundraisers, that kind of stuff. I only get to pledge—join—if they bid for me."

The tiniest bit of hope sprung up for me. "So it's not a guarantee? It's like an audition."

Will was walking, because the sound behind him changed. It slipped into the distance, and I heard a door shut. My guess from the echo following his voice was that he'd closed himself in the bathroom.

"Kind of? But I have a good feeling about it. I'm a legacy, and you remember Tyler Stackhouse? Graduated last year? He's a member. He's going to sponsor me."

Swallowing a sigh, I let go of that little hope. "I guess I'm surprised. I didn't really think about you, you know, doing anything like that."

"It's a good organization. They do a lot of charity work. Dad said you can't beat the connections you make in the OTP."

Forcing myself to smile, I said, "Good luck, then. I hope you get in."

"Hey, Sare," Will said. A new, lower note came into his voice. "What's the deal? Are you okay?"

"Like I said," I told him, "just really missing you. I can't wait until homecoming."

Will went quiet. He seemed to be shuffling in place. I heard footsteps scraping across tile. The sound bounced around him at odd angles. It gave everything a sort of distorted feel, like he was trapped under glass. Or I was.

"Will?"

"I don't want you to be mad," he said.

Now it was my turn to stay silent. My panicked thoughts leapt ahead. This was the breakup. This was the part where he told me that long distance just wasn't working for him. That Hailey shredded her guitar way better than I did mine, and she put out on the first date. Or something. Sucking up the one shred of courage I had in me, I said, "Just tell me."

Hemming a bit, Will made a few uncomfortable murmurs. "I don't know for sure yet, Sare. But if they do bid for me, I don't think I can do homecoming. OTP hosts a charity drive every year right after rush."

I couldn't hide it anymore. I wasn't going to cry on him, but I didn't have it in me to pretend that was okay. It wasn't. Sitting up, I drew in a shaky breath, then said, "I'm not happy, Will. I've been holding on to homecoming since you left. Since before you left, actually. When were you going to tell me you're blowing it off?"

Will sighed. "I'm not blowing it off. We can set another date."

"When?"

Silence. Then, "I don't know yet. Sarah, I'm actually in the middle of something right now. Can we please talk about this later?"

"When later?"

Hurt and anger collided inside me. I shook with it. I wanted to beat the ground with my fists and slam doors. I wanted to grab Will by the shoulders and shake him until he came to his senses. How could he throw that out there so casually?

That date we made, the first night we made love, the one that convinced you that it would be right to go all the way . . . I just had that penciled in. Sorry! Rain check?

Tension played across the line. When he spoke, it was slow and deliberate. "There are going to be a lot of events coming up. I'll want you to be my date. There's the Fall Social that the alumni host, for one."

"And that's when?"

"November."

I could barely breathe. Waiting until the end of September had seemed insurmountable. Now he didn't want to see me until November?

"Maybe we should talk later," I said finally. "I have some band stuff I have to take care of."

"Sarah," Will said. "I might have a weekend before that. I just don't know yet. We're still going to Skype and text—that's not going to change."

I didn't bother to point out that it already had.

TWENTY-SEVEN

Walking into Dave's garage again was like going home and going to the moon at the same time.

I recognized my surroundings, but I didn't belong there anymore. I felt like an intruder. I didn't know how to breathe the air. The couch took up the middle space again. There was an extra guitar in the workbench rack. It practically vibrated with Dave's essence. This was no longer *our* space. It was his, exclusively, and I was intruding.

Dread welled in my chest. We had to get through this rehearsal for East River's homecoming.

Dave nodded toward a plate on his workbench. "Mom made cookies."

"Thanks."

Taking one, I bit into it. Savoring salt and sweet, I did my best to make myself at home. The old couch was broken down as ever. I sank into the cushions, in a shape fitted to me exactly. Unpacking my guitar, I stole looks at Dave as he tuned his.

He really had changed his look. Not drastically. It was still him;

he wasn't wearing a costume. But now he wore his clothes with a dark sort of swagger. A little more skin, a more careless roll in his steps. The few good-boy touches, the button-down shirts, the dress shoes, had disappeared entirely. Gleaming with a new sharpness, he was New Dave, sinfully improved.

Because quiet had too much potential, I broke it with a question. "Have you talked to Dany? You don't have to tell me if you don't want to. I'm just curious."

Coming to sit beside me, Dave shook his head. It was a slow, sinuous motion that carried through as he pulled his guitar strap on. His blue-gray eyes met mine, sharp with intent. "I didn't talk to *her*, no."

I swallowed my bite of cookie and wished for milk. A giant glass of water. An escape hatch to open under me. Dave and I had known each other for so long, but I couldn't remember him ever looking at me like this. Like he wanted me and might actually do something about it. It had always been sweet looks, sugar kisses.

He'd always backed off, even though he'd obviously wanted more. What if he'd let himself get swept up—if he'd stopped thinking and let me see this wanton, open desire—would I have wanted him, too?

Before, there had been a puppyishness about it. Like he was keening at the back door, begging to be let in. It was hard to see that and think it was sexy. But now those puppy-dog looks were gone. Now, his gaze was raw and ravenous. It was open and unafraid—he practically dared me not to notice.

Jane's mouthy warning not to run back to Dave played in my head. Sternly, I told myself I wasn't running back to him. We were rehearsing. We were a band. That was it. That didn't explain why my palms were suddenly sweaty. Rubbing them dry on my jeans, I tore my gaze away from his.

"All right, Dean Whittier said they're going to have a deejay for two hours. We're gonna play the hour in the middle so everybody can slow dance."

It wasn't like Dave didn't know that already. We'd signed the contract for homecoming together. The school had given us a list to follow, detailing song content we could and couldn't use and a bunch of constraints for a band that was seriously unlikely to *encourage moshing, slam dancing, crunking, twerking, or other dance or motions deemed dangerous or inappropriate by the administration.* Even as I signed the contract, I wondered if they had any idea what any of those things were.

Settling his guitar in his lap, Dave strummed a chord and let the notes hang between us. "Are we going to sing anything new?"

"I figured we'd stick mostly to covers and maybe throw one or two songs from the EP in, in the middle."

Shrugging, I tried not to notice the way he watched my every move. The way he leaned toward me subtly. Waves of heat radiated from him. Though he sat no closer than he ever had, I was wildly aware of him.

Dave strummed a few chords. Those notes didn't go to anything in particular, but then he segued into an acoustic version of "Teenage Dream." It only took me a bar or two to catch up, and soon I was playing lead and singing.

There was a good chance that the line about getting their hands on me and my skin-tight jeans was going to break the contract. But the melody was lush and pretty, especially when it was slowed down and arranged for acoustic guitar. The administration probably wouldn't notice.

Just as I trailed off the last line, Dave leaned over his guitar.

"About the other night."

Every part of me tensed. I didn't want to talk about the other night. I didn't want to talk about this at all. I wanted to rehearse, and go home, and sit in my music room while trying not to text Will. That's what I wanted. In my chest, my heart twisted painfully. It was like a hand had gripped it suddenly and rolled it in its fist.

"We have a lot of work to do," I started.

"I was out of line."

That wasn't what I expected to hear. Leaning back to consider him, I tried to read his expression. His face was smooth as ever, his brow furrowed artfully. He looked apologetic, and he radiated sincerity.

It was hard to remember that was Dave's default expression. It was the reason we'd played in so many over-twenty-one clubs. He had a face that people wanted to trust. That's why girls weren't afraid to throw themselves in his path; it was like they instinctively knew he'd never hurt them.

I met his gaze. "Yes, you were."

"I won't lie," he said. "I still have feelings for you. But I'm not going to push it."

That felt more like Dave. And because I needed music now more than anything, I nodded. I didn't want to overthink every single thing. Taking his hand, I squeezed it. His fingers turned in mine—rough, where Will's were smooth. Hard-worked, where Will's were refined.

"Thank you. Seriously, thank you."

Slowly, he let his grasp slip from mine. "We should get back to work."

Singing was easy after that. We found each other in the melodies and the harmonies. After a while, we were even laughing again. Every so often, though, I'd catch Dave unguarded. Watching me, my lips, my fingers. The heat he generated, that was new.

In fact, I caught myself thinking, that was really the only thing we'd been missing before. I'd always enjoyed making out with Dave.

But I'd never wanted it to go further than that. With him, just the tips of his fingers slipping against my waist had been more than enough.

Suddenly, there was heat. A spark. I didn't have to act on it. It didn't sound like he wanted to. But it swirled in my thoughts nonetheless. What if I just hadn't been ready yet? What if Dave really had been the perfect boyfriend?

It could have been a terrible mistake to let him go.

Will and I cooled off for a couple of days. We still sent those duty texts, but they were clipped and impersonal and we didn't call once. There were no Skype visits, and we didn't even flirt on Twitter. It felt like Antarctica between us. I ached in the cold; I only hoped that he did, too.

Then, four days after the disaster call, two dozen Gerbera daisies (my favorites) arrived at my doorstep, with a hand-drawn card.

Will wasn't much of an artist, rendering us as stick figures under a rainbow. His dark, slanting handwriting spilled a poetic apology down the page. He wasn't much of a poet either, but that didn't matter. The PS on the card was perfect. It read, "*Because you once told me these were some happy @#(*! flowers. I love you.*"

They came just in time for our next date on Skype. But there wasn't a switch inside me. I couldn't flip from icy cold and frustrated to ready for my first cam sex like that. Not with just a bouquet of flowers and a cute note. They made me feel better, but I didn't know if they made me feel better *enough*. My nerves jangled until dark. I didn't know if I could do it. If I could go through with it.

Reservations aside, I planned to do it anyway. That's how things had always worked with Will—I jumped, and he didn't let me fall. With his roommate out of town for a robotics convention, Will locked himself up with his laptop and with me. I barred my bedroom door and turned the music up so no one would hear.

As soon as his video call came through, I pounded the trackpad a little too hard. I nearly knocked the laptop right off my desk, and I did send a cup full of markers and guitar picks flying. I scrambled after them, so when Will appeared on the screen, I was nowhere to be seen.

"Sarah?" he asked curiously.

Snatching the cup off the floor, I popped back up, blushing. "Sorry, I'm clumsy. And nervous."

Resting his angular chin on the heel of his hand, he studied me. "Why's that?"

"Because," I said. It didn't explain it, but a vague gesture at him, at me, at the whole situation, filled in the rest. Instead of fading, my blush grew. It had been fun and playful to flash him. This was something else. And things hadn't been right for a week. I wasn't ready for this. We weren't in the same place we had been last time. I wanted to back out, more and more.

Will said, "Well. Funny you should say that."

"Why?" I asked, wary.

His tone had taken me by surprise. Picking up his computer, the video blurred a little. When it focused again, I saw his room at a new angle. On his desk, candles burned, and on the floor was a blanket. A picnic basket. With a teasing smile, he sat down on the blanket and patted the spot beside him. "Come. Sit with me."

With a dubious laugh, I shook my head. "What's all that?"

"I thought about it," Will said, opening up the basket. He reached inside and produced grapes. Apples. And it was when he pulled out the random wedge of cartoonish cheese that I realized all the food in that thing was fake. Waving the cheese around, he looked up at me. "And I realized, as hungry as I am, I'd never eat this shit."

Knitting my brows, I still smiled as I allowed, "Okay?"

Will tossed the wedge over his shoulder. It bounced and disappeared beneath Antwon's desk. Wildly proud of himself, Will leaned in. "Which means, as much as I miss getting with you, I'd rather wait for the real thing."

I exhaled. All my anxiety burned away in an instant. It was replaced with relief, and infatuation and adoration. Still more proof that Will wasn't the guy everyone thought he was. In fact, it seemed to me like any other guy in the world would have gone for it. And screen-capped it. And probably shared it with all his friends.

Not Will. And it was proof that he could surprise me—by doing things like rushing a frat, but also by cooking up incredibly romantic schemes. But that I also absolutely knew him, and trusted him. It made it so much easier to love him. Carrying my laptop back to my bed, I stretched out with it. "I love you, you lunatic. I wish I could just lay here with you all night."

Will smiled at me in the dark. "We can do that."

"Can we?"

Holding up a finger to stay me, he disappeared from view. Shifting the computer around, he propped it—on his desk, I think. I heard two quick breaths, no doubt Will blowing out the candles. Then the angle changed, and he moved the screen around until he was centered in the picture, in his bed.

With a lazy arm splayed over his chest, he turned his head to look at me. "There. Let's sleep together."

I rolled onto my side. Curling a pillow against my chest, I gazed at Will, so far away. He was mostly shadows with a few streaks of light outlining him. I probably looked the same to him. All blue and black and hazy. But he was there. With me, the two of us together again.

"Let's not fight anymore," I said.

Reaching toward the screen, his fingers briefly blotted out the picture. It was like he was trying to stroke my face from a distance. "We probably will. Why don't we promise to always make up, instead?"

A sweet sentiment. I reached out for him, too, and nodded. "Okay. If we have to fight, we'll always make up."

Gentle, Will seemed to search my face. All of the tension peeled away, like we'd found each other again. He looked at me and knew me. I knew him again, and I loved him so much when he said, "We're meant to be, Athena."

I kissed my fingertips, then pressed them to the camera. He did the same, and then I settled down in my sheets. "Shhh," I told Will. "Close your eyes."

He did as he was told. At least partially. Lips moving slightly in the dark, he murmured to me anyway. "Sing me a lullaby?"

"You're too old for a lullaby," I replied with a smile.

"Then just sing?"

That simple request moved so much inside me. Tears sprung to my eyes, but I blinked them back. It was from happiness, from my world shifting back into place.

I tried to remember the first song I'd sung for him, but for some reason, the only song that came to mind was "Everything." I hadn't written it for him, but it had come to me the same time he had. They were twined together in my memory: new music, new love.

I skipped the first verse completely and started with the chorus. That was the most important part, the one that told him I belonged to him, that he belonged to me. They were my lyrics, embroidered with his words. They slipped from my lips, pure and alive.

"We don't have to talk. We don't have to do anything. Be anything. Be everything. This could all be a dream, some impossible dream we once had."

Drifting off with a smile, Will murmured, "Love you, Sare."

And though he was sleeping, I hoped he heard it when I said, "I love you, too."

TWENTY-EIGHT

Because Jane could talk anybody into anything, she got Simon Garza to agree to provide some narration on her movie. Our fearless school paper editor, and part-time voice-over genius, Simon was the perfect choice. Since I had the recording equipment, he and Jane both ended up at my house on the next Saturday morning.

The music room felt crowded with three of us in it. Jane had carted over her ridiculously huge monitor. Hooking it up to her computer, she cursed under her breath as she tried to get the two of them to play together nicely. That left Simon and me waiting patiently for the director to get it together.

Crowding close to Jane, I motioned for Simon to come closer. "C'mere, I want to take a picture."

Simon leaned in, and Jane shot the camera a dirty look over her shoulder. In the middle, I made a goofy face and texted it to Will with a quick note: movies are serious business y/y?

"Can I see?" Simon asked, reaching for my phone.

Handing it off to him, I twisted the cap off my root beer and settled back to watch him play with the settings. My legs draped over the arm of the chair, I waved my bottle at the screen. "It's kind of slow if you don't download your pics every once in a while. But I like it."

"I told my parents if they wanted to make sure I never ended up in a ditch somewhere, they should get me one." Simon sighed heavily. "They just laughed at me. I was wounded."

"That's a PAYGO, dude. My mom told me if I wanted a cell phone plan that cost a hundred dollars a month, I could get a job and fund it myself."

Simon pulled up the Twitter app and snorted. "Don't you get paid for the band?"

An explosion of profanity rose up, and Jane looked like she wanted to kick something. Hard. And repeatedly. Just to be on the safe side, I slid out of my chair and climbed into the other one. My shins were tender, like veal. And Jane wore combat boots.

Sitting right behind Simon, I rested my chin on his head as he scrolled through my timeline.

"Usually just a couple hundred bucks if we play a party or something. And we get twenty percent of the gate at the Eden, but only net, and only out of a third of it, because most people are going upstairs to the dance club."

Simon rolled his head back to boggle at me. "Are you trying to make me do algebra?"

"Short version," I told him with a smile, "it's not much."

I flipped the screen to the next page on the phone. "Check it out, DigitalMozart app. I can write music in that on the go. And Buzz-Tune lets me play a piece of music and check to make sure—"

"Ooh, Instagram," Simon interrupted. He didn't want to hear about music software either.

Before I could call him a phone-spy, he sucked in a sharp breath.

The small screen filled with color first, then resolved into photos. The first shot turned out to be Will, stripped to his boxers again. With his arms tied behind his back. And Hailey in his lap. There was whipped cream involved.

My face burned, and it felt like someone had slapped me. Gritting my teeth, I stiffened as Simon scrolled through what looked like a *series* of these pictures. It told a very slow motion story, a flipbook of betrayal. Why Will was tied to a chair in the middle of a party, I didn't know. Why his next-door neighbor straddled his lap with a can of Reddi-wip, I also didn't know.

My stomach churned. Our silence attracted Jane's attention, and she came over to look. She, at least, had words for the situation. "Oh, fuck that noise."

When she reached for my phone, I stayed her hand. "No, I want to see the rest of them."

Now uneasy, Simon glanced back at me. "Are you sure?"

No, I wasn't. But I had to look anyway. These pictures were public, probably linked up from Twitter, too. Each new shot added another lead weight in my belly. It turned out there were girls stripped down to bras and undies also tied to chairs. And then, when they weren't tied down, they were all dancing.

Sweaty, red-faced, drunken dancing. Shades of blonde and brunette streaked through the shots, girls in motion. In one, Will was sandwiched between what appeared to be twins. Or if they weren't twins, they were doppelgängers. Will had his head thrown back, laughing. All three held plastic cups in the air—the universal sign of club or party dancing.

But what angered me the most was that it always came back to Hailey. Hailey with an arm around his waist. Will with an arm around her neck, kissing the top of her head. The two of them standing on a starlit porch, apparently howling at the moon. That one was tagged #hotasswerewolves.

I felt humiliated. I felt furious. I hated them so much.

"I will drive all night to kick his ass," Jane said. She made the executive decision to close the app and toss my phone onto the far couch. But even that wasn't far enough.

Though bile rose into my throat, I forced a smile. "That's Hailey. They're just friends."

Simon and Jane managed to swivel in perfect time. Their faces were identical: completely dumbfounded. And they both looked like they wanted to school me in common sense.

Now, I felt like an idiot. That whole setup with the fake fruit and the basket and everything, just to play me? All that big, blue-eyed sincerity, oh he wanted to wait for the real thing . . . Probably an easy thing to say, since it looked like he didn't have to wait long.

Wriggling out of the chair, Simon slid to his knees in front of it. With imploring eyes, he looked up at me. "Sarah. As a friend, who's a guy, I want you to believe me when I say this."

"It's fine," I protested.

"That boy is cheating on you," Simon continued. With Jane as his hallelujah choir, he refused to listen to my protests. Instead, he put a hand on my knee and tried to make me meet his gaze. "Guys let girls sit on their laps for one reason. It's the same reason they give random, 'friendly' shoulder massages. It's because they want to get some."

It was so hard to hold my emotions in. Not because I thought Simon was wrong. But because I thought he was right. Of *course* Will was cheating on me. He couldn't make it more obvious. Slow callbacks, slow text backs . . . his online accounts full of pictures of other girls—of one other girl in particular.

The one who answered his phone for him and didn't give him messages from me. The one who giggled in the background when I did manage to get a little face time with him. So cute, with her freckles and her guitar, and her easy access, just one door down. Maybe she was the reason Will wasn't up for cam sex. He could have already gotten the real thing, then called me up just to make the date.

I was so, so stupid. And so humiliated.

Patting Simon's face, I looked from him to Jane. "Guys, really. I appreciate the righteous fury, but it's so not necessary."

Simon blinked. "Excuse?"

"He's rushing that frat. They keep posting stupid pictures of their parties. A couple days ago, he had to stand in a corner in a diaper, with a sign that said, *Ask me about my grandma*."

The sheer force of will it took to keep Jane from rolling her eyes at me was visible. I appreciated the restraint, I really did. Her mouth twisting up in a grimace that couldn't quite make it to a smile, she said, "Would he be okay with it, if that was you in that picture and some other guy in your lap?"

It burned like acid to say it, but I managed to get it out. I even managed to sound convincing. "He would. We trust each other."

"Uh . . ." Jane started.

"I'm going to see him this coming weekend," I said suddenly. I didn't know where the words came from, but they tumbled out of me before I could stop them. It was a lie. A filthy, dirty, 100 percent false lie. But it should have been true. Maybe it could be. I could text Will, or call, or e-mail, or send him stupid semaphore messages on Instagram since he just couldn't stay off it, and say, *How about this weekend? Us together for real. I need this.*

Suspicious, Jane narrowed her eyes. "You didn't tell me that."

I slid to my feet. "We talked about it last night. I forgot to mention it."

My friends watched me move through the room like I was a tennis match. I felt cornered and picked apart. It was bad enough that Will was getting whipped cream rides from Hailey, in full, blazing, hipstamatic color.

I couldn't take Simon's pity. And I didn't want Jane's sympathy. She wouldn't even be a big enough bitch to say, "I told you so."

Pointing down the hall, I said, "I'm gonna grab some sodas. You guys thirsty?"

I didn't wait for them to answer.

The way I saw it, I had a choice. I could text Will once and wait for him to get back to me. Or I could text him 1,200 times in four hours and let him think I was crazy. I settled for once every hour, which was more than splitting the difference.

Though I wanted to fling accusations and demand answers, I kept my cool. At least, I kept it cool digitally.

Jane's doc is coming along, think u'd really like it.

Sleeping late?

That was some party on instagram. More rush stuff?

Where are you?

As the hours ticked by, I grew more and more livid. Each text that went unanswered only fueled my anger. He hadn't been too busy to upload an entire night of debauchery from his phone, but he couldn't be bothered to respond to me.

I must have been pacing too loudly, because suddenly Grace appeared at my door. Leaning in, she squinted at me. "Everything okay? Sounds like you're boxing an elephant up here."

With that simple question, she opened my Pandora's box.

Everything I'd kept in. Everything I'd refused to say to Jane and Simon. Perhaps because I knew exactly how Grace would react. I wanted someone to rage with me. I felt so stupid for trusting him.

Sweeping over to her, I pulled up whipped cream and bondage on my phone and thrust it at her. With a defiant tilt to my chin, I splayed my hands on my hips and said, "You win. You were right."

Grace's expression faltered. She might have even paled a little. I guess I'd forgotten that she was the modest sister. The one that had never owned a two-piece bathing suit in her life and didn't like going to the beach because everyone else did. She'd probably just seen more of my boyfriend than she'd seen of hers in the last four years.

Handing the phone back, she looked at me sadly. "I didn't want to be."

"You want to know what's crazy?" I asked her.

"What?"

My voice rasped furiously. "I'm not hurt. I'm pissed. At him, because he said all the right things. From the very first time we kissed, it was like he *knew* me. I did so many things I shouldn't, because I thought we were soul mates or something. But apparently, he just has a deep, sociopathic ability to figure out what a girl wants to hear."

Stepping into my room, Grace frowned. Concern dotted her brow as she held a hand out to me. "Sweetie, what kind of things?"

As angry as I was, there were some things I didn't want to admit. It haunted me that Will and I cheated in order to get together. I felt that with a raw, rising shame now. What he was doing to me right now, I'd done to Dave. He'd done to Tricia.

Sucking in a sharp breath, I shook my head. "It doesn't matter. I knew what I was doing. So shame on me. And shame on me, because you warned me. Oh my God, you warned me, and I bit your head off about it. I'm so sorry."

Grace folded her hands together primly. "I don't hold grudges."

"So what do I do?" I asked her. "You've been here. What happens next?"

Carefully, Grace said, "Well. First you have to talk to him. Confront him, because you won't be able to move on until you know the whole truth."

Bitter laughter bubbled out of me. "That would be so great, except he won't return my calls!"

"Then, you make a good faith effort. Give him a reasonable amount of time to answer. And if he doesn't ... then consider that his answer."

Before Grace could say anything else, my phone rang. Or rather, it purred, "Hey, Athena." Pointing at it, I told her, "That's him," before turning away to answer.

The connection was terrible. Not only did static run the line, loud music blared in the background. The unmistakable sounds of yet another party roared on, and I wondered, how many parties could one person go to in twenty-four hours?

"Will?" I said. Then I raised my voice. "Will, are you there?"

The line broke up. There was a flicker of silence, then Will's voice finally filled my ear. "I can barely hear you!"

Obviously. Why move to a quieter spot to talk to his girlfriend? It was like he oozed contempt for me. Stalking the edge of my rug again, I knotted my hand in my own hair. "What the hell is going on over there, Will? Have you seen your Instagram account lately?"

Bits and spikes of sound came through the line: "... initiation ... Tyler Stackhouse ..."

"I'm not okay with this," I shouted. Then I hunched my shoulders, looking back at Grace. She was kind enough to be mortified for me. Receding into the hall, she disappeared from sight.

"Wanted to talk to you before you saw those," Will said.

A shriek blared through the phone, and I held it away from my head. Between the music and the people, I wasn't sure I was hearing everything Will had to say. Then again, what could he possibly say that would fix any of this? Nothing. I couldn't think of one single thing.

Short, I said, "Then you probably should have called me back last night."

". . . give me the benefit of the doubt . . . just a couple more things I have to do, and things will be back to normal."

I sat on the edge of my bed. "I don't know what normal is for us anymore."

Will said nothing. The quiet stretched out, and though I could make out the crush of the party on the other end, I wasn't sure the connection was good anymore. Or if Will was just ignoring me. Either one seemed so imminently possible that I just sat there. I waited.

"Will?"

Still nothing. So I pressed my thumb across the face of my phone to hang it up. All my emotions drained out, ushering in a quiet, cottony indifference. Numb instead of pain, and I welcomed it. Staring down at my own toes, I didn't look up when Grace reappeared.

"What did he say?" she asked. She had to; all she could eavesdrop on was my side of the conversation.

Flatly, I repeated what little I'd heard. The benefit of the doubt. Things would be back to normal. He wanted to warn me about the pictures. With each non-explanation, Grace murmured her commiseration. Trailing her fingers along the frame of my door, she waited until I finished talking.

"You know what?" she said. "Somebody incredibly wise once told me, 'You'll get through this. Something better is waiting for you.' I didn't believe it at the time. But I do now. I really do, and I believe it for you, too."

I stilled. Maybe she was right. Maybe something better *was* waiting. *Someone.* I thanked her and waited for her to leave. And then I carefully typed out a few words and sent them into the ether. Can I come over?

Then I counted, one-Mississippi, two-Mississippi, and on three, I got my reply.

Absolutely, Dave replied. I'm always here for you.

TWENTY-NINE

At night, Dave kept the garage door half-open. It let in slants from streetlights and the glow of moonlight. The concrete floor flickered when cars drove by. A couple of lamps on the workbench illuminated a small circle, and the rest of the studio space faded into dark. It was quiet—peaceful. I was glad that my spot on the couch fit as perfectly as ever.

"I was surprised you texted," Dave said, offering me a cup of coffee before sitting down. Pulling his right ankle up onto his left knee, he spread out in his corner of the couch. Arm trailing the back of it, his fingers plucked at the old plaid upholstery. "Don't get me wrong, I'm glad you did."

Curling around the heat of my mug, I nodded. "I appreciate it. I know things have been rough for you lately."

"Actually." Dave's brows lifted thoughtfully. "I've been all right. Better than I have been in a long time."

With a sip from my cup, I peered at him. "I'm glad to hear that."

"I've had some time to sort myself out. Clearing out the studio, breaking out of old habits . . . it's been good."

"You look good," I told him.

It wasn't a lie. No matter how many times I noticed his new clothes, the way he stood now, the way he walked into a room with the calm assurance that he commanded it—it all still surprised me. All this time, this next, best version of himself had been waiting to appear. I couldn't help but wonder if it was my fault it had taken him so long to get here.

Thoughtful, Dave said, "You look tired."

Closing my eyes, I nodded. Weeks of staggered schedules had caught up with me. My face showed all those nights that I'd gone to bed after two just to get back up at six. It seemed reasonable. My last year in high school was mostly a formality. It was imperative that Will do well his first year of college. So I was the one who bent, and bent, and now I was in Dave's garage, slightly broken.

"Do you want to talk about it?"

Did I?

Shifting, Dave slid closer to me. Leaning over his knees, he let his hands dangle between them. The faint light flashed off his thumb ring. The silver was duller now than it had been freshman year but richer. Even now, he idly spun it, like it was a totem. I don't know why it mesmerized me all of a sudden. It just caught my eye and I couldn't look away.

Or maybe I was watching his hands. They were so talented on a guitar. Deft and careful with his restoration work. Animated when he talked. Rough and callused from hard work and hard play, they were strangely beautiful. The ring set them off.

With a smile in his voice, Dave teased, "Sarah, didn't you pay attention in physics? Time and space are the same dimension. You're only as far away from something as you want to be."

Raising my head, I looked at him. Really looked at him. There had been a time once, when I'd been afraid to let him touch me. He'd wanted to be so much closer, but I hadn't been ready. I couldn't imagine where those feelings could lead.

Now I could. Without guitars between us, or even a hint of melody, he was so present. So electric and alive. That was the one thing that had been missing all that time. It was so unfair that it took this—breaking up, moving on—for me to feel it.

I could admit, maybe some of it was that moment at the Eden. When he came out of nowhere, hands hot, eyes burning. It wasn't that I wanted him to act like a Neanderthal. But I'd always felt like Dave could take me or leave me.

It was so different now—now that I realized he *could* hold back, but it was driving him a little crazy to do it. And now that I knew what it would be like. I wondered, would his weight feel different on me? What would the roughness of his fingertips feel like, circling the curve of my breasts?

My thoughts twisted, making my breath hitch. When I looked over, I couldn't help but stare at his mouth. Full and teasing—I knew what it felt like when he kissed me. What if he went down on me? Would he try to catch my gaze when he did?

Dave shifted. His hand on my shoulder was theoretically friendly. In practice, it was more. In spite of his warmth, his ring was cold. He traced it in subtle strokes, just along my collar. Still pretending that touch was nothing more than friend to friend, partner to partner, Dave asked, "You all right?"

I wasn't. I was lonely and confused, and it felt so good to be touched again. Sensation drifted down my throat, swirling lazily and weighting my breath. My body reacted now, entirely on its own. Without thought, it *wanted*; it recognized a signal and it longed to send one back. It anticipated the coolness of that ring on the small of my back. On my hip, pressing in. . . .

Thoughts scrambled, I tried to think of something to say. All I managed was a shake of my head.

Slipping his hand beneath my hair, Dave trailed his ringed thumb across the back of my neck. The metal had warmed. It felt almost liquid; almost like a kiss. The fine hairs there stood up; my skin tightened wantonly. Now it was Dave's touch that was cool. Down the curve of my shoulder, back up again. When silver touched the pulse point in my throat, I found my voice.

"What are you doing?"

Dave's fingers twined in my hair, tugging lazily, then slipping free. Each touch came with plausible deniability. Maybe it was innocent. Maybe he was just comforting his friend. It could have been true, until he leaned closer. "Whatever you want."

Plaintive, I looked to him. "I don't know what I want."

I couldn't help but think that Dave would have never taken one compromising picture of himself, let alone a whole album of them. He would never flaunt his infidelity by posting it where everyone could see it. Yes, Dave could flirt all night and all day, but he always came home with *me*.

Almost casually, Dave said, "Maybe we could figure it out."

Suddenly, words flew from my lips. It wasn't planned; I think it was a reflex. Maybe to ask for permission, or find an escape, I wasn't sure. All I know is that I needed an answer. I needed to hear something solid, that couldn't be stroked away with the cool kiss of silver. "Why did you always hold back with me before?"

His hand stilled. It weighted the back of my neck; warmed it. But now everything that moved was in his eyes. "We had something together on stage. I felt it; I know you did, too. And with the guitars and the lights, I could just let go and feel it. That's what kept me going. You weren't ready, but as long as we had that—"

Stunned, I studied his face. "Are you serious?"

"I've never kissed anyone but you, Sarah. I never wanted to."

"I don't know what to say."

"Maybe we talk too much. Maybe we always did."

Dave's voice dropped, and he dropped his pretense. Catching my chin between his thumb and forefinger, he leaned in and turned my face toward him at the same time. The heat thickened around us. Stormy gaze flickering, Dave seemed to take me in. He didn't stop at my lips; his gaze trailed over my body like a caress.

My breath shortened; his raced to match. I knew he could see the rise of my nipples through my thin shirt. I wondered if he could feel the heat the gathered between my thighs. If he could smell me.

Slowly tensing, Dave lingered there as his breath grew ragged. My lonely body yearned to leap up to meet him. I had places that needed to be kissed. Curves that needed strong hands to shape them.

The moment was full of possibility. It bristled with it, bright and sharp. Trailing his thumb against my chin, Dave strayed dangerously close to my mouth. If I moved, just a little, I'd find Dave's lips on mine. I'd find out what all that music passion felt like when he translated it to flesh.

My breath caught.

Dave turned, not toward my lips, but toward my ear. He murmured hoarsely, "I'm not going to give you another chance to get away."

Headlights streaked beneath the garage door, a brief, blinding flash. It stopped the spiral in my head, before I did something I regretted. Before I hurt Dave again, because he deserved so much better than that. As mixed-up and confused as I was, I really didn't want to lead Dave on. He was a good guy—maybe the best guy.

No. Not again. I'd learned my lesson the hard way: cheating solved nothing. I pressed a rough, chaste kiss against his cheek.

And then I fled.

I woke up to a voicemail from Will. There wasn't much to it, just a hello, and a quick sorry about dropping the call. No apology for the pictures; no explanation for his behavior. I deleted it and didn't bother to call back. It wasn't noon yet, he wouldn't have answered anyway.

More confused than ever, I staggered into school late. Late enough to find out that Jane, in all her benevolent wisdom, had decided to get my mind off things by signing us up for the President's Fitness Challenge.

Nothing said *I'm sorry your life is falling apart—let's avoid it* like putting on a gym uniform three years after taking your last required gym credit.

"I know it's sort of second grade," Jane panted as we jogged in slow motion around the stadium's track. "But they let us off early if we do this shiznit, and I wanna go to the movies."

Each step reverberated up my spine. Though cooler autumn weather had slipped in around us, I was soaked in sweat. It formed a humid V down the front and the back of my *Property of East River* T-shirt. My hair, inspired to new heights of frizz, bounced around my head. I felt like one of the cottony dandelions, right before somebody made a wish.

"What do you want to go see?" I asked. My throat burned from breathing too hard.

Waving a hand, Jane said, "You'll love it. It's a silent Romanian film about—"

"Are you kidding me?"

"You didn't even let me finish!"

Rolling my head toward her, I didn't really *need* to say it. The look did all the work for me.

"I hate you," she muttered.

I tugged at the front of my shirt. Fanning it, I tried to get a breeze against my skin. I couldn't remember the last time I'd felt this grimy. Probably at summer camp—the last place I was desperate enough to shower in public.

"I'm not saying don't go." Cutting a look over at Jane, I sighed. "Go without me."

With a regal gesture to indicate our slick, nasty bodies, she said, "I did this for us."

Any other time, I would have just gone along. This time, though, I was running—literally—on two hours of sleep.

After I left Dave's, I'd locked myself in my room with my computer. Going over old texts and old e-mails, reading old @ messages on Twitter. And then, looking at those pictures again. Those pictures. I finally took Benadryl at four o'clock and collapsed from exhaustion.

I shared none of this with Jane. Instead, I begged off for artistic reasons. "I have a couple songs for the movie that I really want to finish up for you. Will you be mad if I skip?"

"Yes," she deadpanned. "I'll hate you forever. You'll be dead to me."

Throwing my arms around her, I rocked her until we both lost our balance. "Thank you, I love you."

"I love you, too," she said, peeling out of my grip. A smile resurfaced when she shoved me. "Now get your stank off me."

⌣

Later, and alone again, I dialed Will's number once more. This time, when it went directly to voicemail, I left a message. Though I tried to sound okay, it was a struggle. I wanted to scream but recognized that screaming would solve nothing. So I measured my tone and weighed each word.

"Things have been rough the last couple days, and we really need to talk. But I just wanted to tell you that I do miss you. I do love you. I believe in us. Please call and tell me you believe in us, too. I just want to hear you say it again."

I hoped I sounded just desperate enough for it to work.

It was well after three in the morning when I finally dozed off. I guess my body had decided there was no call to wait for. Unfortunately, my mind wasn't so convinced. My dreams were strange and fitful.

In one, there was a party at a mansion on the hill, and I had to have a ribbon to get in. I knew Will was there, so I went looking for a ribbon. Everything I touched, though, turned to ash.

Tossing myself out of bed with the sunrise, I checked my e-mail. I had a note from Emmalee about the varsity banquet and a two-for-one coupon at the Daily Grind. Nothing from Will. I checked my phone. No texts. Or tweets.

And this time, no photos in his timeline or updates to the Tumblr. It was like Will had fallen off the face of the earth. I went so far as to pull up the college newspaper. If there had been an accident, if something terrible had happened on campus. . . .

A quick scan told me that nothing had been reported overnight. Interestingly enough, I did find a tiny little article about Omega Theta Pi's rush season. Skimming the article, I discovered that they would be introducing their newest members that night during their annual BONEFEST party.

Recoiling from the screen, I shuddered. *Bonefest.* Seriously? The article came with a small black-and-white photo of the frat house. It was neoclassical, with white columns and a tall porch—and as ever, a few red party cups speckling the railings. A sheet hung from the upper balcony, hand-painted and sagging.

On it, big, bulgy femurs spelled out the Greek letters ΩΘΠ. Though the "bones" were white, they looked suspiciously like penises. It was so shockingly frat-cliché that my stomach tilted queasily. What exactly would be going on at Bonefest? Did Will think that was funny? Was I wrong about him? About everything?

I paced in front of my windows as I cleared the browser and texted Will again. where r u? v worried. plz let me know ur all right.

Autumn had slipped into the neighborhood, seemingly overnight. Our maple trees had shifted toward golden leaves, waving restlessly against a pale blue sky. Touching the window, I noticed that the glass fogged around my fingers. When I pulled my hand away, a ghost of my touch remained in the haze.

Dumping my phone, I rushed through my shower. If he called, I didn't want to miss it.

By the time I emerged, I was marginally cleaner, and Will still hadn't called. Gathering up my plates from the night before, I tucked my phone in my pocket just within reach. Then I headed downstairs with my head still fighting over the possibilities.

Grace must have heard my footsteps on the stairs. She had always been a morning person, much to Ellie's chagrin. It was like it immediately made her less trustworthy because she never needed an alarm clock to pry her out of bed.

"Morning," Grace said, skimming behind me. She poured herself a tiny glass of orange juice and hovered just at my elbow.

Fixing her with a plastic smile, I replied, "Yes, it is."

"Trouble sleeping?" she asked, sympathetically.

"I slept okay. You?"

"Well enough."

Producing my phone, I sent another plaintive note into the void. "Have you heard from Will?"

And with that question, something snapped. Shoving my phone in my pocket, I said, "If Mom asks, tell her I went to the diner, okay?"

Jane and I loved having breakfast at the diner, but as far as I knew, she was basking in her Saturday sleep-in, her head filled with visions of bleak black-and-white Romanian landscapes.

I was heading to the diner to be alone, but if my best friend randomly showed up to have breakfast with me, it would have been a sign that the universe and I were starting to see eye-to-eye.

I wasn't sure what it meant when Dave showed up instead.

THIRTY

I t was like Dave sensed I was uneasy. I had parked myself at one of the back tables. I wasn't all that hungry, but I ordered a plate of fries and a cup of coffee so the waitress wouldn't hate me.

With my non-breakfast cooling in front of me, I distracted myself by reading the archives of the St. P-Windsor Trumpeteer. It wasn't a website that was thick on details or rich with information. Mostly, it seemed like a place to run ads for roommates and to blurb random campus happenings.

The frats and sororities showed up a lot. The pictures blended together after a while: young, bright faces full of smiles that had obviously been corrected by orthodontia. There was never anything less than an ear-to-ear grin, like they picked off the weak ones who occasionally frowned and used their skulls as chalices.

"If looks could kill," Dave said, slipping into the chair across from me, "That phone would be dust right now."

He was the last person I expected to see.

Turning it facedown, I slapped it onto the table. "Where did you come from?"

"I needed a BLT," he said, shaking a white take-out bag. "Why are you sitting here, not eating breakfast?"

It was sick how well he knew me. That he could take one look at my order and know with an absolute certainty that it was just for display. Plastering a hand to my face, I peered at him through my fingers. "I'm hiding from Grace. She's driving me crazy."

With a smile, Dave dropped his bag on the table. "I get that way about Troy. Weird, huh? They go away to college and everything's brilliant. No more older brother lording his existence over you. You take over his room, steal his old books, get used to his chair at the table being empty."

Relaxing a little, I nodded. "Exactly. Then it's Thanksgiving, and you kind of miss them and their stupid face. And you get all moony until they come home . . ."

"Where they promptly remind you why you were glad they left in the first place."

We melted into laughter. It wasn't the funniest thing in the world, but God, it was so nice to feel something familiar. Comforting to connect with someone on common ground. I let my hand trail down, clasping the back of my own neck. My hair was still knotted in messy braids, and it was nice that I wasn't worried whether Dave liked it up or down.

His expression shifting, Dave considered me for a moment. Then he patted the table as he stood. "Why don't you come home with me? I have a whole queue of movies I've been saving for a rainy day."

Trailing my fingers down my shoulder, I nodded toward the window. "Sunny as can be."

"I'll feel bad leaving you here to mope."

Already, I was gathering myself to leave. With mock outrage, I nudged him. "Hey, I was sitting here *ruminating*, thank you very much."

Dave waited for me to head for the door, then fell into step behind me.

"Did you know that literally means to chew your cud?" he said. "That's why cows are called ruminates."

Pushing into the pale, cool morning, I laughed as I pulled my jacket closed. "Most of us forgot our SAT vocab."

"I don't believe in forgetting," Dave said. There seemed to be a special weight to those words, but I didn't examine it. Neither did he. Putting a hand on my back, he looked up the street in search of my car. "I walked here," he said, somewhat suggestively.

"Okay, okay," I told him. "I'll give you a ride. Jeez, quit begging."

Suddenly, everything felt so easy with Dave. We knew each other so well, and not just metaphysically. Three years was plenty of time to get to know somebody. To understand their quirks and their flaws. To care about them in spite of them.

It seemed so petty now, to hold a wrong coffee against him when I hadn't even tried to correct him. And so backward that I'd just been waiting for him to make a move. It hadn't ever occurred to me that I could make mine.

Now we were heading back to his house to "watch movies." On the surface, that's what we meant. I also knew that if I sat too close to him, he'd put his arm around me.

Flashes of Will's bare skin stroked by a parade of sorority girls filled my thoughts. It was like they were imprinted there, carved into the folds of my brain.

Jessa Holbrook

Pulling my phone out, I stopped beside my car and sent a text. One that meant more than the others. One that Will should understand was necessary and vital. As long as he was okay, I thought. But he was almost definitely okay. St. P-Windsor was too small for something tragic to happen without having it splashed all over the school website.

i'm really worried about u + really worried about us. i NEED u to call me

I hit send. And then I waited, five seconds, then ten. I waited so long that Dave sprawled his arms on the roof of the car and drummed it with his fingertips. "Hey, Sare? I didn't wear a jacket ... can we, uh?"

"Yeah, sorry. Just letting my mom know where I'm going."

Unlocking the doors, I climbed behind the wheel and set my phone to vibrate. Starting the car, pulling into the street, we were up to forty-five seconds and counting. My conscience squirmed, remembering a time when I had sat in front of Dave, daring him to sense that I was texting another guy. Daring him to notice that my attention had turned elsewhere, that I was thinking bad thoughts. Now I dared Will to sense the same thing.

A minute. Two minutes. No reply.

Ten minutes.

Forty-five.

Two hours.

No reply.

Most of the time I'd spent at Dave Echols's house had been in the garage.

I'd been inside the house, of course. Bringing cookies to his mom for Mother's Day, or during their annual Fourth of July cookout. But Dave and I had always been focused on our music, which happened in the garage.

His Blu-Ray player lived in his bedroom.

Perfectly Dave, the room was soothingly decorated in hues of green and blue. Neat bookshelves lined one wall, and his desk was immaculate. There was more music equipment packed into corners, and a few special guitars hanging on the wall. There was only one chair, though—a hard, high-backed one for his desk.

We sat on his bed. The whole room smelled of his clean cologne, the bedspread especially so. The mattress was warm and broken down in the middle. Gravity insisted on sliding us next to each other. I felt comfortable here, and I didn't pull away when Dave put his arm around me. Nor did he mind when I leaned my head against his shoulder.

Wildly, intimately aware of him, I stirred through the bowl of popcorn we shared between us. He dipped his hand in after mine. Our fingers tangled together, slick with butter, gritty with salt. They hooked and looped, so familiar and so tentative at the same time.

My pulse pounded ever louder, filling my ears and blotting out the sound effects of the movies. So it was easy to get distracted by Dave's touch. His scent. By the fact that I was surrounded by him in a way that I never had been before. My gaze drifted from the movie, up to the model solar system dangling from his ceiling. All the planets had a haze of dust on them. They'd probably been there for years, just part of the landscape that he'd never changed.

A phantom vibration skimmed my thigh. Subtly, I pulled my phone out, but the screen remained blank. It was an imaginary sensation, one that pricked at me as I replaced the phone and settled against Dave again. Warm in the curve of his arm, I wondered if this was just the person I was. Not very good at being faithful, not very good at being alone.

Dave shifted, pulling me subtly closer. Our hips pressed together, and his fingers chased mine lazily. Slipping and looping, his thumb grazed my palm. My nerves stung, mixed between dread and anticipation.

If something happened, if something was happening, it wasn't an accident. I had no defense. I had nothing except a phone full of unanswered texts and photographic proof that my boyfriend had let other girls touch a lot more than his hand in the last week.

Where was he?

As Dave rolled the warm edge of his ring against the inside of my wrist, I couldn't stop wondering. Where the hell was Will? Why wasn't he answering? Was he hurt or was he cheating? It wouldn't be the first time for him—it wouldn't be the first time for me, either.

Just then, Dave turned toward me. There was no pretending anymore. He wasn't watching the movie and neither was I. If I faced him, the only thing between us would be a breath. We would kiss.

Adrenaline pumping, I pulled away from him.

"God, you should please just hate me," I told him. "I'm sorry. I can't do this."

His stunned expression said it all. But I couldn't care if this made me look fickle or confusing or terrible. In fact, I knew it made me look terrible. But I had to avoid making another huge mistake.

I had to see Will. To fix it, or to break up with him—it didn't matter. No more pretending that things *just* happened. They didn't; I hadn't tripped and fallen into Will's arms that first night. And I hadn't innocently followed Dave home today.

They were choices. My choices.

It was time to make one.

THIRTY-ONE

The nice thing about a highway like I-70 is that it was a straight line that stretched out to either horizon.

I couldn't make a wrong turn, I couldn't get lost. The pastureland that framed the road was stubbled now. Endlessly flat, with no trees or flowers, blooms or blossoms to take my mind off the black ribbon of road. With nothing to look at but yellow stripes and the setting sun, my thoughts rose in orderly floods. Tonight, I would find out once and for all what was happening with Will. With the two of us.

The road was so flat, but my emotions coasted and crested at alarming intervals. Thinking about those Instagram pictures sent me into a blind rage. But realizing that it might all be over soon sent me to tears. Cycling through fear and certainty, despair and anxiety, I kept coming back to those pictures.

To Hailey, always in the background, since his very first day at St. P-Windsor. I felt like I knew her face as well as my own by this point. I couldn't even hate her, because I knew how Will Spencer worked. If it wasn't an unexpected kiss in a theater catwalk, it was a seduction by firelight as boats bumped softly in the distance.

What had seemed so thrilling in the moment now showed its flaws. What if I hadn't been the one to walk down to the water that night? The boathouse was a popular destination. Emmalee and Simon proved that readily. If not me, then who? Who would have sat down in that blanketed boat and reached for Will's root beer? Did it even matter? Had *I* even mattered?

Tricia's sad assessment played on repeat in my thoughts. *I think he just hates to be alone.* She knew him longer and better than I ever had. Maybe I should have pressed more. I should have dug into his past instead of immediately fantasizing about a future.

Fumbling blindly, I dialed Will. This time, instead of ringing, it went straight to voicemail. He'd turned his phone off. Turned me off, and shut me out. Tonight was his disgusting party. A kegger to celebrate nothing but getting laid. His big celebration at his brand-new fraternity. I felt wild with anger. I felt sick.

If he was sleeping with somebody else, wouldn't she be there? Wouldn't she be the co-star in the next set of Instagram humiliations he uploaded for all the world to see?

Putting my foot on the gas, I flipped my turn signal and passed the vintage VW Bug that had straddled the right-hand lane for the last four miles.

I called Will again, one more time before I pulled into his college and walked into his frat house to demand some answers. All he had to do was call me back. All he had to do was answer. But no. It went directly to voicemail again.

"I don't know when you're going to get this," I told him. I narrowed my eyes when I passed a blue information sign, St. Philip-Windsor College, twenty-three miles. "But for your sake, I hope you get it in the next half an hour. I'm coming to see you. I'm almost there, and I want answers. If nothing else, you owe me an explanation. I'm not going to let you wish me away."

With that, I hung up and merged back into the right lane. God, I sounded crazy. As soon as I hung up, I realized it. If Will was that guy, if I had been wrong about everything . . . what was I going to do about it?

The craziest thing of all was, I still wanted him. I wanted all of this to be a misunderstanding. Drifting into a trance with the hum of the road, my thoughts turned over once again. The things that had happened with Will had happened for a reason.

Tears welled again. My skin buzzed, the same tone as the road—my body, my heart, believed in him. Even as my thoughts shattered, scattering in all directions, my heart remained steady. And it felt so very much like I was losing him that I spiraled down once more.

As dark settled over the countryside, I sped toward the college. Toward Will. To a whole different kind of destiny. I had no idea what to expect when I arrived. All I knew is that it would be both terrible and spectacular.

I didn't want to park down a dark side street, but I had no choice. Cars lined Greek Row, headlight to taillight. Girls without jackets ran across the street in packs, blending into clouds of polo-shirted, shorts-wearing guys. Lights spilled from open windows and open doors. The air bore a trace of acrid pot smoke, blended in with the pervasive scent of cheap beer.

The streets weren't well lit, but I wasn't afraid. There were too many people milling the sidewalks, darting in and out of the houses. The night was alive, and people were friendly. I must have said hi a hundred times before I walked a whole block.

It seemed to be a big night for everybody in a frat. Sheets and signs hung from a lot of the mansions. As I ducked my head and hiked toward OTP, I passed one sign that artlessly pleaded for passersby to *Save the Boobies.* Of course, both the *o*s had dots right in the middle. They couldn't risk somebody missing the subtle point they were making or something.

Next door to that, *Do It for a Dollar.* That one featured a pole-dancer in silhouette, copied straight off a tacky trucker mud flap. I quit reading them when I stalked past *Sporting Wood.* I didn't know if it made me feel better or worse that Bonefest was practically literary compared with the competition.

When I finally saw the OTP house at the top of the hill, my knees jelled a little. I had just driven four hours to get here, and now I was afraid to go inside. Shadows moved past the windows, bodies dancing and twisting with abandon.

Heavy, bass-driven music pumped into the night. On the front lawn, a handful of guys stood around, watching in awe as a couple of girls cartwheeled in front of them. Even I was impressed by the blonde who managed to do a one-handed back handspring without spilling her beer.

As I passed them, I nodded and tried not to feel wildly out of place and hideously overdressed. My tunic and leggings looked like a burqa next to all the betty shorts and skimpy halter dresses. It was like they couldn't tell their breath frosted the air. Maybe they had so much liquor in them, they actually *couldn't.*

Hurrying past them, I jogged up the front steps.

"Hey, hold on."

A guy guarding the door held out a hand, stopping me in place. His gaze dropped down, and at first, I thought he was looking at my chest. Then I realized he was studying my wrists. My wrists? Uncomfortably, I crossed my arms over my chest. I wasn't sure what the deal was, though glancing around, I suddenly noticed what I hadn't before—people wearing orange paper bracelets.

"You gotta go see Nurse Kayla if you want a drink badge," the guy told me finally. Though his job seemed to be greeting people and relaying this information, his voice slurred. Slumping against the doorframe, he craned to look over his shoulder, into the house. "Think she's in the kitchen."

"Thanks, I will," I said. "Hey, have you seen Will?"

The guy slowly leaned his head back. He looked like I'd asked him to figure a couple of equations. With another look over his shoulder, he finally shook his head. "I know he's in there. Try in there."

A train of brunettes streamed out of the house, fingers linked, voices high. Bumping past me, they chirped a string of apologies before disappearing into the dark. Their laughter and their perfume sweetened the air, leaving an impression of them behind.

There were so many girls here; they were all so gorgeous. I felt like a plain brown bird as I pushed my way into the party. Hands held cups above the fray, people danced in rooms packed so tight, it was hard to make out individuals. Every time I saw a guy with dark hair, my pulse stopped.

I figured my best bet was to make a circuit through the house. No matter where I went, people crushed into me. It wasn't deliberate or malicious. There were just too many partiers and too little space to contain them. Jostled and bumped, I barked out a startled cry when someone splashed their drink on me. It was sticky sweet and fruity; it clung to my skin even as their apology slid right off.

I tried to wind my way toward the edge of the room. If I could stay close to the wall, I'd have a better view. Except I didn't. It was just a crush of humanity, all pounding away to electronic drum lines and digital sirens. Catching a guy in an OTP hat, I leaned in close to be heard. "I'm looking for Will. Will Spencer, have you seen him?"

Turning his hat around, the guy hopped in place, scanning the crowd. Then he shrugged and pointed me the way I just came. "Think he's in there!"

Since I knew he wasn't, I thanked Hat Guy and kept pushing my way through. As I crossed a threshold into a room full of framed member pictures, I stopped dead. Standing at the other end of the room, talking with her hands, was Hailey. She hadn't seen me—and I didn't want her to. Sick to my stomach, I slumped against the wall.

She was prettier in person. Always in pictures, she'd been cute. Cute with her freckles and her sometimes pigtails, a kind of adorable that was only threatening because it was so unpracticed. Seeing her in the flesh made my heart drop. Her hands moved like a dancer's as she talked. Her body undulated with it, round hips rolling with subtle motion.

It was like she had her own field of gravity. I watched two different people abruptly stop to talk to her, even though it was obvious they'd been headed elsewhere just a moment before. Even *I* wanted to get closer to her, and that terrified me.

There I was, sick with jealousy, and I still just wanted to be near her. How could Will have ever resisted that?

I couldn't walk past her, so I turned around. Trying to pick my way through the room I just left, I caught my breath. Beneath a swinging chandelier, Will dipped a girl back and kissed her throat. My heart stopped, and I actually caught myself on a stocky guy who was unfortunately standing too close to me.

He didn't seem to mind. In fact, he patted my hand and leaned in. "You okay?"

"Sorry, I lost my balance," I said.

That was an understatement. It was like I'd stepped into quicksand. Sinking fast, and no way out. Tears sprung to my eyes. When Grace had talked about Luke cheating on her, I had sympathized. But I had never really empathized. Now I felt the crushing blow, a sledgehammer to the chest.

Everything broke at once. A crippling nausea swept through me. Somehow, I'd been prepared for him to be cheating on me with Hailey. Who was *this* girl? How many girls had he slept with since he got here?

Just then, Will surfaced and the girl gave him a playful shove. When he turned, I realized—it wasn't Will at all. What was even more disorienting was that I did recognize him. It was Tyler Stackhouse, a guy from East River. Will's sponsor or whatever. I didn't remember them looking so much alike.

Relief loosened my limbs. I felt so clumsy and uncoordinated as I swam through bodies to get to Tyler. Clapping a hand on his shoulder to catch his attention, I smiled when he turned around. Recognition lit his face—that's how small East River was, apparently. The beautiful people recognized the art geeks, even though we ran in none of the same circles.

"Sarah! What the hell are you doing here?"

He sounded *delighted*. And more than a little bit drunk.

All of a sudden, I was engulfed in heat and sweat and a waft of unfamiliar cologne. It took a second to realize that Tyler had thrown his arms around me and picked me up. Hysterically, I wished for Jane to appear.

Because I was insane, I smiled up at him. "Looking for Will, actually. Have you seen him?"

Tyler thought about it, then clapped a hand on my back. "Totally. Right this way."

The girl Tyler had just been kissing looked so confused. Her lips parted, and I swear, she issued a sound that could best be described as *meep*. Turning back, Tyler winked at her. "I'll be back for *you* in a minute."

I don't know what magic Tyler had. When he walked through

each room, the crowd parted. He was the Moses of OTP, apparently. We passed through a carpeted hallway, then walked right into a wall of sound. The music was so loud here that I felt it on my skin. It buzzed and pulsed.

Rave lights flashed patterns on the wall. It was darker in here; beer and sweat and the raw possibility of sex hung in the air. As my eyes adjusted to the light, Tyler pointed me in the right direction. There, in the middle of the dance floor, was Will. Plastered between two blondes, he danced with his eyes closed, and with a cup in each hand.

My stupid heart leapt up, so happy to see him for the first time since August. And then it plummeted, because he was letting those girls grind against him. No matter how oblivious his expression, his body wasn't acting on its own.

"Thanks," I told Tyler.

"Get a wristband," he replied cheerfully. "Join the party!

Melting back into the crowd, Tyler went back in search of his meeping blonde. I had no intention of joining the party. My slow burning fury from the drive up here was building. My skin felt too tight to contain it. I had had enough. Squaring my shoulders, I shoved my way through protesting dancers to get to Will.

When I reached him, I grabbed his arm and pulled it to get his attention. His eyes snapped open. One of the party lights swung around, streaking white through the icy blue field of his gaze. Was it shock? Was it fear?

For the first time, I couldn't read the emotion in his eyes. And just in case he was having the same problem, I threw my arms out and raised my voice so he could hear me over the crowd.

"What the hell is wrong with you, Will?!"

THIRTY-TWO

The explosion that had been building inside me went off. I didn't care that we were surrounded by people. Let them listen! Let them hear it all. After all the excuses I'd made for Will, I was done. I was done pretending I was okay with any of this. No more sitting there, silently, hoping everything bad would magically improve.

"Is this why you're not answering your phone?" I demanded. My hands flew wildly, gesticulating at *everything* around us. The partying, the house, the brand-new friends and conquests that demanded all of his time at all hours of the day. "This is all just so important that you figured, what the hell, Sarah can wait. Screw Sarah!"

Embarrassed, Will crowded closer to me. Taking my arm, he lowered his voice instead of raising it. "Can we ta—"

"We can talk right here!" I laughed at him incredulously. "I mean, you do everything in front of these people, right? You get naked in front of them. You let them take pictures of you getting lap dances. I mean, if they're close enough to watch you screw around on me, aren't they close enough for this?!"

Hardening, Will cut a glance to the left and the right. His pale face had already been flushed from dancing. Now splotches of scarlet filled in between the pink. Even the tips of his ears were blushing. I was viciously glad about it, too. My mouth just kept going, every thought in my head spilling out.

"Are you embarrassed? Oh my God, I'm so sorry. I wouldn't know about that—oh wait, except I do. Because you keep posting to Instagram, hi, this is me letting Sorority Sasha lick whipped cream off my chest! Oh, tee hee, never mind the completely obvious boner I have—I always get that way when a girl ties me up in public!"

The music didn't soften. The crowd didn't stop with their partying, but the people close to us began to shrink away. Ringed by dead space, I knew we were a spectacle now. I just didn't care.

Will did, though. Trying to gently guide me away, he looked flustered when I refused to let him pull me off the dance floor. Now he clenched his teeth, a muscle flickering in his jaw and a darkness crossing his eyes. "Keep your voice down."

He couldn't have chosen a worse thing to say at that moment. "Why?! You have no problem broadcasting your dirty little frat-boy escapades all over the Internet for the world to see. Why should I?! In fact, let me get my phone. We should upload this moment to Instagram."

Scrabbling for my phone, I felt crazed. "You pick the tag, what should it be? Hashtag stupidgirl? Hashtag thoughtilovedher?"

Will closed a hand over my phone. For a moment, it looked like he might drag me out of the party—by my wrist, by my hair, didn't matter. Instead, he peeled the phone out of my hand and jerked his head toward the stairs. "I'll give this back upstairs."

Then he turned his back on me and stalked away. Stunned, I stood in place for a second. My balance was gone entirely. My rage wasn't spent, but somehow, Will had taken the control from me. Without raising his voice, or even defending himself. He just stopped it dead, as if he were the only one who decided the course of our fate.

Infuriated, I started after him. As I cut through the crowd, a girl laughed as I passed her. It wasn't mocking; it was admiring. When I whipped my head to look at her, she threw me a thumbs-up.

"Make him pay, honey," she said. "You can do better."

That's when reality crashed in around me. My anger popped like a bubble. It wasn't that I didn't have the right to be furious. But with that chipper bit of encouragement from a stranger, I suddenly saw myself from the outside. To someone who knew nothing about me, I was the raging, crazy, psycho-hose-beast girlfriend.

I'd heard plenty of stories about her before. She got drunk at parties and called her ex a hundred times in a single night. She bashed out headlights and keyed her initials into car doors. She set fire to comic book collections and threw her ex's stuff into the street to be run over by Mack trucks.

Blood pounding in my ears, I grabbed the rails and hauled myself up the stairs, two at a time. The crowd was thinner up here, people actually having conversations in the hall. Waiting for the bathroom, generally escaping the bacchanal below. At the end of the hall, beneath a big oil painting of an old man in a suit, Will stood silently with his arms crossed and his jaw jutted.

Every inch of him radiated anger. Almost wary to approach him, I made myself walk in his direction. If nothing else, I needed to retrieve my phone so I could slink home, humiliated and shamed. The closer I got, the tighter the knot in my throat. It threatened to cut off my air entirely. When I was a few steps away from him, Will pointedly turned and walked into one of the rooms.

He stood at the door when I got there. Silently, he waited for me to walk inside. Then he slammed the door and turned to me. He had every right to yell. Somehow, it seemed much more frightening that he didn't. Hard eyes and hard voice, he cut through the air to return my phone.

"Now it's my turn," he said coldly. "What the hell are you doing here?"

Clinging to the phone like a totem, I said, "Catching you."

"Catching me what?" Eyes bugging out, Will took a few steps back. "Partying? It's Friday night, so what if I'm partying?"

I had to gather my wits. Screaming hadn't helped. It wouldn't help. And if this was the end, I wanted it to be clean. I wanted to do it right. I wanted to salvage something from this.

"I've been calling you for days," I said. I hated that my voice cracked; I sounded so weak. "Texting you. Tweeting. E-mailing. Will, you disappeared on me. And you did it right after . . . right after this."

It was sadly way too easy to pull up the pictures that had haunted me. Holding the phone out to him, I scrolled through his Instagram feed pointedly. Picture after picture.

"So what was I supposed to think?"

Still angry, Will brushed the phone out of his face. "That I was rushing OTP. Or are you missing the twelve other guys in those pictures doing the same thing?"

"Dancing with two girls at the same time? Like you were five minutes ago? That's what everybody's doing? Letting people post footage of you with Hailey in your lap? Letting her answer your phone? I mean, where were you? Why is it that every time I *did* get to talk to you, Hailey was in the background? Just tell me the truth, Will."

Will looked away. "The truth, huh?"

This was it. I steeled myself for it. I already knew from my reaction to the not-kiss downstairs that it was going to obliterate me. But I needed it.

"Hailey," Will said, turning his eyes back on me, "is dating Nate Beresford. The president of Omega Theta Pi. She introduced me to him; he's the one who convinced me to rush. I'm sorry I haven't been around as much as I've wanted to. They took my phone. They took my computer. I spent the last four days cleaning the toilets around here with a toothbrush."

Leaning back against the door, I slowly deflated. Will didn't sound defensive. He sounded tired. And beneath that, hurt. It was glaringly obvious to both of us that the trust we thought we had between us wasn't nearly as strong as we thought. Sliding my phone into my pocket, I said, "You blew me off for them. You haven't even tried to reschedule our visit."

"I have midterms coming up," he said flatly. "I wanted to make sure I had the whole weekend free for you."

"You have plenty of time for a club that thinks Bonefest is a good theme for a party."

Will glanced at my wrist. Then up to my face. "There's a nurse in the parlor trading drink badges for a blood stick. We're registering people for a bone marrow drive. You know, to match up for people who need transplants?"

Was that the truth? It seemed to be. "That's . . . I mean, that's a good thing."

"Did you not see the signs all up and down the street? Houses are collecting for breast cancer research, for the Audubon Society—it's service week, Sarah."

"Then why does it look so . . . so . . ."

"Sleazy?" Will asked. Then, he replied with a shrug. "I'm not going to apologize for wanting to hang out with these guys. I'm not going to apologize for whatever fraternity issues you have, I'm not. I don't ask you to apologize for hanging out with sanctimonious vegans."

"That's so unfair."

Spreading his arms to encompass the whole night, he said, "And this wasn't?"

For once, the moment I took before replying was to think. I could rail against him, throw myself at him, beat on his chest. Or I could be mature enough to just let it go. Possibly let us go. It felt like my heart was split in two. Like the rest of me wanted to follow suit. But I forced myself to stay calm.

"I'm sorry I made a scene," I said. "I'm sorry about that, Will. But I won't apologize for the rest. Fine, they took your phone. It's not your fault you can't get in touch with me. Okay, I believe you that Hailey is just a friend. But they didn't make you post those pictures online. They didn't force you to dance with girls in lingerie."

Frustrated, Will pulled at his own hair. "It didn't mean anything, Sarah."

"It was disrespectful to me. To our relationship . . ."

"They're just party pictures," he snapped.

Rising up, I asked, "Okay, would you be okay with me taking pictures like that with somebody else?"

Will hesitated. "I'm not playing theoretical games with you."

I had to tell him. I had to make the point. It felt like there was the slimmest chance that we might be okay, but I knew that would only be true if we were honest with each other. I wanted him back, but only the right way. No more wondering. No more waiting, hoping, no more telepathy, because that obviously didn't work. I loved Will; I wanted him. But only if we started communicating with each other like we'd sworn we were going to. Approaching him, I held out a hand, "Okay, then not theoretically, what if Dave told me he wasn't ready to give up on me?"

The weight of the air changed in a second. It was suddenly clear and cold, and Will stiffened. "I'm sorry, what?"

"What if he invited me to his place to watch movies? What if he reached for my hand, and I wasn't sure I wanted to pull away. Why would I? The last time I'd seen my boyfriend, he was on the Internet in his underwear, with a couple of incredibly beautiful sorority girls twerking all up on him."

Anger bubbled up in Will's voice. "Are you kidding me? I'll kick that guy's ass."

I shook my head. "No. No you won't. You're going to stand here and look at me. And you're going to tell me you're okay with all that. Because you think I should be okay with proof that you've done so much more."

It was Will's turn to deflate. A look of embarrassment crossed his fine features. A quiet sense of victory filled me. I'd knocked him just enough out of his own head to take a look at where we both were right now. It wasn't a pretty place, or a happy one. And he finally got it. Felt it and cringed away from it; tasted the same bitter acid I'd been tasting for weeks. Finally. I was so relieved.

The music boomed away beneath our feet, filling the quiet with a sort of pulse. It stretched on and on, but it felt like it was pushing us closer. Insisting that if we couldn't fill the silence, we should close the space between us.

He stepped first. I followed, smoothing a hand against his chest. Staring at my own fingertips, I murmured to him. "I love you so much, Will. It's scary to be that vulnerable. I know you feel that, too. I know I can't expect you to hole yourself up in your dorm room and never come out.

"But you still have to think about me. Think about the things you're doing, think about how they make me feel. It was bad enough that you were letting those girls touch you. But my God, Will. All my friends saw those pictures of you. They've been walking around for weeks, thinking I'm an idiot for putting up with it."

Leaning in, Will pressed his brow to mine. Instead of gazing into my eyes, he closed his. He covered my hand with his and took a long, slow breath. Then, he finally said, "I'm sorry. I wasn't trying to hurt you."

Tears rose up again, hot and fast. This time, they were made of relief instead of heartbreak. It was a good apology. This felt so much closer to right. Voice quavering a little, I said, "I know you weren't."

With finality, Will continued. "I want to be with you. Only you. Is that what you want?"

Swallowing hard, I nodded.

"I tried to be cool about it before," he said. "Not anymore. You can pick the band, or you can pick me. And if it's not me, then . . . I'll fucking suffer, but I'll be happy for you. I will. But you're keeping that guy on base, Sare. You left a door open, and he walked right in."

He was right. That's exactly what I had done. It was humbling to realize that I had been selfish enough to take advantage of that. Both letting Will tolerate it and running to Dave when things with Will got too complicated.

It terrified me to say goodbye to Dave. To give up Dasa. But I had been holding on to both of them for the wrong reasons, maybe even long before I fell into Will's arms in the boathouse. In the twilight recesses of my own thoughts, I had to admit that all I was doing by keeping the band together was holding us both back.

Smoothing my hand down Will's chest, then slowly wrapping my arms around his waist, I pressed into him. I rose up onto my toes and turned my face against his neck. Breathing him in, I sighed. His spice filled my senses. The patchy, painful numb slipped away now that we were touching again.

His pulse raced, and I kissed the warm skin on top of it. Once, then again, as I swore to him, "The band's done."

Hands slipping over my waist, Will took a step back. He pulled me with him, nosing against my temple, my cheek. Nudging me to turn my face up to his. When I did, he brushed his lips against mine. But instead of feeding me a kiss, he murmured into my mouth instead. "I promise I'll think about you. First. Always."

That promise melted into me. It spread through my veins, sweet as any drug. And when he kissed me, I forgot that I had driven four hours in a blood haze to get to him. That I hadn't washed my hair; that I probably looked like the rabid lunatic that had possessed me for the last couple of weeks.

Because when he kissed me, I woke up. Our rhythms blended together again; I looked in his eyes and I realized everything would be okay. This is what I wanted, and I had it on *my* terms. I knew now that I was strong enough to walk away if I had to. That I could stand up for myself and expect more. Better. I really was here in his arms because I wanted to be. Not because I needed to be, or was afraid to be somewhere else. I had the strength to trust him—and myself—enough to give it a chance to be exactly right.

Swaying to music that was ours alone, we moved through the shadowy room together. Will marked me, his kisses hot brands down my throat, his hands tattooing possessive strokes along the length of my back.

Raising my hands to unbutton his shirt, my fingers trembled. I bared his skin, wracked with hunger and with need. The fabric smoothed over his shoulders, reminding me how beautiful he was. Carved and sculpted, so finely made it took my breath away. But not so much that I couldn't whisper to him, "If we fight ..."

"I promise we'll always make up," he replied.

Then he took me back to his room and proved it.

THIRTY-THREE

I woke up next to Will again, and it was a new day. Not just because night was over and the sun was rising across the campus. Things felt different; they felt better. I sat at the window, finger-combing my tangled hair and watching St. P-Windsor come alive.

Some students had weekend classes. I could make them out by their jackets and backpacks. They hurried as they walked, straight lines like ants along the pavement. Others were making their way home after all-nighters. Their clothes were wrinkled. They shivered in the cool morning light and buzzed aimlessly in this direction or that.

This was Will's world now. When he woke up, the sun didn't come through his window—that's what he saw when it set. Brick and ivy and cobblestone in places, a street full of sprawling mansions that pretended, on the outside at least, to be Greek temples. On the inside, they were worn, the furniture was well used, and none of the dishes matched.

"I'll fix you some breakfast," Will said.

He emerged from the bathroom freshly shaved, his hair askew. It looked like he'd tried to wet it, smooth it. All that had done was send certain defiant strands of it sticking straight up. Comfortable in thinning sweatpants and his St. P-Windsor pullover, he tugged me into his arms for a kiss.

Lingering on my lips, his hands roamed my back, perhaps memorizing my shape again. I did the same, because I wanted to soak him up. When I drove home, I wanted to smell him on my clothes. I wanted to remember every inch of him, the way he looked in the morning: sleepy, handsome, mine.

"C'mon," he said again, nudging me toward the door. "We'll see who's awake. I'll introduce you to everybody."

And he did. We found the frat's president, Nate Beresford, and Hailey-the-girl-with-the-guitar already in the kitchen. When Will and I came in, Hailey flung herself off Nate's lap and right at me.

Her voice was smoky, kind of coffeehouse sexy. So when she exclaimed that she was so glad to finally meet me, I was both flattered and a little turned on. She smelled like apple shampoo, and her eyes were a shocking green up close. When she let go of me, she punched Will in the arm, hard.

"I heard what you did, dumbass," she said. "Stop being a dumbass."

With that, she murdered my jealousy. They had anti-chemistry, a brother and sister vibe that practically poured off them. Then she rolled those green eyes at him and went back to sitting in Nate's lap.

Embarrassed, Will slipped an arm around my waist. "Nate, this is my girlfriend, Sarah."

"I figured." He smirked over Hailey's shoulder.

"I'm gonna show her around," Will said, leading me away. The house was still littered from the party. The pervasive scent of beer and sweat permeated the walls. In the hallway, Will stopped to introduce me to the guy who had played bouncer the night before.

Waving a finger at me slowly, he said, "Hey, you were looking for Will, right?"

"I was," I said, trying not to smile. Apparently he hadn't been drunk last night. That's just the way he talked.

With a nod, he shook my hand. "Hope you found him, man."

Will and I escaped to the next room before we started to laugh.

Hand-in-hand, Will and I walked the campus. Though I'd taken so many virtual tours with him, it was different in person. The trees were taller; all the colors were richer.

In the distance was a bell tower I'd never seen before. At the turn of the hour, it played a rising scale. Then, suddenly, it lapsed into a few bars from the Harry Potter theme. Bursting into laughter, I looked at Will in surprise. "Does it do that every time?"

Grinning himself, Will shook his head. "Not every time. Sometimes it's just chimes or hymns. Last week, they played "The Imperial March" from Star Wars, though."

My heart soared. Until that moment, Will had been away at some imaginary place. A world completely separate from me. Now we'd shared one small thing that could have only happened in person, and it all became real. More certain now than ever, I squeezed Will's hand and pulled him down for a kiss.

"We're going to do better," I murmured to him, dizzy as he pulled away slowly.

He promised, "A lot better."

Falling into step with him again, I leaned my head against his shoulder as we started across the campus green. The gothic buildings that framed the quad glowed pinkish in the light. Their edges looked regal instead of threatening.

Soaring above the spires, a clean, blue sky stretched out in every direction. It was endless and perfect, and so full of possibility.

"I was thinking," Will said, glancing at me. "Maybe I could come home next weekend. It's not that far. I could make it at least once a month. If you want me to."

Because we'd made a vow to communicate better, I didn't pretend it wasn't necessary. I wouldn't fall back into old habits; I needed to see him more, and I wasn't going to pretend I didn't. Instead, I wrapped my arm around his and beamed up at him. "That would be amazing. I'm going to try to line up some solo shows. Let me know when you're going to be in town, so I can schedule around that."

Incredulous, Will drew his head back. "Are you nuts?"

"Um . . ." Confused, I smiled crookedly. "I guess?"

With a snort, Will tugged me into motion again. "Don't schedule around me. Maybe I want to see my hot-ass girlfriend owning the clubs. Did you ever think of that?"

"I hadn't."

"Well, you should." He arched a brow at me.

A blush stole to my cheeks. That floating-away infatuation came back, but this time, I didn't drift so high. Reality kept me closer to the ground, and reality would get us through our time apart. It was good to be with Will again, and *really* with him. We were together, and it was going to take some work. But it was worth it, every time he flashed that wicked smile my way.

"You know what the best part of that will be, Will?"

"What's that?"

"Going home afterward with my favorite groupie," I told him.

Then I jumped into his arms and sealed that joke with a kiss.

THE END

EPILOGUE

The Debut Stage at Furnace Hollow Music Festival belonged to me. I had a MUSICIAN pass dangling from my lanyard, an electric guitar in my hands, and the whole crowd surging at my feet. Lightning bugs flickered in the humid, hazy night—sparks like the cell phones that people held up to record the show.

Overhead lights pulsed with color, streaking upturned faces in the audience with confection colors. In the summer twilight, I ripped a strip off a brand-new set of songs. The speakers blared, the bass drummed in my bones.

I'd learned a lot of things in a year and a half. The first was that leather looks great but it smells like death when you sweat in it. The second was that people will hype right up for a song they've never heard, as long as they hear a song they love first. And the third was that Will Spencer was a total junkie for live music festivals.

Even in the audience, he was unmistakable. Neck looped with a VIP pass, he was a laser-bright oasis in a seat of agitated energy. Lifting his chin to say hello, he swayed with the back beat. I felt the same beat in my hips, but thankfully when you're on stage, no one can see you blush.

Hailey bounced next to him, her cup in the air and Will's black straw hat on her head. I hated that thing, so if she accidentally took it home, my heart wasn't going to be broken.

OTPs took up a whole row, frat brothers and their girlfriends, flavored with all of my peeps. Jane and Simon and my sisters all came. Mom and Dad, too. They wore earplugs and stayed in the safe side of the crowd but were no less excited. They waved like it was my first day at camp when I looked toward them.

There was nothing like stage energy. It made me feel sexy and crazy and wild. I stood a thousand feet high—people sang because of me. They danced for me. They were there to hear *me*.

My throat raw and my voice raspy, I gave everything back. Every single bit of it, in every single note, in sweat and song and a thunderous crash of music to signal the end of the night. By the time I sang my last note, my ears rang. A deafening white noise enveloped me, the sweet, strange reward for rocking it out and rocking it hard.

The crowd was still roaring when I ducked backstage. Since this was one of the smaller stages, a series of connected tents gave us a little privacy and someplace to come down off the performance.

Blessedly, they had iced bottles of water waiting, right next to industrial fans. Planting myself in front of one, I slung my guitar over my shoulder and pulled out my phone. Will had texted me about the crowd before I went on. I loved getting his impressions of a show from the outside.

When my phone came on, it blew up with texts. From Jane and Will, and a couple of new musician friends who'd just come off their respective stages. All interesting, but there was one mixed in that made me shiver.

The avatar was a generic CW pretty boy picture, snagged from the web. The name next to it was simply HIM. Dismissing all the other texts, I dragged his to the front. It read:

Got a little time for me tonight?

Almost guiltily, I threw a look over my shoulder. It was ridiculous, of course. There was no one backstage but musicians and roadies. Some volunteers, the usual. As far as they were concerned, I was just another girl with a guitar. They'd have to look at my lanyard closely to identify me; it wasn't like they could read my mind—or my phone's screen.

I texted back. Sorry I was on stage, just got this.

Though his reply was almost instant, it seemed to take forever. I had to move, to escape the sensation that everyone was looking at me. That they could see the heat spreading under my clothes that had nothing to do with performing.

Question stands, he said.

I don't think I have time, I texted.

Make some.

Trying to escape the backstage maze, I darted through the chaos, barely looking up. As I backed through the flaps into the outside world, my thumbs flew. My boyfriend's here.

I hit send and burst into the humid night. Turning beneath the glow of floodlights, I took a deep, savoring breath. Good scents rushed up to meet me, funnel cakes, frying sausages—patchouli and sweat, even the sweet smoke from a bonfire down in the camping section.

Suddenly, everything went dark. Warm hands darted out from behind me and covered my eyes.

Another scent washed over me, familiar and warm. This one turned me liquid and hungry; it matched a beat that was more primal than the one emanating from the stage.

Dragging my lower lip through my teeth, I clutched my phone to my chest. I didn't need to see it. He was about to reply to me personally. Cheek grazing my hair, his voice stroked my skin expertly. It slipped into me, taunting me with things I couldn't have—at least, not yet.

"I don't care about your boyfriend," Will Spencer said, his murmur low and teasing.

"You should," I said. Even though I was still playing along, I couldn't hold back a smile. "He's here with all his frat buddies."

With a wink, he said, "I think I can take him."

Then without warning, Will dipped me and stole a kiss. Slipping past my lips with a curling, velvety tease, he marked me with a promise. His mouth could do miraculous things. I just had to get him alone to enjoy it.

We did not pass go. We did not collect cheap beer down in Music Village. We went directly to our hotel room. As soon as we closed the door, Will pushed me against it.

I didn't care about the noise we made. Or about the contents of my purse when I tossed it into the wherever. All I cared about was Will's tongue in my mouth and his hands on my skin. We were good about calling and Skyping, writing and calling, but it wasn't the same.

"Too many clothes," I told him, tearing at his t-shirt. It stretched as I dragged it up his chest. The dark trail of his hair pulled my gaze down. Across rippled abs and deep-cut David-esque lines, down into the jeans that hung casually from his hips. Like any present, I couldn't open him fast enough.

He rasped a rough kiss against my throat, his fingers working my jeans open. "I miss your skirts."

"It's good to work for something you want," I teased. Thumping my head back against the door, I yanked his shirt over his head, then lunged for another kiss. To punish me for teasing him, he darted away, sinking to his knees. He thought he was going to get away with something down there. I let him think it, dragging my fingers through his hair and watching him conquer my skin-tight jeans.

When he went to kiss my knee, I tightened my hand in his hair and tugged him back up. Not hard, just enough to get him moving in the right direction: toward my mouth. The scent of his skin swirled around me, sweetened with cologne, darkened with sweat. Shaking my head, I told him, "Fast now. Slow later."

Even though he widened his eyes, as if to chastise me, I just laughed. We had all night to explore and play. In a little while, we could stretch out and count each other's freckles. Maybe spend some time basking and cuddling, and whispering stupidly adorable things against each other's lips. We'd get back to basics; we'd fall asleep together. Wake up entangled, fall in mad, crazy love again at first light.

But right now? I just wanted him—on me. Inside me, and all over me, until I couldn't tell my end and his beginning.

"You're a monster," he said, and picked me up.

Arms around his neck, I asked, "Whose fault is that?"

In response, he spun us around. I laughed, startled. The sudden motion made me dizzy, and his bare skin against mine only enhanced that. I drugged myself on his kisses, laughed against his mouth as he carried me across the room. That he could pick me up and carry me anywhere made my skin hum. To be fair though, everything about him made my skin hum. His kisses, his teases—the way he dropped me on the bed, just to dive after me.

His expert hands twisted in the thin fabric of my panties. Any other time, he should have taken some time to appreciate the fact that I'd gone out of my way to floss my butt with decorative underwear.

This time though, he got a pass. Anything to get him onto the bed with me and in my arms where he belonged. With a quick twist, they were gone. Thrown to parts unknown, probably to stay there forever. I sent silent apologies to future occupants of Room 234.

Because Will refused to be entirely tamed, he licked a stripe up my belly. His mouth was fire. Skimming along my ribs, then up the curve of one breast, he followed taste with touch. As he moved over me, I forgot to hurry, just for a minute. Instead, I let sensations roll through me. Hot. Hungry. Eager.

One smooth hand skimmed my belly, then cupped my breast. Thrumming inside and out, I almost let him get away with the slowdown. But then he made a foolish mistake. Edging his teeth against one nipple, Will dared to smirk at me. Deliberately thwarting me, because Will was just evil like that.

So I fought back.

He wore his jeans just loose enough that I could streak a hand down the front of them. Springing up to greet my touch, his erection fit perfectly against my palm. Stroking it through his boxer-briefs, I traced its length shamelessly. Unlike my orderly body, his was happy to leap up and beg.

"I don't think so," Will said, sliding up to nip at my throat.

He faltered when I dipped down again, wrapping my fingers around him. He was thick and hard; I knew his shape intimately. I knew what Will liked, too. A stroke, a little bit of a twist. His eyes rolled back as he groaned, thrown completely off his game.

Victorious, I tangled one of my legs around his, trapping him against me. It was my turn to look right into his eyes, to watch his face as I reminded him just how much he'd taught me. And maybe how much I'd figured out on my own.

In places, my fingers were rough from playing the guitar. In others, they remained satiny smooth. Alternating between them, I savored the way his breath turned shallow. When we first met, I was the most uneasy goddess at the party. Now I felt like I ruled him comfortably.

Those sounds he was making, they were for me. Because of me. Of course he knew how to drive me crazy. But now I knew how to return the favor.

"I warned you," I said. Then I shut myself up with a gasp, because I forgot one important thing: Will Spencer played to win.

He stroked a thick finger into me, his thumb washing over my clitoris at the same time. I still felt like a goddess. Only now, it was one that melted into pooled, glowing gold. New gravity pulled me down. It centered all the nerves in my body into that one spot, curling my toes, racing my heart. My hips rose to his touch because I needed more. I wanted to be full of him, plowed into the sheets and buried deep.

At the same time, I still wanted to best him. So instead of a race, we had a game of dirty, dirty chicken. Pressing into him, I stroked him faster, shifting my grip until I felt his pulse in my palm. Friction and heat put rhythm into his hips.

In response, he stroked another finger inside me, answering my pace with the same. He pressed his brow against mine, and our eyes locked. We traded crooked smiles and grimaces. When he forgot to move, I raced forward. Drawing low moans from him felt like success. It roared in my blood, and then just as fast, he'd make me forget everything but his touch. Skin pink, fresh with sweat, the humidity rose between us.

The whole room warmed, scented with sex and laughter—and frustration. When I'd said fast now, slow later, I didn't actually want to finish with just our hands. When we came, I wanted everything: his weight on me, his lips on mine. I wanted to be drunkenly in love and wildly out of control—everything fast and hard, yes, but *together*.

I missed him. All of him.

"You win," he murmured, and captured me with a long, deep kiss. When he surrendered, I almost cried. That connection, the one that had pulled us together in the first place? It was still there. So strong, alive and electric. He pulled his hand away, clutching my wrist to stop me mid-stroke. Suddenly, everything was still urgent but fluid too.

Winding around him, I held on tight as he slid us up the bed. Covering me completely, Will pressed kisses along my throat, lingering where my pulse raced. Gracelessly, we wrestled him out of his jeans. They caught on his heel and we both had to wrench around to finally strip them off. But once we did, it was so worth it.

Skin-to-skin, we fit together perfectly. My curves softened his angles, and when I chased his kiss, he let me catch it at exactly the right moment, Fingers winding into his hair, I looked into the cool, clear blue of his eyes and smiled.

"I missed you," he said.

With a brash shrug, I raised my head to steal another kiss. "I know you did."

"Fast now, slow later?"

"Let's do what we always do," I told him, even as I reshaped myself beneath his weight. "Just go for it and see what happens."

And why not? From our very first kiss, we hadn't done things the easy way. Or the simple way. Sometimes, not even in the best way. But all that struggle had led somewhere wonderful.